ABOUT THE AUTHOR

Peter Gray has been writing in various guises since he was twelve years old and he has never been able to stop. From plays to magazine articles Peter has produced a plethora of work.

His first 'Sam Series' book "A Certain Summer" has had excellent reviews, one from TV presenter and ex England soccer coach Bob Wilson who grew up in the same area and could easily identify with the character in the book.

With many short stories, articles and celebrated Mummers Plays plus many touring productions under his belt. Peter is always busy writing something or other. He has also acted in and directed some of those productions and one such production played at Warwick Castle for six full seasons. He has also written several scripts for advertisements, mostly with a humorous theme as well as many live shows for the stage. He has now embarked on a new series of Adventure Novels of which more details can be found on this website at www.petergrayauthor.co.uk.

He currently lives in the Highlands of Scotland.

ALSO BY PETER GRAY

A Certain Summer
Sam's Kingdom
With Feeling

FROM THE AVALON SERIES

The Drums of Drumnadrochit
Auld Clootie
The Brollachan
The Black Clan
Caledonian Flame
Plague Witch

Bethran
Seer of the Picts

by
Peter Gray

Tricky Imp Publishing

Bethran, Seer of the Picts

First edition first published November 2020

Tricky Imp Publishers
Caithness, Scotland.
Email: books@trickyimppublishing.co.uk

A CIP catalogue record for this title is available from
The British Library.

ISBN 978-0-9572668-9-6

Cover design & artwork by the author.
Additional internal artwork by the author.

More Information at:
www.petergrayauthor.co.uk
www.trickyimppublishing.co.uk

Printed and bound in the UK by 4 Edge.

Introduction

This introduction is designed to give some insight into the people of the north that we came to know as the Picts. My story takes place around the year 690 AD and though as the reader you understand that the date is early, the Picts and their culture not corrupted by Christianity would not use or understand this dating system. This is the first of many issues to poleaxe a writer delving into something that is for the most part, unknown.

The time in history we tend to call the 'Dark Ages' was far from dark. It was much more vibrant and enlightened than past historians have given it credit for. As we learn more about the time, historians and scholars are beginning to see that the early history of Britain was dynamic. The only darkness seems to cover the Picts themselves.

Writing about an ancient civilisation is always going to be difficult, and if the writer wishes to capture some authenticity of the time, then a great deal of painstaking research has to be done. If the subject is a civilisation that is surrounded in mystery, conjecture and flawed guesswork, not to mention, very little documentary evidence, the task can seem impossible.

The Picts are such a race, a people that seem to be interwoven with the thickest mists that can roll off the Highland mountains or drift in from the North Sea. They are an enigmatic illusion to some, and a legendary warrior class to others. To me, they became a fascination, and I knew I had to strip away most of the layers of fiction before I could find out what was underneath. What I did eventually find, was a fabulous jewel of Scottish history that is even more interesting than the historians would have us believe. The first revelation was the fact that though we now call them 'Picts', (Roman: Painted People) there are only three Roman writers of the time that used this term and one was Julius Caesar. He wrote that they 'dye themselves with woad, which produces a blue colour, and makes their appearance in battle more terrible. They wear long hair, and shave every part of the body save the head and the upper lip.' It is now known that Julius Caesar never went further north than the Thames, and it is likely this story was given to him by one of his generals as an explanation for why these savages were taking so much overpowering. Rhetoric, not historical accuracy is probably what Julius Caesar was working with. There are also hints in Roman commentary, that the Picts called themselves Kalti, but I can find nothing to support this. The word has more than a passing resemblance to 'Celtic' so it could have been used as a 'catch all' term.

A more common name used at that time would have been 'Cruthin' yet even that word seems to be used to describe all people not conquered by the Romans. That could apply to others, not just the Picts. We don't know what the Picts called themselves, so what did they see themselves as? Possibly the truth lies in the fact that the Picts as we know them were separate tribes, each with their own overlord and maybe even regional kings. This would give each one their own identity and their own personal name, obviously, these would probably not survive. It was only later that the Picts became a sort of confederation of tribes, and even then, it is doubtful that they would see themselves as a unified nation. The problem becomes greater when no written evidence survives, and it is likely that their extensive stone carving did the talking for them. Unfortunately, the most learned historians and scholars still know next to nothing about the symbols of the Picts.

So, I decided to think, as a Pict of the time may think. To the individual trying to scrape an existence from some of the harshest landscapes of Scotland, his personal identity would reach no further than his family and his settlement. To a warrior of some standing, he would be accountable to a lord of some sort and to that lord, he would see himself as a vassal of a king, but of a king of the tribe, not of a nation. Even if a king proclaims himself, king of the Picts, would that mean anything to anyone but the most important warriors of the day? Probably not, so here I look at the mediaeval feudal system and overlay it onto the Picts. It fits quite snugly, all except for the church, which was something that came fairly late, particularly to the northern Picts. Even as Christianity made its way into modern day Sutherland and Caithness, the newly converted people saw the saints as important, this could mean that the idea of a single god was still difficult for them to grasp.

We now know too, that these people were far more advanced that previous historians had considered.

Farming was important, and many types of crop were grown. Some Picts were wealthy and prosperous, they had fabulous artwork and jewellery, they also traded far and wide. They fished the rivers and the sea. They built large houses in wood or stone and were masters of stone carving. Their metalworking skills were equal to any other tribes of the period and they built forts and earthworks. They strengthened the stone ramparts by vitrification[1], a method of which we have still not been able to replicate. Their soldiers were highly skilled, well equipped and horses were part of their armies, which were feared by their neighbours. In summary, they were just the same as their close neighbours and no more or no less advanced than any of them. The only real anomaly is the name the Romans gave them. Painted People? There seems to be no evidence that they were tattooed, painted or otherwise decorated in any way. Their own carvings show nothing that could possibly be associated with such a decorative trend and yet if it was an important aspect of their culture, it would have surely been reproduced on their artwork. This leaves me thinking that a mistake in translation of the word Picti could be the cause as translations of modern Latin announce Picti as meaning spangled. Picta translates to picture, so could it be that the word was misused or even disparaging name given to what the secretary to Emperor Chlorus, Eumenius saw as a drab people? Certainly, I see no reason to use the name as anything other than a denomination that is a generalisation, of a people that may have had no name for themselves.

Another explanation is that the word Picti, may not mean what we think. Pict also comes from ancient British languages and means 'the wheat growers'. Did the Roman soldiers hear other British people calling the Caledonian tribes 'Wheat Growers' and see similarities with the sound and so use it themselves? We just don't know. It is clear that any Roman writers of the time can be discounted and many of the details written can easily be proven to be inaccurate.

As to their lands, here I have to surmount another problem. Place names as they stand today have only slight hints to their heritage and after the Viking conquest, a great number of place names changed to Nordic parlance. Then there is later Gaelic influence and Scottish too. This means that even if we assume a particular village had survived from the Pict times, which is unlikely, its name could have changed many times. With this in mind, in this story, the names of the settlements are based on early naming procedures[2] with the inclusion of some inventiveness on my part. I have included some idea where they stood in the glossary but settlements came and went. The Picts were probably semi-nomadic, having winter and summer pastures in different places. We know in some areas, higher pastures were grazed in the summer and lower ones in the winter, in short, they would have to travel with their livestock under the influence of the seasons. Of course, some farmed fertile, sheltered land and probably stayed put but generally, the pattern would resemble the herding systems of later generations.

In summary, the people in the story are fictional but based on the little we know of the Picts. The places are also in the main, fictional but placed where settlements would exist, or where habitation of that period is known to have existed. The details are based on what little we know of their culture, their lifestyle and their achievements. In all aspects of this work, I have tried to paint a complete picture of the Picts but using the English language to tell the story, and a little imagination to fill in the missing pieces, of which there were many. I hope after all that, you thoroughly enjoy the story.

Peter Gray, February 2020

Chapter One – The Journey North.

On the deserted track that wound its way along the coast, two Jackdaws were trying their luck with a crow who had found something that looked reasonably edible down by the cliffs. The crow knew a Jackdaw had no chance against him, but two of them? That was different. He sensed that before long he would either have to move it, or lose it to his cousins. The odds changed again when a buzzard flew over and the crow picked up his prize and moved off to find somewhere quieter to take his meal. The two Jackdaws hopped over to where the carrion had been to see what was left, but they heard a noise and they too, took to the air. The sound was being made by the most successful predator in the Highlands, a man. He was making his way up the steep track on tired and aching legs, being helped along by his right hand, which was gripped tightly around his long staff. As he reached the top of the rise, a view opened before him of yet more hills, more of the rough track, and yet more distance that he had to travel. He

13

stopped and glanced over to his right, over the endless sea stretching into the east. Behind him and to the south-eastern horizon, could be seen the landmass that he knew as Fortriu, with its mountains in the distance. He sighed deeply, and once again turned his gaze to the north. His tall figure readied itself for the task ahead. A task that had made his life worthwhile and he narrowed his eyes. His leathery skin wrinkled to the task and formed furrows on his tough, weather-beaten face. He removed his hat for a moment and rubbed the long, grey hair before replacing the headwear. His hands were as dark as his face, both discoloured from many years of exposure to the weather of the far north, the salt of the sea, and the harshness of the climate. Every year he made that same journey, and every year it seemed further to walk. It was as if that rough, stony road was being stretched, pulled out along its length to make the journey more arduous each time he travelled it. He considered resting and taking some food, but he had promised himself he would reach the next settlement for his stop. After all, they would feed him for free. The standing stone that had announced he was entering the Kingdom of Cat was a good day behind him and so he knew he was coming to the end of his journey. He raised his staff and set it forth, following its movement with his feet, and urging himself on, towards the settlement he knew would soon come into view.

It did, but not before doubts had entered his head that he had mistaken where he was. The settlement was first seen by several stacks of light smoke swirling into the ice-grey sky that loomed overhead. The half dozen or so buildings soon came into his vision and he was relieved to see that there was life still there. So often, these small settlements were not repopulated once their occupants moved out to winter grazing, many buildings would be left empty until the land reclaimed them. Very few existed long enough to be named. Even fewer were considered to be permanent. The one he now entered was no more than a summer base for the half dozen families that grazed their animals there, but it had existed for at least four years, yet it still did not have a name, or at least the man knew of no such name.

As this tall stranger entered the settlement, two people nodded to him and one particular man looked up from his work and gave a slight smile.

'Bethran, is that you?' The tall stranger walked steadily towards him and with no change of expression replied,

'Tis I, well met Callin.'

'Well met old friend,' replied the man, and they amicably knotted their right arms in a time-old gesture. 'I'm thinking you need food and drink.' said the man, seemingly genuinely pleased to see him.

'If you have any to spare, it would be gratefully received,' replied the stranger as he sat on a low wall close to the main building. To the others of the settlement, this stranger was unknown by sight, but they were quickly becoming aware that this was Bethran, due to his imposing demeanour and his unique garb. He was a traveller, a wise-man and a seer and he had a reputation that was well known along the coast, if not his features. Many sought him out for news, some for knowledge and a few for advice. Bethran was a good man but nothing came for free, though everyone knew this and accepted what he could bring to them was well worth any food or drink they could provide. Callin knew Bethran more than most, he had known him for at least twenty summers during which Bethran had walked that coastal road, bringing knowledge and news to isolated communities as he moved. Callin had once travelled with the man when he was in the employ of one of the tribe elders. He had accompanied Bethran on a journey south some years ago, accompanying a betrothed daughter of one of the elders to her future husband in Fidach. The child had been promised to cement a bond between the two tribes and she had been escorted by a sizable retinue which had included Callin and the seer. That was so long ago, and now as Callin looked at the weary traveller, he saw the years had not been kind to him. Bethran was of forty or so winters old but looked much older. In the seer's eyes, this was not such a bad thing as it gave him the look of immortality. Some who did not know him well considered that he was almost a hundred winters old. The people of Camma thought that he could be a thousand years old, as he knew so much about the world in which he travelled. For now, he was content to sit and eat, replenishing his stomach, ready for the continuation of the journey. Not before he told the settlement any news of the world, he could impart. For now though, he sat at a bench in a rough building, and ate a bean stew and a little stale bread. The stew was poor and cold, but the weak ale was much more to his liking. It was to be found in many settlements on this coast, made from barley, mixed with herbs and heather, and then added to water to make a very welcome addition to his diet. A few settlements had their own recipes for this ale, but Bethran looked forward to any of them, and as he lifted the mug, he smiled for the first time that day. He drank greedily and wiped his mouth on his sleeve. Callin entered the hut.   'There is a drop more ale if it suits,' said the man.

'It suits very well,' grinned Bethran, pushing the empty mug to his friend. Callin once more half-filled it and handed it to Bethran sitting opposite. He knew this was when he would hear anything worth hearing.

'What of the war?' he asked.

'There is no war,' insisted Bethran as he took a greedy gulp of the ale.

'So, is there to be one?'

'No, too many mouths talk but say nothing. People speak of war because they fear it, but there will be no war.' and he wiped his mouth once more. 'It would not concern you if there was, wars are never fought on clifftops.'

'I know that well enough,' replied Callin, looking down to the floor a little sullenly. Bethran knew in that instant what Callin was thinking.

'You are considering taking up the spear again?' and he gave a slight laugh, 'forget it, war is not the same as helping tribal elders defend their land.'

'I know that well, but we were trained to fight by Lord Cullcoil, he is a decent man in that respect.'

'Lord Cullcoil and his fighting master know little of warfare, and…' Bethran paused a moment, 'you are not of an age to survive such a conflict, leave wars to younger men,' and he drained the mug once more. Bethran knew Callin was an able warrior, but he was now older, and slower, and war only favours the victor.

'The spoils of battle can be great,' replied Callin as his spirits rallied, and there was an eagerness in his features, 'and Lord Cullcoil is a great man.'

'He is a good leader, true, but there is a higher authority than he, and Lord Cullcoil is not the one to say if there will be war or not.' Callin let his expression become dark once more. 'I know your life here is not easy,' continued Bethran, 'I also know that the last two winters have taken their toll on the people but...' he shook his head, 'the wages of war are nought but death.' Callin stood.

'So you think this life is any different?' there was a bitterness in his voice, 'there are six fewer children in this group than last year.' He turned to Bethran. 'We lost two to illness, four to the cold and two strong lads were lost in the snows.' He slowly shook his head. 'Death stalks the land whatever we do, there is no escape from its grasp. At least on the battlefield we have a fighting chance.'

'You are wrong about your view of war,' insisted Bethran leaning on the table and looking down into the empty mug. 'When the Irish came over the mountains eight winters past, the army that marched to stop them was two thousand spears strong. The Irish fled back to Athall and our army returned without any bloodshed, yet-'

'You have told me the tale before,' interrupted

Callin.

'And I shall tell it again to any that think war is profitable,' insisted Bethran. 'Of the two thousand that left, just half returned, a thousand spears died without casting a blow, without drawing a sword. Soldiers cannot fight the weather, they cannot defeat starvation. Swords and spears do not harm the lord of death.' Bethran was used to telling stories. He didn't so much embellish them as make them palatable to the listener. 'That dark warrior rides his mystic horse into battle,' he continued, 'knowing his foes cannot defeat him, yet he can defeat all.'

'You speak of death as if he is a soldier,' frowned Callin.

'In some ways he is,' replied the seer, 'his weapons are other people's ignorance, his armour is man's stupidity.'

'I know you too well for your speeches to have any effect on me,' replied Callin with a forced smile.

'You must make your own decisions, my friend,' shrugged Bethran, 'but be sure to open your eyes wide as you do it,' and he stood.

'Will you stay the night?' asked Callin. Bethran nodded then said,

'If I left without sitting by the fire with the others, I'm sure they would chase me away when next I pass through.' He allowed a smile to his friend.

The evening was spent pleasantly enough and as he had said, Bethran sat around the fire with those who would listen to his words, and many were eager to know news or even gossip about their lands. When the stories were exhausted, the seer pulled his blanket around him and laid by the fire, until it died and left the hut in darkness.

The next morning, he rose early and after goodbyes and a gift of bread and ale from the people who he had entertained the previous evening, he continued north.

He began to reappraise his opinion that the road was becoming longer. Indeed, the journey all the way from Seal Bay in the south, to his destination in the north had once taken him just ten days, and that with stops overnight at several settlements. This time it would be twice that, even with boats to cross two of the estuaries. Either the road was indeed becoming longer, or he was becoming too old for the journey. As he stopped to rest once again, and the track fell away to the sea, he wondered how many more summers he could continue to make this journey. Could he actually survive without it? His knowledge of the seasons and his participation in several ancient rites seemed everything to many of the people of the land. But then again, there were other factors making his services redundant.

The track here took him down to the shore, to the edge of the sea and he stopped for a moment watching the gentle waves lap up the rocks making a soothing sound as they flooded over, and then slid back to where they had started from. He looked north and continued on. He realised the next stop was a larger settlement that he knew as Lliefoot. This settlement had become permanent, or at least as permanent as a village could be. It had existed for as long as Bethran had trodden this path, due mainly to the fact that the people of Lliefoot had become prosperous. There were several reasons for its wealth, the main one being the gold that could be found in the river, and the river too was alive with fishes, which had become a good source of food and income. There were four large long-huts with several smaller huts gathered around them. These were mostly workshops with an older style round-house on the edge of the settlement. This was mainly used as an overwintering site for the cattle once they had been brought down from the hills. Down by the mouth of the river, there were several more huts of various styles and shapes that were mainly used for boat repairs and salting of fish. Across the river were a few scattered buildings in poor repair. This was the original settlement that had all but been abandoned for the more fertile land to the south. Many crops were grown too, and several stockades could be seen nearer the trees where some livestock was kept. At certain times, even horses could be seen, usually when Lord Cullcoil stayed in the settlement.

With the inclusion in more recent years of a metalworker and a smith, the settlement seemed a busy place where all manner of items could be made or purchased. Bethran was to make the second of the long-huts his first stopping point, and for good reason. This was where the settlement's elder was usually to be found, along with his wife who brewed fine ale. As Bethran walked through the settlement, he noticed, but tried to ignore, the various villagers who spotted his unmistakable shape traverse the path, and bowed low to enter the door of the long-hut. Inside, he drew in the heady scent of the bog myrtle that hung in abundance from the roof of the hut, a dual use herb that kept insects away, but was also used in the fabulous Lliefoot ale. The main room of the hut contained the four elders of the settlement, sitting and discussing the rite that Bethran was there to undertake. Every year, around this time, the people of Lliefoot took to the shore to perform a ritual that they believed kept evil from their homes. There was a legend that far out to sea, was a monster that lurked and swam up and down the ocean looking for villages to swallow up. The only way to keep it from coming on land was a rite of fire, and Bethran was asked to perform it. He didn't believe in the ritual, but it was just another profitable service he provided on his journey north. That night, the elders would gather the people with torches, and they would follow Bethran down to the water's edge where he would invoke the protection of Lyr, the sea god, to keep all evil monsters from the land. Once the rite was performed, the people would cast their torches into the sea and a bonfire would be lit by a 'Forced Fire' ritual. The bonfire was a large, hazel twig representation of a sea monster, with kelp and moss draped over it for effect. Forced fire, or 'needed fire' as some called it, was practiced all through the kingdom to ward off spirits, and sometimes for healing. Only at this occasion had Bethran seen it used as a ward against evil. Bethran wasn't even sure that the ritual still held its old significance to the people, for the new religion was creeping over them and the old gods were being retired. If anything was sure to bring them out to the gathering however, it was the copious amounts of Lliefoot ale which had become part of the celebration.

Once Bethran had eaten his fill, he readied himself for the rite on the beach, but before, he would make the long walk up the high edifice which guarded the little settlement from the harsh tongues of the north wind. It was quite a climb, but he needed to be away from prying eyes, for he had something he had to do. Luckily, the sun became visible through the clouds and when he thought it was at its highest, he looked around to be sure he was alone and pulled a linen bag from his pack. From that, a woollen sack was retrieved, and he removed a bronze disk that was his whole world, the means for him to survive. It was a simple-looking instrument, engraved all around, with many small holes around its edge and three pegs protruding underneath. He placed it carefully on a rock by the path and aimed the inscribed rod in its centre to the sun. From there he placed several small bronze pegs in the holes and watched the shadows they made on the disc. His eyes were unblinking for several moments until he gave a sigh and a nod. He was on time and he quickly packed the disc back into its bag and returned it to the pack.

That evening, he knew people would come to him to cast the bones and tell them what the future held. Did he believe it? No, he didn't think he did as he packed away the instrument, but if it brought solace to the people, what harm could it do?

Back down in the settlement, the villagers were readying for the evening, more work going into the feast prior to it, than the actual rite, but there was a sense of goodwill and joy. By the time the feast began, Bethran had spoken to some old friends and met some new ones, but it was clear that the settlement of Lliefoot was a happy and prosperous place, so different to many of the places he had visited previously.

As the sun slowly set, the rite was begun and Bethran took his place on a large boulder and spoke to the gathered crowd.

'Good people of Lliefoot,' he began with a theatrical sweep of his arm, 'we are gathered here this night, to give thanks to Lyr for keeping us safe this past year, and to place ourselves at his bidding once more. We offer these trifles to his minions…' and he paused as three young girls broke up bread and cast it into the waves, 'in the hope that he will continue his protection. Great Lyr, lord of the seas and oceans,' he continued turning to face the sea with his arms open, 'we bring the power of the flame to light our way…' and many villagers walked past him and cast flaming torches into the waves, 'in the hope that you will see our flame and remember us.' Then Bethran could hear the many mumbled voices giving their own prayers to the god of the sea. Once it had subsided, Bethran turned back to face the village and announced, 'Lyr has heard our prayers, light the fire,' and he stepped off the rock and made his way towards the bench that held the ale. Several of the young men began to rub the previously prepared wooden stakes together to make heat. It would take time, and so most of those at the beach made their way back to the settlement proper. Once the forced fire was placed in the kindling and the wicker sea monster was aflame, a cheer would erupt and the celebration would continue. Bethran had seen it all before, these past seven summers he had performed this rite, ever since the old Pellar of Lliefoot had died. The rite had always been performed on the longest day, but as Bethran had to be elsewhere on that venerable eve, the date had changed. Many said evil would befall them for changing the ritual, but it hadn't. In truth, the settlement had become more prosperous, and even the trade had increased. That was why the Seer was popular, that was why he now had a queue of villagers waiting to extract some words of wisdom or hear his portents for the future. They were eager, even though each one had to 'gift' him for the pleasure of course.

It wasn't a task he disliked. He saw the night at Lliefoot as one of the highlights of the journey, though he always felt worse for wear in the mornings. The moss-covered monster suddenly erupted into flame and the villagers cheered with singing and dancing around the whole settlement. The younger people rushed back to the blaze and ran around the conflagration with screeching and cheering. Bethran smiled to himself and finished off yet another mug of ale, if he ever decided to take root, Lliefoot would probably be the place.

He awoke with a feeling of utter exhaustion and it took some considerable time before he was feeling well enough to break his fast. That came by way of bread and cheese, washed down with a mug of peaty water straight from the river. It was a wide, powerful flow that was tinted brown from the peat washed down from the mountains, but the villagers maintained that this gave their ale the distinctive body and helped with the brewing process. Brewing wasn't something Bethran was interested in, just the result of the labour. He strolled back to the settlement and made arrangements to cross the river, not before he spoke to the elders to assure them he would pass through on his way south some days hence. Then he climbed into a boat to be taken across the river to the other bank. He looked back towards Lliefoot before he crested the hill on his journey north.

He knew the next part of his journey was difficult. The track went up and down the fissures of the rocky coastline, sometimes overlooking a precipitous drop to the sea below and strong winds could make this part of the journey dangerous. Today though, there was little wind, and the sky was grey with leaden clouds that seem to hang like the roof of a long-hut. He continued on, over a massive outcrop of rock topped with thick heather where very little other flora grew, but mountain hares were abundant. So were the buzzards that preyed upon them.

As he continued on, he began to see a small settlement in the cleft of the rocks, another, that to his knowledge had no name. Here there was only a single trail of smoke rising, and the roofs of the other three huts had not been repaired. He passed through the once busy settlement and called out, but saw no one. He continued on up the steep path to the top of the high cliffs and yet again took his rest there. He looked up and down the coast and knew his destination was just two days away. He thought he would be there on time but he would consult his instrument at midday. When the sun returned, that was what he did. He once again took the bronze disc from its wrappings and consulted it, concerned that if the weather changed, he may not see the sun again for some time. There was a little guesswork this time as it was well past mid-day, but he knew his art well enough.

The next settlement he came to was another riverside stop that the people called Birchbay. There was a small river that cut through a valley where birch trees grew in abundance. The settlement was inland somewhat due to high tides flooding the bay proper. There were six or seven stone and wood built huts with a single long-hut made almost entirely of stone set into the hillside. Smoke issued from the turf roof. Birchbay was not as prosperous as Lliefoot but it had certainly grown a little since his last visit. A new building of stone had appeared at the side of the river that seemed to have a large, wooden wheel fixed to it, and two wooden barns beside it. Some land to the north had been cleared and looked like an overwintering space for livestock. Bethran strode up to the long-hut and made himself known.

'Bethran,' smiled one of the younger men by the door, 'is it that time of year already?'

'It is indeed,' smiled Bethran, grasping the man's arm, 'and you look even healthier than last I saw you,' he paused, 'and stronger. It seems both you and Birchbay are doing well.' Bethran turned to look around the settlement.

'We survive,' nodded the man, 'but come, you must meet the others,' and they entered the long-hut to speak with the elder. The elder of Birchbay was probably younger than Bethran himself, but he bowed in reverence to the man non-the-less.

'Good to see you again, Bethran,' nodded the elder.

'And you Sinran,' replied Bethran as he sat, 'I see the settlement is doing well and you are building along the river.'

'We are,' nodded Sinran, 'we are building a new mill. When last you came this way, we spoke of a wheel powered by water to help with the milling, it is almost complete...' he hesitated and Bethran thought he knew what was coming, 'but, we cannot get the wheel to continue to turn.' He sighed and glanced to one of the other men.

'What Sinran was about to ask, is,' cut in the younger man, 'would you cast your eyes over the machine? We are lost in the complexity of the workings, and the smith that helped us built the wheel has run out of ideas.'

'I know nothing of these machines,' shrugged Bethran.

'But you have seen one, have you not?' asked Sinran.

'I did see one, two summers ago, but that was in Fidach, and I did not speak to the people that constructed it,' insisted Bethran.

'But you saw it working?' asked Sinran with a pleading look. Bethran stared at the man for a moment and then made a sigh.

'I will look at the machine but I cannot promise that I can make it work,' he eventually said.

As he walked with the others, several of the villagers joined them. This was a part of his life that Bethran was worried about. He was expected to know everything about everything. This tall, thin man who looked older than his years had to perform miracles wherever he went and if he didn't, his reputation would fall and his means of making ends meet, with it. He felt worried. This machine was nothing to do with the movement of heavenly bodies, or the seasons or anything that Bethran knew about. The smith should be the expert here, but from what he could see, the smith had done nothing more than put several strong men turning the wheel, then letting it go to watch the thing grind to a halt. Bethran looked at the wooden wheel first. It was the span of a tall man and was made of timber and iron, similar to the one he had seen some years previously. The bottom portion was in the water and it was connected to the building by a thick wooden shaft. By now, a crowd had gathered and so Bethran stepped inside the building to be away from those fascinated glances. He looked at the shaft coming through the building. It had a stone wheel fixed to its centre and another wheel lying flat below it, balanced on an upright shaft. Wooden pegs protruded from the back of both wheels and he thought it was very similar to the system he had seen before, if a little smaller. Bethran asked the men to turn the water wheel again, and he watched the stone wheels inside move, and then gradually slow down to a full stop. They were not even touching each other, and yet they would not turn by the power of water. Bethran saw that the problem must be the water power, it just wasn't enough. He retraced his steps outside as the gathered crowd moved to let him pass.

'The water has no strength,' he said at length, 'there has been little rain and the level and strength of the river is too low.' He turned to the elder and stared.

'But even when the river was higher, the wheel did not turn under the power of the water,' insisted Sinran. The Seer looked back at the wheel and then down to the water. He grasped his grey beard in his hands and thought deeply, he went back into his memory and tried to picture the mill wheel in Fidach. Then it came to him. The water ran over the top of the wheel, not under it. He let go of his beard and turned to Sinran.

'The water must run over the wheel, not beneath it, a channel for the water must be built to run from further up the river and the wheel must be raised from the water.' He saw several of the closest people droop their shoulders, this wasn't what they wished to hear. 'The other option is to move the mill to where the water falls from height so that the channel may be shorter, but…' he paused, 'the amount of water must be great so the river may need to be dammed to supply a suitable flow.'

'But that could take many moons to complete,' sighed Sinran.

'It could, but what worth is a mill that does not mill?' replied Bethran. A few of the villagers mumbled as if the god of corn had just spoken.

'We could still complete it before the oats are ready,' suggested the younger man, 'if we set more people to work on it,' he added looking at Sinran. Bethran gave a shallow nod as Sinran turned from the two men to look at the faces of the gathered crowd.

'Very well,' sighed the elder, 'we will begin in the morrow and look for the best site for the mill, the smith can help us dismantle the wheels,' and he led them back to the settlement.

'That is not quite what I expected,' sighed the elder deeply, and Bethran too, felt uneasy about the incident. If he was wrong and the wheel still didn't move, well, he didn't wish to think on that outcome at all.

He stayed the night and set out early in the morning, telling the elder he would pass through in several days to see how they were progressing. To himself, he considered missing out the stop completely, though the river crossing at Birchbay was the only safe crossing for some distance.

The rest of the journey was undertaken beneath a clearer sky, and the sun shone enough for Bethran to take several rests that day. He knew he would be at his final destination by nightfall, and so at mid-day he took the final reading from his bronze plaque before he arrived. He was on time. It was just two nights before the longest day and the celebration he was to attend. As he continued up the gently rising track, he met two travellers coming the opposite way and after exchanging pleasantries and any news, he moved on and crested the top to see the open plain that announced the lands that were known as Camma. Camma was really three separate settlements that formed a mutual bond. The easternmost sat atop the cliffs and was home to metalworkers, boat builders and fishermen. The most southerly was a large farmstead with several buildings around a larger round-house. He passed through this and on to the landward settlement, which was the most populous. Three square long-huts sat in its centre with various buildings, stalls and huts around it, with four or five enclosures, some of which contained livestock. Two horses could also be seen which set this settlement apart from other such places, by wealth and social status. Just below the crest of the hill stood the heart of Camma, a larger building that was partly set into the ground with two or three smaller buildings attached to it. This was a prosperous community that gained mutual assistance from all the others due to it being the base of Lord Cullcoil. As Bethran walked up the hill toward a small stockade that surrounded the main building, he looked to his right and saw the hillside covered in small standing-stones. In two days hence, Bethran would start the Camma celebrations there, and he decided with some determination that he would not get drawn into anything to do with mills and their design, or anything else that wasn't his business for that matter.

Chapter 2 – The Summer Festival

'Bethran, a joy to see you again,' beamed the stocky man.

'Well met, Lord,' smiled Bethran as they embraced. The man gestured for Bethran to sit and then he called for ale, which was brought quickly and placed on a bench in front of them. Bethran looked over at the man. He looked well, and time was treating him kindly. His full beard, greying but trimmed carefully in the fashion so much worn by the powerful and wealthy, gave him the look of a man who knew about life. Lord Cullcoil was a shrewd man, he had been a great warrior, and his father who had been the so-called King of Cat had taught him well the ways of trade and diplomacy. This had ensured that Cullcoil had retained his grip on the area and enjoyed respect from his peers. The Kingdom of Cat was a large area but the population and numbers of settlements was low, which meant that the administration of the area was easy, but it was less profitable than other kingdoms. It wasn't even a kingdom any longer, the eastern peoples had come together in a confederation to form a larger kingdom, yet there was still a healthy rivalry between the heads of those kingdoms. Cat was seen as a backwater by many of the southern lords, but Cullcoil knew well that Cat was the trading bridge between the Kingdom of the Boar, and the rest of the mainland. The Boar Kingdom lay across the water to the north and was a group of islands occupied by a fearsome tribe. All but one of the islands was ruled over by Dalmar, who was a suspicious sort, and there was a stronger rivalry between him and Cullcoil, mainly over the single island that belonged to Cat. Nevertheless, the two kingdoms traded heavily and Cat became the trading middle-man for commerce further afield. Some trade went by boat, but pirates were not unknown, and this meant that sea transport was expensive.

'How goes life in the south?' asked Cullcoil in a jovial voice.

'As usual, there are mixed fortunes, some profit, others fall by the wayside,' replied Bethran, taking a drink of the ale.

'And what do you see of our people?' asked the Lord. Bethran glanced carefully at Cullcoil, he knew that he meant the people of Cat and not *all* the people of the four kingdoms. He took another drink and drew in a breath.

'I am sure your eyes see the same as mine, some are struggling, others do well, the same as Fortriu, the same as everywhere,' and he set his gaze steadily on the man. Cullcoil nodded knowingly. He picked up his mug and emptied the whole pot down his throat. He burped loudly and wiped his mouth on his sleeve and placed the pot on the bench.

'And what do they talk of?' he asked at length.

'Everyday matters for the most,' shrugged Bethran. He knew what Cullcoil was up to, but he decided to get him off the subject. 'Most are worried that a war is coming,' continued Bethran, but Cullcoil simply laughed.

'A war,' he said dismissively, 'that is all they talk of,' he laughed again. 'Why do people who spend their days farming, concern themselves with war? Have they too much time on their hands? Do they not have enough work?'

'With respect Lord,' interrupted Bethran, 'It is as much their business as kings and warriors, for it is they that will be asked to die on the battlefield too. It is they that will have to give what they can ill afford for the army.' Cullcoil let the point sink in, he grunted then said,

'I suppose so. Your words are always worth listening to Bethran.'

'You knew the truth of those words before I spoke them,' smiled Bethran, 'you are just trying to gauge if they will eagerly fight for you,' he paused, 'which means there could be something in the rumours,' he added.

'No,' insisted Cullcoil, and he stood. 'Even if the Great King was to raise an army, he would not ask for Cat people,' he paced a little then added, 'we are too far away for a march into the south.'

35

'Then why are you troubled?' asked Bethran. Cullcoil looked over to him and then sat down once more. He leaned over and topped up Bethran's mug, then said,

'I had a messenger from Lord Dalmar two moons ago, the messenger was here to bring news and to take messages back, but...' Cullcoil looked hard at Bethran and was wondering if he should speak, he couldn't guess how Bethran would take it. 'Well,' he eventually sighed, 'there is a well-known seer on the islands, you have probably come across her?'

'Yes, Derile of Limm,' nodded Bethran, 'she is good from what I hear.' Cullcoil nodded and leaned forward, resting his forearms on his knees.

'I spoke with the messenger from the islands at length, and after a little ale had freed his tongue somewhat, he began to tell me of less official news. It seems that Derile has been making some very disturbing predictions.'

'Such as?' asked Bethran, with some interest.

'She told of fire from the sky, she says that the gods are unhappy with the new religion and they plan to punish us.'

'The same happened in Fortriu,' nodded Bethran, 'but the new religion has grown and now people ask their white saints to protect them. Nothing has changed except the name of the gods.'

'There was more,' added Cullcoil, and he frowned deeply.

'More?' asked Bethran, and the Lord nodded.

'She predicted pirates would come from the east

and burn their fields, she said that these pirates would ride on the backs of dragons, their black wings flapping at their sides, breathing fire and belching pitch.'

'Sounds dreadful,' smiled Bethran, but Cullcoil wasn't joining him in the humour. Bethran dropped the smile and raised his brows. 'You know that prophecies are views of what may happen,' insisted Bethran trying to placate the man, 'not necessarily what will come to pass.'

'You have taught us that, yes,' nodded Cullcoil, and he frowned even more deeply. Bethran saw something else in that furrowed brow. Not everything had been told.

'There is more?' asked the seer and the lord just nodded. He was thinking something through, and then he decided to tell Bethran everything.

'Just after the Hawthorne Moon Festival, two trade boats were sailing south down the islands, they were calling at most of the shore settlements, but a mist fell,' explained Cullcoil, 'they decided to turn for the land but one of them was lost in the thick fog. The second boat dropped anchor as they were not sure where land was and didn't want to be dashed on the rocks. They must have drifted out to sea, for as the mist cleared a little, they noticed a group of rocks jutting out of the ocean. This gave them an idea of their position and direction to sail, but just as they were underway, they saw something further out to sea in the thicker mist. Thinking it was the other boat, they moved closer.' Cullcoil broke off the story.

'And?' asked Bethran, but he could see there was

anxiousness behind the man's steel-blue eyes.

'They saw,' he paused and opened his eyes wider, 'or at least, they think they saw a sea dragon, just as the seer foretold.'

'There have been pirates in those waters for many years, this is nothing new,' insisted Bethran.

'Pirates riding dragons?' asked the Lord, casting a frown Bethran's way.

'Not as such, but I have heard stories in the south of Dragon Boats seen on the eastern sea, many have witnessed them,' insisted Bethran.

'And did you believe those stories?' asked Cullcoil with a penetrating gaze.

'Some, not all,' replied the seer shaking his head, 'but for now, a few sightings of strange boats on the eastern sea, does not seem like an important issue either. For many years the peoples over the sea have landed on the islands to trade.'

'Yes, they have,' agreed Cullcoil, 'but not as often as they have in recent times, and not in dragon boats. Those have always been trade vessels. If these are scouts for some greater fleet…' and he sighed deeply.

'Is this why you want to ready your people for war?' asked Bethran.

'I would have thought that you of all people would take another seer's visions seriously,' replied the lord. Bethran gave the slightest nod and said,

'We see things, some are difficult to interpret, but if I told you every dream or vision I had, we would all be in an eternal panic.' Cullcoil stood once more and walked to the door.

'Well,' he said looking down to the nearest settlement, 'we should talk of this again, but for now,' he turned to Bethran, 'I am to ride to Dunwhin, I have business there, more cattle thefts.' Bethran nodded and knew it was time for him to take his leave. He walked from the hut and into the glare of the exterior of the long hut. As he made his way down to the settlement, he recalled hearing that Dunwhin had an old fort on the hill above the settlement. He had never been, but he was sure he had heard of it. Was Lord Cullcoil repairing the old ramparts there? He shrugged it off and went to find the elders of the settlement.

The main settlement stood on a low plateau of flat, fertile land, over a thousand paces from the rocks overlooking the sea. There was no river here, but an excellent spring sat on the hillside which supplied all three settlements, though the easternmost settlement could take water from a small burn. On the side of the highest rise was a swathe of standing stones, the highest reaching no taller than a man's thigh. They were irregular in shape and size, laid in rough rows down the gentle slope. No one knew why they were there, but it was assumed the ancients saw the site as important. Though the importance was now lost, the people of Camma held a lavish celebration every year on the longest day of the summer. Bethran was always on hand to provide an accurate confirmation of which was the longest day and to begin the celebrations which ran over two days. Most people knew roughly which *was* the longest day, but Bethran had a powerful instrument which could tell the exact day without error. Bethran had also been questioned about the standing stones, but though he had studied them and noted that at least one lined up with the sun on the longest day, he had little idea why the ancients placed them there. Not knowing was a thorn in his side, as people expected this wise seer *to* know. After a long and hard study over the many years he had visited, he just could not grasp the meaning, if there was a meaning in the Camma stones. He looked over them once more, and spent some time walking through them, now and then trying to line them up, but he saw nothing. At around midday, he took his bronze plaque from its wrappings and placed it on a stone that sat in the centre of the settlement. The stone had three holes bored into it to allow the tags beneath the instrument to fit snugly into them. He checked the alignment with the sun and noticed that there was a slight deviation of the shadow thrown from the single pin he had placed in its edge. He knew one more day would see that shadow line up with the all-important mark. He knew that meant tomorrow was the longest day. Several people watched him, but once he had confirmed the day, he expanded on his actions by placing several other pins and making some gestures to throw anyone off the scent. He could never give away the secret of the bronze dial. He would become as redundant as those standing stones if anyone knew how it worked. Once he had completed his task, he made his way to find some food and to rest, ready for the evening in which many would sit and listen to his tales.

Bethran took it upon himself to sleep among the standing stones that night and as he lay, looking up at the stars, his brain went into deep thought about the nature of the heavens. It had always been a fascination to him, and though he didn't understand the working of the world, neither did he believe the legends or the current thinking of scholars. In the south, the new religion was taking hold, and these so called 'Christians' had their own mystics and seers that were called monks. These monks had access to vast libraries of books, written in an ancient language, the language of the Romans, and Bethran had been so interested in what the books held, he had learned the basics of the Roman language. He still hadn't found anything that could explain the workings of the world. The books explained everything as the work of their god, and that seemed less plausible than the stories of their own gods. He had done many experiments and had tracked the movement of the sky, and though he had some theories, the whole conundrum baffled him. He eventually drifted off to sleep, but his dreams tormented him.

Bethran stood on the highest rock on the clifftop, and out to sea he saw a bright light in the sky. It was coming closer, and it was glowing enough to dazzle him. As it neared, he saw it was a dragon, a large dragon breathing fire and swooping down. It was being ridden by a warrior who was dressed in flaming armour and wielded a spear tipped with a monster's tooth. In his fear, Bethran pulled back his staff, and as the dragon flew over him he swung the staff and knocked the rider from his mount in a torrent of fire. He stood after being knocked over from the conflict and looked back out to sea. What he saw terrified him. A massive fleet was sailing toward him from the horizon. A fleet of dragon boats full of pirates.

When he awoke in a cold sweat, the dawn had not yet broken and so Bethran, still shaking from his dream, walked down to the cliff edge overlooking the sea. Once there, he sat on the highest part of the cliffs, crouched, and wrapped his blanket around him. He sat there, his eyes fixed to the horizon, and watched. He watched until the sun pushed itself from behind the rim of the ocean and burst forth its light in a gold fan to bring new life to the world. Eventually he stood. His legs complained, he had sat there so long. He stretched his body, and once again shivered at the thought of his dream. Had he seen something that would come to pass? Were the standing stones really dream stones? Or was it just because of the story that Lord Cullcoil had told him? He shivered once more and went to find something to eat.

With Lord Cullcoil still away to the north, the festival would be overseen by one of the elders of the main settlement. This surprised Bethran and showed how concerned the Lord was. He usually resided in Lliefoot, yet he had been in the north for some time by all accounts. Bethran put these thoughts aside as he had to prepare for the ritual that evening. At midday, his task was to confirm the accuracy of the longest day. This was steeped in ritual and Bethran would be expected to play his part as it had been done for countless generations. He didn't relish the theatricals he had to undertake but he went about it in good humour. Firstly, he found a private place given for his use by the village to prepare. He reached into the pack and pulled out several items that were required for the ritual. The first was his bronze plaque, which as well as being the most important item of his tools, also made a good mirror. Its polished surface, slightly convex allowed a fairly close up reflection of his weatherworn face. Then he pulled out a small leather bag which contained beads and woollen strings with other decorative items. There was also a delicate chain made from bronze links with silver wire intertwined, tiny decorative beads threaded in now and then. There was also a silver torse. The torse was a fine item of twisted metalwork that would be worn upon his head, the chain around his neck. The torse wasn't really silver. It was made from polished pewter but at some distance, it looked silver to the untrained eye. Years ago, he would have allowed some young maid to thread the coloured beads and polished shells into his beard, then braid and tie them with ribbons. Now, Bethran had made alternate ways of decorating himself for the festivals he attended. The beads and shells were ready threaded onto twisted hair and hooked into his beard and onto the chain around his neck. They were made from plaits of long hair, his own hair as it happened, and so looked natural. It made the preparation much quicker and easier than it would normally be. This didn't mean that he looked upon his task as trivial, far from it. He had even enhanced his look by new and novel additions over the years. His clothing was becoming a little too worn for the ceremonies, and so he had taken to hooking all manner of fabrics and trinkets to his gown before beginning. The final touch came from a small pot, stoppered and waxed to seal it. He broke the seal and pulled the stopper in the hope that the contents hadn't dried out. They hadn't and he pushed a finger into the black, oily substance inside. He resisted the urge to sniff it, as the main ingredient was fish oil, which was mixed with ground charcoal and flour. This substance was then carefully applied to the outer extremities of his eyes. He peered down into the reflection cast in the bronze disc. The black around his eyes gave him a demonic look which he liked. That look seemed to go down well with the populous but he was always quick to remove the outlandish accessories after the ceremony was completed. He would probably be asked to start one of the main games later, and he could ply his trade as a seer and a teller of stories too, so he kept the costume and the face paint for the main act only. He was always popular, as his stories were not the ballads from history, they were tales of his adventures, which meant they were not just true, they were about him. Many he knew would ask about the rumours of a war, and some would ask about the new religion and what he thought of it, but on the whole there would be enough scope for him to have a little amusement too.

One of the elders came to fetch him when the time was upon them and Bethran followed solemnly holding out the bronze disk in his outstretched hands. He carefully placed the plaque into the holes on the stone and inserted several of the pegs, though there was only one he was watching, the one that cast its short shadow onto a predetermined mark on the disk. He waited as the silent crowd gathered round him with a good space between. He closed his eyes and raised his head slightly. It was part of the show, but without that show, would they believe in it? He considered they wouldn't. As the shadow on the disk came close to its position, Bethran bent a little and then raised his arms in an exaggerated pose.

'Hear me people of Camma,' he called with a menace in his tone. 'I am come here to witness the passing of the sun across the sky. I am come here to measure that passing and to tell if the gods are happy with what you have achieved. I can tell you that this summer, they are.' He allowed his arms to fall to his side, and he scanned their faces with a grim expression, the dark-ringed eyes making him seem dangerous, as well as all knowing. 'People of the Kingdom of Cat, people of Camma,' he continued as he still looked upon them. 'It is the height of the summer, it is the zenith of the year. Let the celebrations begin.' It was an instant transition, from a reverent silence to a bedlam of noise and activity in the blink of an eye. There was cheering and clapping and music seemed to issue from every part of the throng. People made their way to the food and the ale and Bethran remained in his position until they had cleared. Only one remained, Morcott, one of the elders. He bowed with a satisfied smile and then turned to join the others. Bethran then left to disavail himself of his outlandish garb and to clean his face. He now had time to spare and so he walked to the cliff edge once again and looked out to sea. His dream seemed trivial now, but he still wondered if it was some portent of things to come. He knew there were other people who lived over the ocean to the east. They sometimes sailed to the islands of the Boar People. They traded and then left, but the islanders made no doubt to any that asked, that these people from the eastern sea were warriors, and indeed, some were said to be pirates. It was also rumoured that these people sailed in dragon boats in times of war. So was his dream due to the stories that he had heard? It seemed without sense that a foreign sailor would make the perilous journey over the sea to pillage from people that had nothing worth stealing. Maybe they would come for cattle, there was a great deal of theft of cattle even on the mainland, it was part of life, but the pirates wouldn't be able to take the cattle back with them on their boats, would they? That didn't seem possible. He shrugged to the horizon and tried to forget about it.

Back at the settlement, he took bread and cheese and sat on a low stone wall to eat and watch the celebrations. As he finished, a young boy brought him a mug of ale, climbed onto the wall and sat beside him. His feet barely touched the floor, he was so small. Bethran nodded and drank the ale in two large gulps, and then laid the pot by his feet. The boy sat looking at him and made Bethran a little uneasy, simply because most of the villagers saw him as unreachable, or even a person to be afraid of. Bethran had never added to that notion, but neither had he tried very much to dispel it.

'What is your name lad?' he finally asked.

'Drost,' replied the boy, 'son of Drost.' Bethran knew the elder Drost, he was part of one of the elder's families, a quick-thinking, intelligent man who was seen as a future leader of the settlement. 'Will there be a war?' asked the boy.

'I do not think so,' smiled Bethran.

'The elders think there will, they think the Lord will raise an army soon.'

'Your lands are too far north for the Irish to come,' explained Bethran.

'Why do you call them Irish?' asked the boy with a frown.

'That's what I have always called them, why?'

'My father told me that the Irish live over a sea to the west.'

'Well, that is true, they live over a sea, but they also live to the west, over the mountains,' explained Bethran.

'At Dunat?'

'That place is just part of their kingdom,' insisted Bethran, 'some people call them the Dal Riata, where I am from we just call them Irish.' The boy looked puzzled. 'There are so many tribes, they all have names, it is much easier to give them a single name,' added Bethran impatiently, 'and as they speak Irish, we call them Irish.' The boy still looked puzzled and began to swing his legs.

'So why do they want war with us?' he asked, eventually.

'As I said,' sighed Bethran, 'I do not see a war

coming this far north, and as to why they would war with us, that is complicated.' Bethran sighed once more. He didn't think that the boy would understand the reasons that he himself couldn't fathom.

'Is it because they speak Irish, because they do not understand us?' Bethran thought on this, the boy was astute for one so small. Of course it was more complicated, but it was one of the reasons that compounded the problems. He shrugged and said,

'It could be,' and he stood and walked away, taking his mug to try to get it refilled.

The festivities of the day were now well underway and the ritual of placing the bronze plaque on its stone completed, Bethran could be himself and join them in their rejoicing. His only other task was to start and oversee the 'Game in the Stones'. This was probably not the reason the ancients had built their field of stones, but it was what the people of Camma now used them for. It was a kind of fertility rite and a way of finding a partner. It didn't always work, but the game was popular and indulged by anyone who was trying to find a mate, or even a lover in some cases. The idea was thus, all the participants would choose a stone on the outside to begin the game, and stand by it. Then, a drum made from a hollowed log was beaten and each person could move in any direction one stone to that beat, the process repeated allowing each person to head to a target. The idea was to land by the same standing stone as the person you had chosen. There was nothing official about this process, it was just a game, but everyone enjoyed it, as of course, much flirting and sexual playfulness could be practiced without repercussions.

When the sport was finished, Bethran went to the main hut to help the elders set out a bench with sacred foods for another ritual after dark. This particular ritual was symbolic, an act of putting back to the sea and the land, that which they had taken throughout the year. Helping in this preparation was his way of finding out gossip, and what the people were actually thinking. As darkness fell, Bethran returned to the rear of the long-hut where he would make his predictions for the settlement. These were not really anything to do with 'seeing', Bethran just used his eyes. If the crops around the settlement looked good, he predicted a bumper harvest. If he saw pretty young girls giving the boys lots of eye contact, he predicted many births in the spring. If the animals looked healthy, well, the pattern of his predictions went on like this. Rarely did he give them negative predictions unless he was convinced they were pursuing a problematic course. Once this was done, he removed himself and sat by one of the fires and listened to the music that was being played, with a mug of ale of course.

He had been dozing when the commotion started. He awoke and looked about him, but could see only as far as the firelight allowed. He stood and walked to the direction of the noise and found a gathered crowd. Burning torches, held by several people in a ring with others behind them, showed two of the elders with a young man with some kind of tether around his neck.

Bethran pushed his way to the front and listened.

'I swear I did not touch it, on the bones of my dead ancestors, I did not touch it,' cried the man.

'You are the only one who cannot be accounted for,' insisted the elder called Drost. The other elder was certainly a generation senior of Drost and his name was Morcott who now spoke.

'Then why can you not tell us where you were?'

'I did, I told you, I was in the copse by the track,' insisted the man. Bethran saw that as well as the tether, his hands were bound behind him.

'You say this, but no others saw you, and why were you down there when the celebrations are here?' asked Morcott.

'I was alone, I just went for a walk,' replied the man, his head now bowed and his face showing pain.

'Is there no one who can vouch for you?' asked Drost. For a moment, there was a flash of something in the man's expression, and he looked to his left without raising his face into the darkness beyond the crowd. Bethran looked to the direction, and he saw movement. He looked back to the man.

'No one,' replied the man, looking back to the floor with a sense of inevitability in his voice.

'Then there is nothing to be done,' announced Morcott, 'you have stolen bread from the sacred altar, bread to be cast for the gods, there is only one punishment.' There were a few sighs and shaking of heads in the crowd, probably more from disappointment of the sullying of the celebration than any regard for the young man. 'You will be allowed to make an offering to the gods and then you will be thrown from the cliff,' continued Morcott, and the man was shepherded away. Bethran saw him look back into the assembled people before he was escorted into the darkness. The crowd dispersed with murmurings, and eventually he stood alone in near darkness. He turned to where the man had been looking, and walked over to the huts in that direction. One by one, he listened at the door of each until he heard a noise. He banged once and entered. He saw a woman seated on a cot and she looked up as he entered. Her eyes were damp, and her face was distressed.

'You know the man who has been accused?' His voice was harsh and unforgiving. She looked at him for a moment and then looked at the floor with a slight nod. 'I assume you are not of his kin?' he asked in the same tone. She shook her head after a hesitation. 'You were with him when he was supposed to have stolen from the altar?'

'No,' she announced, looking directly at him. Bethran crouched beside her and with a menace in his voice said,

'That boy is going to be thrown from the cliff, not because of an arranged meeting with you, but because he wants to protect you.' He looked around the hut and made an assumption. 'You are married and you do not want your husband to find out?' She stared at the floor but said nothing. Tears began to fall. 'Then, hope your silence remains in your dreams, for I think he could come back to haunt you,' and he stood.

'I cannot say he was with me,' she whispered, 'if

51

my husband were to know, he would throw both of us from the cliff.'

'And you would deserve it,' scowled Bethran, 'but at least you would just be an adulteress. As it stands, you are a liar, a coward and an adulteress.' He turned to leave but stopped at the door, looking back at her. 'It matters not, your husband knows.'

'No, no, he cannot,' she cowered with a terrified face.

'Then who stole the bread from the altar? Would it have not been safer for a common thief to take food from one of the benches by the fire-pit?' He watched the realisation twist her features, and he left.

'I value your words Bethran,' began the elder called Morcott, 'but no one has been found to confirm it was not he.' They were gathered by the clifftop, again the area lit by torches and a small crowd around them. The punishment of the man was about to begin and his arms were still tied, but the tether was removed.

'He did not take the bread,' insisted the seer.

'Then you know who did?' asked the elder. Bethran considered saying he did, but he had no proof, so he decided against it. He had promised himself he would not become involved in other people's lives and yet here he was, waist deep in it.

'No, I do not, but I know *he* did not take it.'

'Did you see him by the copse, or did someone else see him?' asked Morcott and then Drost asked,

'In short, Bethran, have you any proof?' Should he tell of what he knew? There didn't seem any point, the woman would deny it and it would make a long-term problem for the village.

'There is nothing I can give you as proof,' began Bethran, 'but I am sure this man is not guilty of the crime he is convicted of,' and he pointed directly at the man.

'We all value your council Bethran, but without proof…' Drost trailed off.

'Is this man known to you?' asked Morcott.

'No,' replied Bethran, 'I do not even know his name.'

'Tyr,' spoke the man in a dejected voice. All looked at him as he had been silent for this time. 'My name is Tyr.' He spoke it as if no one had previously asked, as if they would throw him from the cliff without even knowing who it was they had sent to his death.

'I do know, it was not…' Bethran paused and nodded towards the man, 'Tyr, who stole the bread from the altar. Why would someone steal from the altar when so much other food is easy to take? Tyr does not look as if he is starving, or even hungry. Can anyone explain it?' For a few moments, Bethran's words seemed to make sense. There was silence, but there was no other explanation for the theft.

'We do not need to explain it,' announced Morcott eventually, 'everyone has someone to say where they were at the time the bread was taken.'

'Then I suggest you toss him from the cliff and dash his life on the rocks,' nodded Bethran, and he turned to leave, 'but he did not do it and whoever did, will never be found if this man dies,' and he made his way to the main fire pit to find ale and some food.

As he ate and drank the fine ale, he looked at the abundance of food around him. No one would go hungry on such a day, so why would anyone steal food when there was so much to be had? It was clear whoever had taken the loaf from the altar, had an accomplice to say he was with him, and the crime had been designed to catch Tyr, not to steal bread. That led to one person and one person only. The husband of Tyr's lover. He tried to forget about it. It wasn't his business and no one would thank him for intervening, except probably Tyr himself. But then again, Tyr would be now be a pulp on the rocks with the tide washing over his body.

The incident certainly had an effect on the celebrations, but the final act of the night was about to begin. Two bonfires had been lighted close together and as soon as the flames were high enough, several prepared logs were thrown onto them, and smoke immediately began to swirl. The unmistakable scent of Juniper became apparent, and the smoke swirled all around the area. Cattle could be herded mewing in the darkness as the drover brought them towards the fires. The people of the village gathered around the flames and held torches, making a narrowing funnel towards the fires. When the smoke was at its thickest and those nearest the fires were becoming blinded, the cattle were herded down the avenue of torches between the two bonfires. There were only five cattle, specially brought down from the summer grazing for the ritual, and they were complaining loudly now, not wanting to go through the smoke and between the fires. They were coaxed by the drovers with sticks, and eventually they dashed between the bonfires as some people were heard to be saying prayers. Once the cattle had run through the gap in the two fires, many of the people followed suit as they plunged through the Juniper smoke. Juniper was a very important magical plant, and even Bethran took a turn through it. There was more drinking and dancing after and the cattle were grouped together, ready for their journey back up to the summer pastures. Bethran joined in the merrymaking and eventually decided to retire, but that night he decided not to sleep among the stones. He found a place beside a large boulder, close to one of the smaller campfires. As he pulled his blanket over his shoulders, two men approached. One of them was Drost.

'I am sorry to disturb you Bethran, can we speak?'

'It is no disturbance, what ails you?' replied Bethran, and he sat up and leaned against the boulder.

'The elders decided that the man Tyr should not be put to death,' nodded the man. The second man seemed to nod in agreement, and the seer considered he must have been one of those responsible for the change of heart. 'We thought deeply on your words and considered that if you were so sure of the man's innocence…' there was a pause, 'your counsel is not to be blown on the breeze like fire smoke. There must have been a reason you came forward.'

'We are to spare the man's life, but he is to be banished from the village,' added the other man. Bethran nodded sympathetically, he knew that for the man, this was probably a death sentence anyway.

'I am glad you have spoken to me,' said Bethran, 'please convey my thanks to the elder council,' and the two men walked off into the shadows. Bethran settled down to a more comfortable position and thought deeply about the affair. He hadn't asked if the real thief was caught, he knew the man would never come forward, but the simple fact that Bethran had allowed himself to be brought into a matter that didn't concern him troubled his mind, and caused him to sleep fitfully once more.

The morning was once again bright, and the sun was above the horizon when the seer sat to eat bread and cheese. There were few people about and he knew, even though the incident with Tyr had dampened the evening, much ale had been drunk. A few early risers could be seen going about their daily tasks, and fires had been lit for cooking and to warm those who felt the early chill of what promised to be another fine day. Lord Cullcoil had not returned from his trip north, and Bethran had no way of knowing how long he would be away. The time to head south was upon him, and staying longer could make him late for his last visit of the trip, not official this time, something for himself.

Chapter 3 – The Stranger

Bethran was considering missing out Birchbay and heading inland so as not to have to deal with the issues of moving the mill, but he realised that the little community would have advanced little in their work yet. The mill would take time to dismantle and build on a new site, whereas a trek inland would put half a day on his march south. For this reason, he stayed on the main route that brought him into contact with something he would have rather missed. Just outside the little settlement, with the bay clearly visible in the near distance, he noticed a man crouched by a tree to his right. The man looked up when he saw Bethran and stood with some trepidation. Bethran gripped his staff tightly and felt for his knife through his clothing. One could never be too sure on the road. He soon relaxed as he recognised the man as the person who had been banished from Camma. He ignored the man as he walked on.

'Thank you for saving me, Bethran,' called the man looking downcast.

'I didn't save you, the elders did that,' barked the seer as he continued without giving eye contact.

'But if not for your intervention, I would-'

'There was no intervention, I just told the truth,' grumbled Bethran, 'I dislike people making assumptions without facts.'

'But-'

'Do not presume,' interrupted Bethran once more, 'to think that I gave a damn about whether you lived or died.' He stopped and turned to face the man who was now following him. 'I saw injustice. For other reasons, you deserve to be thrown to the fishes,' he hissed and then continued on his way adding in a quieter tone, 'in any case, come the winter, you will wish you had not been spared.' Bethran picked up his usual steady pace in an effort to be rid of the man, but he heard the footsteps of the stranger quicken. After some moments, Bethran stopped and rounded on the man. 'What are you doing?' he asked severely.

'I… I am following you.'

'Why?'

'I, I do not know what else to do,' stammered the man.

'You cannot follow me, I have nothing for you and you will not receive any aid from me,' insisted Bethran, 'I have much to do so be away with you.' Bethran waved his hand dismissively, as if the man was a midge or a wasp.

'But where should I go, I only know life at Camma?' pleaded the man.

'Hmph,' exclaimed Bethran, and he turned to continue his walking. 'You should have considered that before you laid down with the wife of another man,' he continued in a harsh tone.

'Then…' began the man, but he paused as he followed on some ten paces behind, 'may I ask where it is you are travelling?'

'No, you may not,' demanded Bethran, 'I will tell you that the next settlement is Birchbay and that is all,' growled the seer keeping his pace fast, 'but is unlikely you will get a welcome there.' The man probably knew as well as Bethran that a stranger dressed in a ragged shirt and old breeches without blanket or footwear was likely to be a beggar or a felon. He would be whipped out of the village if they had a mind to. He must have considered that too, for his pace slackened and Bethran knew he was pulling away from the man.

'Would you help me to speak to them?' he eventually called. Once again, Bethran spun on his heel and scowled deeply at the man.

'I owe you nothing, you decided that you would risk everything for the touch of a woman who was not yours, and you must make your own way or perish.' The man cast his glance to the ground and then slumped onto the track.

'You are speaking the truth,' the man sighed, 'I have wronged many, and for that, my punishment should stand. I should throw *myself* from the rocks.' The man staggered to his feet and made his way towards the cliff top.

'Your punishment was for stealing from the altar,' began Bethran, 'which I know you did not do, what would have been your punishment for your real crime?' The man stopped, turned and with a dejected reply said,

'The same, if the husband did not cut my throat first.' Bethran watched him turn to face the cliff and sighed, he was correct. His punishment would have been just as severe, particularly if the woman had been the wife of someone important. Bethran looked behind him towards Birchbay and then back to the man.

'I will see if the elders of the settlement have anything for you,' he eventually said, 'but I have grave doubts that they will help you. Do you have any skills?'

'None,' shrugged the man, but Bethran took this to mean that he didn't understand what he meant.

'What did you do in Camma?'

'Do?' questioned the man, 'you mean to earn my keep?' Bethran nodded, so the man continued. 'I was a drover once, but I took to building walls for the stockades and the huts, I can work with wood too, but I have no tools.' Bethran nodded at this once again and then said,

'There is a crumbling ruin of a beacon tower some fifty paces ahead. Stay there and I will get someone to fetch you if they agree.' He once again looked down the track towards the village. He could see swirls of light grey smoke here and there in that peaceful setting, and he slowly turned back to the man. 'If you do not hear anything by nightfall…' he glanced towards the cliff edge and sighed, 'well, you will have to make your own decisions after that.' He turned to continue down to the village as he heard the man thank him for trying. Bethran whispered to himself. 'I believe the cliffs here are suitable to end a life.' He frowned at his own ambivalence for Tyr, yet he didn't think that the man would be there when anyone came. He looked so distraught that he wouldn't be surprised if the man jumped to his death long before nightfall.

'On your way south so soon?' asked the smiling face of Sinran as Bethran entered his hut. They grasped arms and the seer sat to the bench as the elder poured ale.

'Aye, 'tis a long journey and my bones ache more each year,' he replied as he lifted the mug. 'I have some other business before I reach Fidach. Health and prosperity,' he added, lifting his pot towards Sinran.

'Health and prosperity friend,' replied the elder, and they both drank. 'If I did not know you so well I would think you were in some hurry coming back this quickly, was Camma not to your taste this year?' asked the elder.

'Camma was good,' and he paused as he thought how to broach the subject of the man on the hill. 'I just need to be on the lower plains in the next few days.'

'You never took a woman I believe, is this a change of heart?' grinned Sinran, 'when a man is in haste it is usually at the call of a woman.' Bethran looked deeply into the eyes of the elder and gave a friendly frown.

'Who said I never took a woman?' he asked, but

61

Sinran just shrugged. 'The truth is, I once loved, but she was promised to another, so it wasn't to be,' his face became serious. 'After that, well...' he gave a long pause and then added, 'but in a way, I am to meet a woman, Moiri of Keln has made me new clothes for the winter, and I am to meet her on the south side of the ferry.'

'I see,' smiled the elder, 'then you must keep that meeting, I would not want a man to be kept from his warm clothes.' Both nodded with knowing smiles, then drank from their pots. Bethran remembered about the man on the hill.

'I notice that work has not yet started on the mill,' he said.

'No,' sighed the elder shaking his head, 'we do not have the people spare for the work, and it is a large undertaking. We will have to move it over winter ready for next year's harvest.'

'Hmm,' nodded Bethran, 'I may have a solution for you,' he added, but there was doubt on his brow. 'I came across a young man at Camma who knows a little about building. He could be of use to you.'

'This is not a wealthy village, we could not feed an extra mouth over winter,' insisted Sinran.

'Then it will be more reason for him to finish the task so much quicker,' smiled Bethran. Sinran thought for a moment and then tugged gently at his short beard.

'He would have to work alone. The smith could help with the moving of the wheels, but all other work he would have to complete himself,' explained the elder. 'Why would he come here from Camma?' asked the man with a frown. Bethran glanced to the floor, then looked the man in the face.

'I shall not lie to you Sinran,' he said at length, 'this man, Tyr is his name, has been banished from Camma.'

'Then that changes things,' frowned Sinran, 'I'll not have a rogue here. What was his crime?' Bethran thought carefully before he answered.

'He was falsely accused of theft, but when I spoke to the elders and explained it could not have been him, they spared his life but banished him.'

'But if he was innocent, why banish him? Was the real thief not punished?'

'The real thief was not found,' added Bethran, raising his brows.

'Then how did you know he had not done it?' asked Sinran.

'Because,' answered Bethran with a deep sigh, 'he was abed with another man's wife…' he paused for a moment, 'but to his credit, he would have rather been thrown from the cliff than reveal this truth. I found of it because I observed her tears after the event and pressed her on the subject.' Sinran stood and walked to the door of the hut and shielded his eyes from the glare outside. He seemed to be deep in thought, and then he turned and came back into the hut.

'The people of Birchbay would never take this man to their hearts, I see no point in trying,' he explained.

'The people do not need to know, this is between you and Tyr, when his work is done, he leaves,' insisted Bethran adding, 'he has time to make his plans, you get your new mill ready for this year's harvest.' Sinran pulled at his beard again as he thought it through. He gave a slight nod, then said,

'It may work. I will speak with the others and let you know.'

'There is no need to involve me further,' insisted Bethran as he stood, 'I will stay the night and then leave if that suits?' Sinran nodded agreement. 'This man Tyr,' continued Bethran, 'I have left on the hill by the ruined beacon, if you need him he will be there until dusk.' Bethran was about to add that if it was later, they would find his body at the foot of the cliff, but he didn't. He nodded to Sinran and went to find food.

Late in the afternoon, Bethran had been 'seeing' for a pregnant woman. She was curious to know if she would have a son. No woman wished for anything than a son, and Bethran didn't like to disappoint, so he preferred to give a prediction that suited the customer. To this end, he used several methods in the hope that one would give the answer he wanted. He had cast the bones for the woman, but it was inconclusive, and he said so. He then practiced ceromancy, which was divination by melted wax or tallow. He preferred this method as he felt the subject was closely connected to the method, therefore it was more accurate. This time he saw the answer he was looking for. He told her that the child would be male, he also suggested that a second child had a good chance of being male too. The woman seemed happy and offered him a good loaf for his time. As he stored away the loaf in his pack, he saw Sinran approaching. Bethran nodded and stood.

'I suppose that your skills do not reach to men's minds?' smiled the elder.

'Nay, I cannot read thought if that is your question?'

'I was thinking of your friend Tyr,' explained Sinran.

'My friend, he is not. He is a stranger, and I can add that I do not like him in any way,' insisted Bethran with a scowl.

'Well, that is good, for I think he is struck by the moon,' began Sinran. 'I sent for him and spoke at length to explain what we wished him to do.' Bethran nodded, but the frown remained. 'He looked over the mill and seemed to be taking in the construction, but when he saw the wheel he began to grin like a fool. He clapped his hands and went inside. He was no less like a loon inside. He danced around and said that he would do what we wished but we must allow him to work in his own way.'

'Then that is good?' said Bethran as a question.

'It would be if the man was working at that task,' shrugged the elder, 'but for some time now he has done nothing but cavort around in the river.'

'I need to see this,' frowned Bethran once more, and he headed off up the riverbank to the little mill. There, as Sinran had said, Tyr was waist deep in the river, moving rocks and stones from here to there and making it look like he knew what he was doing. Bethran considered that Sinran could be correct. The man was moonstruck, and that was why he had gotten himself into so much trouble.

65

'Ah, Bethran,' called the man with a large grin when he noticed the two men watching him. He waded back to the shore and fell.

'Are you ill?' asked Bethran.

'No, not at all,' replied the man still grinning, 'the cold of the water steals the feeling from my legs,' and he began to rub his naked legs vigorously.

'I mean in your head, not your legs,' grunted Bethran.

'Oh, no, I feel I have reason at last, this...' and he pointed to the mill, 'is wondrous, never have I seen such a thing.' Bethran glanced at Sinran, who raised his brows.

'I gather your task was to move the mill to higher ground,' said Bethran.

'Ah,' exclaimed Tyr finally able to stand, 'yes that was the idea but...' he hesitated as if his mind was not on the task ahead, 'but I also asked to allow me to do it my own way.' Bethran looked over to the elder who gave an exasperated nod and Bethran looked sternly at the young man.

'I suggest, as you have been given a chance here, you do not make another mistake with your decisions,' and he turned to walk back to the village. The light was fading and he and Sinran entered the settlement as fires were stoked, and oil lamps were lighted.

'So do you think he has lost his wits?' asked the elder.

'I am not sure what goes through his mind but rest assured, I will not blame you if you throw him in the river with rocks tied to his neck,' groaned Bethran.

Sinran laughed and replied,

'He could be a source of amusement for a few days, we can always send him on his way with a little food after that.' They parted company, and Bethran looked to the sky. He didn't see rain anytime soon, but he considered that as the darkness fell, the morning would not be such a sunny day as of late.

Bethran ached as he awoke from a more restful sleep than lately. He sat up and stretched his limbs. He was cold, laying in one of the grain huts, and he noticed more than one rat scurry away. Outside, his guess had been correct, the sky was clouded over and there was a breeze from the sea lifting the tops of the highest waves a considerable way up the shingle. The tide was in, and the few fishing boats had already left to ply their trade. The sun was lifting itself from out of the sea, poking through the only cloudless part of the sky and would soon be lost, as it climbed its way across the heavens. The village was quiet, and though there were a few people going about their business, he noticed a few were either making their way to the mill, or returning from it. He carefully readied his few possessions and decided to ask what was happening at the mill.

'What is going on upstream?' he asked of a young woman and nodded towards the mill in the distance.

'I will be damned by the mother goddess if I know,' she shrugged, 'that stranger from Camma has gone and built a wall across the river, is that what all Camma people are like?' Bethran didn't answer. Instead, he made his way towards the mill and he could soon see that most of the village were there. On closer inspection he could see exactly as the young woman had said. A low wall of rocks and stone lay at an angle in the water, barely showing above the surface. It didn't reach the other side, but it was over halfway across. He walked through the small crowd and found Sinran. He was speaking with one of the other elders.

'What has he done now?' asked Bethran with a disappointed tone.

'Done?' exclaimed the elder with a shocked look. 'Done? He has worked a miracle, that is what he has done.' Bethran was impressed with the man's workload. It was obvious he must have worked through the night to complete the two walls, for there was a second, lower wall leading to the wooden wheel.

'I am not quite sure what-' began Bethran frowning, but Sinran interrupted.

'Then watch, Donault, move the stone,' he called to one of the younger men. The young man jumped into the water and with help from another man they moved a large stone that was placed in the way of the wooden wheel. They stood back and for a moment, nothing happened, but gradually, the wooden wheel began to turn.

'He has directed more water from the flow of the river to push against the wheel,' laughed Sinran, 'it seems your friend is a miracle worker.' Bethran considered reminding him that Tyr was not his friend, but at that moment, he thought better of it.

'Where is he?' he asked instead.

'I have sent him to eat and sleep. He was sleeping in the mill when we arrived,' explained Sinran, still smiling and watching the wheel picking up speed. Bethran nodded, watched the wheel for a few moments, and then went to find Tyr.

'You said you had never seen anything like it,' said Bethran to Tyr. The man was eager faced even though he was obviously suffering from lack of sleep.

'That is true, but when I looked at the workings of the machine, I knew that the water passing through the wheel was not enough to turn it.'

'How? You do not even have a river in Camma.' asked a bemused Bethran.

'I cannot fathom how my mind worked on the matter, I can only tell you that I saw walls. Walls that would take water to the wheel, walls that would make the water deeper.' The man smiled and finished off a mug of something or other.

'You are telling me that the idea for the walls came to you, and you have never built such a thing before?'

'Yes,' nodded the man. 'I do have such thoughts from time to time, but I have never had a chance to do anything about those thoughts,' smiled the man, 'I once told old Jenko, a farmer at Far Camma that if he had a spike driven through the shaft of his mattock, it would not break as often. He told me I had been drinking too much parsnip ale and I should leave thinking to the gods.' He paused, 'So I did not have a chance to try it out, but I know it would work.' He burped after the last words and looked contented.

'Hmm,' groaned Bethran. He was lucky, that's all, a man who on occasions thought of something that might just work. It didn't mean that Tyr was a clever lad. He had proven he was the opposite by sleeping with a taken woman, but then again, that was lust. Thought from the loins, rather than thought from the head. He had to admit, however, that the wall in the river was clever, particularly as he couldn't have seen the mill in Fidach, which had a very different design, moving water to the top of the wheel.

'Well,' sighed Bethran eventually, 'you may think what you have done is clever, but you would be wrong.'

'How so,' smiled Tyr, 'I have earned a little respect from Sinran the elder and many of the settlement have spoken to me since.'

'Sinran took you on to move the whole mill,' frowned Bethran, 'that would have taken you several moons to complete. Now you have made the wheel turn, it does not need to be moved.' Slowly, the smile faded from Tyr's face, he looked down to the mug and pinched his lips together.

'Oh, so now I am out of work?'

'That, it seems, is an accurate assessment of your situation,' replied Bethran. He stood and looked down at the young man. 'But that is your problem now. I have to move on, good luck to you Tyr.'

'Could I not come with you?' asked the young man.

'No,' replied Bethran with a dark expression and a shake of the head. 'You are ill-equipped, I have no extra supplies for you and how would you pay your fare when we reach Northferry?' and he turned to leave.

'I think the elders may pay me a little for making the wheel turn.'

'And when the winter comes, what then?' growled Bethran, 'those poor rags you wear will not keep the ice phantoms from your bones, stay here lad and see if you can get other work from your reputation,' and he walked outside. Tyr followed, and with an eager voice said,

'I could be your apprentice. I know how the disc works.' Bethran stopped and spun around to him with a deep frown.

'You think you know, but you do not and...' he paused, 'an apprentice to what? My trade will soon be a memory when the new religion sweeps north.' His face softened as he continued. 'People who follow the white Christ have no need for my skills, they have it written in books in the language of the Romans.'

'Then can we not change to this religion?' asked Tyr and then added, 'would that not give us both a skill?'

'It is clear,' laughed Bethran, 'you have no idea of what you speak, the old gods have power, the new Christian saints have their own power. These are not things to trifle with.'

'I do not truly believe there is power in any of these things, so it does not matter to me.'

'Then you truly are a fool, for without belief, you cannot make others believe,' frowned Bethran, he walked away to fetch his things and say his farewells.

It was not far down the track before Bethran heard the familiar sound of footsteps following him. The

71

footfall was keeping its distance, but Bethran knew it was Tyr. Without looking back or stopping, he called out,

'Stop following me, I will punish you if you continue.'

'I am not following you, I just happen to be walking in the same direction as yourself,' came the reply and the footfall suddenly became quicker as the man ran to catch up. Bethran stopped and looked at the man.

'What do you want from me?' he asked. 'I saved you from death at Camma, I find you work at Birchbay, what more can I give you?' The man looked dumbfounded for a moment. He sighed and looked out to sea before staring straight into Bethran's eyes.

'For the life of me, I do not think I want anything,' he looked down and shook his head slowly. 'My mind has always been full of confusion, I have thoughts that none other seem to have. Many times I have tried to talk with others and every time I am considered to be a dreamer, moonstruck, the village curiosity, just because no one understands that I...' he seemed lost for words for a moment and then a light came on behind his eyes. 'The woman, the woman I loved in Camma, you will not believe me if I tell you that it was her company, not her body I craved.' Bethran shook his head slowly. 'She was the cleverest person I had ever met.'

'She is a woman,' insisted Bethran, 'many men say that a woman's mind has not the capacity for deep thought,' and though he was testing Tyr, Bethran's face betrayed something in its features.

'I know that is said, but she taught me about the sky, she said she watched it every night,' went on Tyr, 'she said she drew out its pattern on parchment. She explained things to me that I just did not have the understanding of.' Bethran nodded at this. 'That was why I wanted to be with her,' he paused for a moment, 'true, she had other interests and her body was as soft as a young mouse, but for me at least, the things she talked of made me realise that piling stones and repairing tracks was such a foolish thing to do.'

'Did you care for her?' asked Bethran in a soft voice. The man looked to the floor and then shuffled his feet.

'Yes, yes I did,' he said with conviction, looking into Bethran's face, 'and though I knew we could never be together, I would have gladly gone to my death on those rocks rather than not have known her.' Bethran took a deep breath and held it for some moments. When he eventually exhaled, it came with words.

'It is well known by many of our people that some wise women and cunning women have a gift that goes further than seeing. Some have the ability to see things that are hidden to mankind. Unfortunately, only a few of these women are given the chance to show what they see, and it sounds as if your...' Bethran paused trying to find the correct word, '...friend, was one of these women.'

'I'm sure of it,' nodded Tyr, 'her husband forbade her from even speaking about things he considered were an affront to the gods. He would punish her if she spoke to others about it.'

73

'That is the way of things, the new religion has the same view, only men can truly speak to their god it seems,' announced Bethran with a sigh, and he continued on his way.

'So may I accompany you?' asked the man a little more upbeat than usual.

'No,' was Bethran's sharp reply. Tyr frowned and fondled something he was carrying.

'But why not? You are the only other person I have met who thinks of the deeper things.'

'Do not presume to know my thoughts,' growled Bethran, realising Tyr was carrying shoes, very worn and tired shoes but footwear nonetheless. 'You would certainly be wrong.' After another twenty paces he added, 'But I am glad you told me about the woman, it does explain a few things about you.'

'So give me one reason why I cannot travel with you?' asked the man.

'One reason?' asked Bethran, stopping and turning on the man, 'what if I gave you five, would you leave me alone?'

'Maybe,' replied Tyr, slightly crestfallen.

'One,' announced Bethran holding up a bent finger, 'you talk too much, two, you look like a beggar and that will not do. Three, I have business I have to perform along the way. Four, I do not have silver to pay your way at the ferry, and five...' Bethran looked as if he was struggling for the last one and then it came, 'five,' he repeated, 'you stink like a rutting goat's arse.' Tyr raised his brows as he watched the frown of the seer intensify. Bethran then turned and continued. 'And you carry your shoes rather than wear them' he added as an afterthought.

'That is six reasons,' put in Tyr.

'So you can count,' called back Bethran, dismissively, 'I once knew a dog that could count.'

'Well...' began Tyr as he followed on, 'as to the first point, I can be quiet, I am usually quiet. I only talk when I am joyous.' Bethran flashed him a scowl. 'The second point, I do admit that I am a little worn, but that could be improved with a little work and a needle.' Bethran shook his head at this, but kept on marching. 'The third point is quite easy. I could help with your business, which was what I suggested earlier.'

'Then I refer you back to reason two,' hissed Bethran to this.

'I see your point, but I do not see it as insurmountable,' replied Tyr. 'The fourth point is easy, I will simply walk upriver to the nearest crossing.'

'Which would put you three days behind me,' laughed Bethran, and he turned a quick glance as he said, 'But that suits me.'

'And as to the fifth point,' announced Tyr to move quickly away from the fourth point, 'I have never been that close to a goat, but I am sure my smell is no worse than any other person.'

'I am on the road a great deal,' began Bethran in a matter-of-fact way, 'which means my contact with others is minimal. It is also the case that I rarely sleep indoors and when I do, it is usually on a floor rather than a mattress or a cot.' He was walking so quickly now he had to take breaths between sentences. 'I also bathe. I bathe in the rivers or in the sea and my clothes are washed whenever I can.'

'Well, we all have our strange habits, but how does that relate?' asked Tyr, genuinely bemused.

'When I reach a settlement, I can smell it. Each one has its own particular smell. Camma, probably because it does not have a river, is the worst. You are probably the worst of the worst if you fully understand my meaning.'

'Well,' shrugged Tyr, 'I would not know about such things but I doubt that anyone could claim to having no smell.' Bethran suddenly stopped. He unfastened the lace on his clothing and pulled open his shirt and his linen coat and pulled the material so far to one side that he revealed his upper chest and armpit.

'Look,' he said, 'this linen is clean, now look at yours.' insisted Bethran but Tyr looked downcast, he knew there was no point because all he was wearing was a shirt, and that was torn and very dirty. There were herbs and even salves that could repel certain odours. Wood smoke was one of the best, but Tyr wondered if Bethran had a particularly accurate nose. Could he smell things that others couldn't?

'So, I could...' began Tyr but paused before continuing as Bethran fastened his clothes, 'probably smell less and bathe more...' but he stopped. He didn't really think bathing could be the answer. If it was, why did others who bathe and wash still smell? If he was to travel with Bethran, he would just have to accept he was eccentric and give concession to that.

'As to point six,' continued Tyr looking at the

shoes, 'I was given them for helping with the wheel in the village, I just have not had time to put them on. I was trying to catch you up.' Bethran was silent. 'And,' added Tyr a little more quietly, 'did you really know a dog that could count?' Bethran shook his head as he walked.

'Yes,' he eventually said, 'many years ago, a friend had a dog that was a failed hunting dog. The man liked the animal however, and said it was able to count. When I argued that a dog could not count, my friend sent the dog...' Bethran paused suddenly. Why was he relating the story to this person he didn't even want with him? 'Stop asking questions,' he bawled. Tyr recoiled slightly, and after a few moments asked,

'So is there anything else?'

'I could go on all day,' growled Bethran as he continued walking, 'but truly, I just want to be alone.' Tyr was now beginning to see that the man was just a travelling hermit. He saw it as his task, to make Bethran a more friendly and personable character. It would be a difficult task, he knew, but he would try. Why did he find this task so important? He realised at that moment, the more time he spent with the seer, the more he liked him. He quickly sat on the track, pulled the footwear on and tied them the best he could. He then set out to catch Bethran up once more.

Chapter 4 – Beyond Lliefoot

Bethran would not relent from his refusal of allowing Tyr to join him on the journey south. There was much more to it than stubborn insistence, for Bethran it would have meant a complete change of lifestyle. He was a man of few words and he didn't want conversations. He wanted the solitary walk, the connection with nature, the watching of the seasons working their magic on the land. He observed the birds, the noises they made and the way they flew. It was an excellent way of making predictions, particularly weather predictions. He watched the snow hares, the otters and the deer, their actions as he walked could tell him much. With someone talking most of the time, these subtle notes would be lost. They would just become swallowed up in the idle chatter of someone who has no idea of what is happening around him. He was a loner and a thinker. What did he want with company? It was his whole life, hadn't he walked this route for these past many summers, bringing news, predictions, and solace to people generally cut off from each other? It was more than his life, it was his calling. Would he feel empty if he were to stop doing it? That was another issue he would have to think heavily on. Times were changing, and the Christian religion was coming north. It was already in Fortriu where he spent the winter, it had spread south and the Great King was embracing it too. It made no sense to him, but others saw something in the ways of it. Maybe it was the monks, they were learned men, and they were convincing in their approach. He knew of two villages that had taken on the new religion, simply because the monks showed them better farming techniques. In the south, a small fishing settlement had converted because the Christian monks paid for a wooden wharf for their boats. This religion certainly had access to gold and silver. None of the churches they built were short of trinkets, even though the monks constantly wittered on that they needed no money to exist. It didn't stop them adorning their altars with gold. Where did that gold come from he wondered? For now, there was little impact in the kingdom of Cat, and some of Fortriu still looked to the old gods and the Great Mother in times of need. Bethran considered that he could probably make this same journey for three or more summers before he became like the old stone towers of their ancestors, part of the past. He was so deep in thought about the coming of the end of his time, that he had completely forgotten Tyr was still following. He had ceased answering him for some moments, and so when Tyr asked him if he believed in the Great Gyre Carlin that ran through the land, he was pulled from his thoughts. He thought he had asked if he had seen the Gyre Carlin, and he became agitated with the questions.

'What would make you stop talking?' he sighed.

'I was just asking. I did not know how you actually felt about the legends.' Bethran realised he must have been heavily sunken into his daydream and misunderstood the man.

'What legends?' asked Bethran with a deep frown.

'Well, all of them, in particular the Carlin that made the mountains and the rivers.' Bethran sighed yet again and said,

'The stories must come from somewhere, our ancestors must have passed the tales down for a reason. That does not mean that the details are correct.' He glanced quickly to Tyr. 'When a man caught a large fish in the marshes near Southferry, he realised it was the biggest salmon he had ever seen. It was stranded on a mud bank and the man could not reach it. He had large wooden plates made from hazel twigs that he used in the winter to walk on the snow. He put them on his feet and waded into the mud to land the big fish. He told his friend who went to the spot to see if it was true, but when the friend told his wife, he left out the part about the wooden plates. His wife told a drover, and the drover saw the prints in the mud that looked like the fish had walked over the mud flat with large feet, two hand spans across. He told his brother who swore that a man from up river had caught something similar, the shape of a mermaid. By the time the story reached the settlement of

Pebbles, the simple salmon had become a large mermaid. When I first heard the story two days north of Pebbles, the thing caught on the marshes was said to be twenty paces long and took six men to kill it.'

'People exaggerate,' shrugged Tyr.

'Exactly,' replied Bethran casting him another glance, 'so give the story of the big salmon another few hundred summers and it will become a fire-breathing monster with burning coals for eyes and a tail that stretches across the eastern sea.' Tyr nodded as Bethran added, 'It does not mean that the story is false, it just became altered,' added the seer.

'A lie then?'

'Not a lie as such, just something to make you understand the meaning behind it,' replied Bethran. He paused to try to think how best to explain it. 'This part of the year,' he began, 'during the time of the big sun, the summer, when the weather is mild or warm, the Carlin is said to be a maid, a Bride, she can take on the form of the wild beasts or become a great stone. In the time of the little sun, during the winter, when all is dark and cold, she is an old hag, casting boulders around in anger. We even have spells to keep her mischief at bay.'

'So the Gyre Carlin, forming mountains and glens, started life as a shrivelled old maid that dropped a stone somewhere,' announced Tyr, 'that does not seem convincing.'

'No, well yes,' stuttered Bethran, 'my point is, the Gyre Carlin can have a different form depending on the story.'

'Which means it is not true,' insisted Tyr. Bethran

dismissed him with a hand gesture and continued walking.

'That is not quite what I meant, I am wasting my time,' he grumbled.

'I understand it,' explained Tyr as he followed on, 'I just find it hard to believe.' He thought for a few moments, then added, 'People exaggerate, I know that, but most of the legends are just so incredible, they do not relate to anything we can see.' For a moment, Bethran realised that this young man did indeed have a bright mind. He was looking at the world in different ways. He didn't just accept what he was told, he questioned it. That was like he himself. Take nothing for granted and question everything.

'But if they were ordinary and mundane,' explained Bethran, 'they would not be worth telling, for no one would listen to them. Who would sit around the fire and listen to a bard tell them about a cattle drover or a fisherman, going about their toil and daily tasks?' Tyr nodded.

'I see your point, but...' Tyr halted and then raised his finger to the sky, 'I wonder if that is why the new religion is growing?' Bethran stopped and turned.

'What?' he asked with a questioning look.

'Do the Christian stories and legends make more sense? Are they about everyday life?' Bethran laughed and then turned and continued south.

'Not at all, from what I have heard of their stories, they are more outlandish and more unbelievable than anything concerning our gods.' His laughing subsided, but his smile remained. 'Magic and sorcery abound from each tale, and the telling of them is tiresome and overlong,' he added.

'So why are people changing to that religion?' asked the young man.

'I cannot tell you,' replied Bethran, shaking his head, 'the Christian monks will tell you it is because their religion makes no distinction between social standing.'

'And you do not believe that?'

'Can you read the Roman language?' asked Bethran, answering a question with a question.

'No,' laughed the man.

'Then why would you convert to it?'

'Do not the monks tell stories like our bards?' asked Tyr with a frown.

'They do, but those stories are of penitence and are lifeless.' He shook his head as they continued bending into his strides. 'They tell stories about saints, these saints are ordinary men, like soothsayers or seers but they do not predict, they do not perform magic, they just suffer.'

'They suffer?' asked Tyr, he was now the one frowning.

'That is what it seems to me,' nodded Bethran, 'they suffer to become saints.'

'Does that make them immortal?' asked Tyr.

'In a way, yes, but their god gives them an immortality I would never want. Though, there are so many similarities to what we believe in, they even use the same festival days as us.' The two men were quiet for a moment as they negotiated a deep cleft in the rocks where a river ran. They crossed over a low rock bridge and climbed up the other side for some considerable height. On the top, the two men rested, and Tyr was awestruck.

'What is this place?' he asked. Ahead of him spanned a great moor, there was rock and heather, yet not a single tree stood.

'The Gyre Carlin's bed,' smiled Bethran. 'On the side that touches the sea, a vast bed of rock pushes proudly upwards, and it is said that after the Carlin made the mountains of Cat, she was so tired that she fell asleep here, the rock rose up to rest her head.' Tyr looked back to Bethran, aware of the irony of the subject matter.

'It is bleak up here for sure,' replied Tyr.

'The people of Lliefoot say it is impassable, nearing the shortest days of the year and is covered with thick ice.'

'Where is Lliefoot?' asked the young man.

'Beyond the moor to the south, half a day's travel along a treacherous path. There are two deep valleys and two rises, then, we will be on the plains north of Lliefoot.' As they regained their breath, Bethran realised he was speaking with Tyr freely and easily. Rather than finding the man irritating, he was beginning to feel comfortable with him. He shook himself from his thoughts.

'I must continue. I have to be in Lliefoot by dark, I do not want to spend a night on the Gyre Carlin's moor.'

They made Lliefoot before dark, but the journey

had been difficult. The wind had risen and there was little conversation due to its strength. The track had been arduous and dangerous, with drops down the cliffs and loose shale here and there. The sun had gone down as the settlement came into view, and the smoke hung heavily over the roofs of the huts. As they reached the river, Bethran found, and shook the bronze cattle bells hung on a thick post to warn the ferryman, and before long, a shape could be seen on the far bank. A hand was raised and a small boat set off to ferry them across.

'What will the ferryman want?' asked Tyr, looking worried.

'I will see to that, I have something for him,' replied Bethran, knowing food was no good at Lliefoot. The settlement always had food, they had ale too, so paying a ferryman came down to trinkets or tools and Bethran bartered so often, he always had something of interest. As they climbed out of the boat on the other bank, Bethran handed the man an iron blade, it wasn't the finest craftsmanship, but to a fisherman, the blade just needed to cut and stay sharp. The ferryman smiled and nodded to Bethran, and the two of them walked to the settlement some two hundred paces further on. Tyr was impressed by Lliefoot, it was everything Camma wasn't. There were trades here that Camma didn't have, and there were almost as many huts as the three Camma settlements combined. Even at this time of the season, there was livestock in the stockades, and fish hung to dry at the eastern end. There were smells and sounds at every turn, and Tyr thought Lliefoot a pleasing place. The river was a fascination to him too, and he wondered if a mill could be built there. Did the village need such a mill? It was certainly an industrious place, even without it. Bethran went off to speak with the elders and Tyr did as he was told for once and sat at the seaward side of the village and watched a few fishermen working on their nets in the fading light. By the time Bethran returned, it was almost dark, and the seer led him to one of the smaller huts. Outside it they sat at a bench and enjoyed a good stew and a mug of ale, the like of which Tyr had never tasted.

'This is good,' he announced, placing the near empty pot on the bench.

'Certainly the best in the kingdom, and probably the best this side of the mountains,' nodded Bethran. They finished their meal and then Bethran unrolled his blanket and wound it around himself. 'You need to find a fire to sleep by, without better clothing, you will feel the cold,' frowned Bethran. Tyr nodded. He knew it was going to be hard for him unless he could find something to make his way in life. As he huddled by a small fire near the centre of the settlement, he considered his future. Being with Bethran was better than being alone, but he knew that the seer had little to help him along and he would have to use his wits or he would suffer. The night wasn't too cold, and he slept well, but he awoke to a steady drizzle just before dawn. The fires were out and so he found a little shelter by the ferry in a stall close by. The problem was that he was now damp. He shivered himself back to sleep and shivered himself awake soon after. Huddled under that stall with his arms around his bent legs, he tried to make plans. He would have to wait and see what cropped up but as things stood, this life on the road was going to be tougher than he first thought and as Bethran had said, he would have to make his own way soon. The winter would certainly crush him.

By the morning, he was thoroughly cold, but he didn't complain and he sought out the heat of the first fires that were lit. His breakfast would have to be taken from the food he had been given for his work on the Birchbay Mill, as the hospitality to travellers did not include a second meal. Anything more would have to be purchased, though Bethran was well enough regarded that he was given hot pottage and oats with a tankard of spiced water. The rain was still falling, though it was more of a mist than a drizzle, and the seer thought about the route he would take south. If the rain continued, he would probably make more stops as, once his clothes were wet, it would be important to try to dry them at night. He walked outside the small hut to see Tyr sitting cross-legged under the eve of a larger hut. He looked bedraggled, and Bethran tried to convince him to stay in Lliefoot until the weather improved. He insisted he would leave with the seer and asked about the next destination.

'There are little enough settlements that will be occupied at this time of the season, particularly on the vast plain below the hills,' explained Bethran, 'there is a small settlement on the little river they call Lode, but I do not remember what it is called.'

'Will it be occupied?' asked Tyr.

'Oh yes, I recall they have few livestock and most of what they eat comes from the small patch of fertile land in the valley above them.' The seer seemed to be trying to remember the settlement in detail, 'It has grown by three or four huts over the years and the sea teams with fishes at that point. They have to walk across a marsh though to reach their boats, as the settlement is some way from the shore.'

'Then can we reach it before night?'

'We can be there by midday,' replied Bethran, 'and thereafter we must continue to Tall Bridges before nightfall.' Tyr shrugged and tried to put a brave face on the idea of walking so far in the drizzle, but by the time they set out, the brave face had gone, it was replaced by shivering and a poorer frame of mind. As they walked, he warmed a little, and the shivering ceased, though he knew it wouldn't be long before it retuned, as the wet was intensifying with a more sustained drizzle.

By the time Lliefoot was a memory some distance behind them, horses could be seen on the plane heading north. At closer inspection, it proved to be two horsemen with a pack animal at their rear.

'When they draw closer, stand off the track,' announced Bethran.

'There is no need to tell me, I know warriors when I see them,' replied Tyr. As they closed in on the riders, Bethran and Tyr stood off the track to allow the horsemen to pass unhindered. Though they were wearing leather helmets, perfectly shaped beards could be seen. Under their capes, good quality clothing was also evident, and the horse blanket of the first one was richly embroidered with fine stitching on it. The second man was not so well equipped, but seeing their swords at their belts, it was clear these were important men.

'You there,' called the first one to Bethran. He looked up to the man and said,

'Yes, my lord?'

'How far to Lliefoot?' The voice was clear, and the accent was similar to his own. These men had ridden some distance.

'Not far,' replied Bethran, 'across the plain and you will see the smoke of the village.'

'Who are you?' said the second man looking at Tyr. Before the young man could reply, Bethran answered for him.

'He's my servant, we're going to Tall Bridges to find him some better clothing,' but he sensed the man was going to question him further, so he continued, 'I'm Bethran of Seal Bay.'

'I have heard of you, you are the seer, are you not?' asked the first man.

'I am my lord.'

'If the weather was more pleasing, I would have asked you to read my future,' he paused, 'but on a day like this, I would rather have a pot of Lliefoot ale than find out my wife is planning to kill me,' and he laughed turning to his companion, the drizzle running down his clothing. The other man laughed with him, Bethran smiled and bowed his head.

'Farewell Bethran,' continued the man, and his horse walked on. The second man nodded back to Bethran but stared at Tyr for a moment before he too moved, followed by the pack animal, loaded heavily with several packs. Spears could be seen hanging at one side, and armour bundled on the opposite. When the animals had passed, Bethran continued on the track and hurried off south with Tyr close on his heels.

'Some do not like to see strangers on the road,' growled Bethran, 'we need to find you some better clothing and quickly.'

'Do you think they are going to raise an army in Cat?'

'No,' replied Bethran, 'they may just be collecting tribute from Lord Cullcoil, or they could be delivering important messages.'

'Or asking him to raise an army,' suggested Tyr.

'Cullcoil was right, you people are too preoccupied with war, there is to be no war,' Bethran insisted, and he spurred himself on ever faster.

They stopped to dry out their clothes at the little settlement at the Lode River, but before Tyr dried his shirt, he washed it in the river to try to make himself more presentable to Bethran. When he returned to the darkness of the tiny, smoke-filled hut where they were resting, the man who occupied it was showing Bethran some small rocks. He was older than Bethran and his hair was thin but wild. His face was wrinkled and deep fawn, like leather, but his eyes were blue and bright. His fingers were thin and crooked, but they worked as well as a young boy's.

'This is a very nice one,' said the man holding up a palm-sized grey stone. His accent wasn't like any Tyr had heard before.

'Hmm,' agreed Bethran with a nod, 'I will certainly take that one.' He looked over some of the others and pointed several out. 'That one, this one and those two,' he paused, 'and I want that tiny one too.' The man scurried off to the corner and brought a small sack and placed the stones Bethran had chosen into it.

'What are they?' asked Tyr, slightly bemused.

'Picture stones,' smiled Bethran. He pulled one out of the bag and showed it to Tyr. It was small, no larger than a small pin brooch, but on one side was a delicately traced out picture.

'I have seen nothing like it,' announced Tyr, opening his eyes wide. 'Is it some kind of beast?'

'We think this one is a beast that lived in the ocean,' replied Bethran, still smiling.

'The workmanship is unmatched,' insisted Tyr glancing over the delicate tracery of the image. He looked up at the old man, dumbfounded that his misshapen fingers could create such a thing. 'You are very skilled,' he added. The man laughed heartily.

'Tis not the work of me,' he coughed, 'a greater hand than mine carved this'un.' Tyr looked at Bethran, who still wore a grin.

'They come from the sea, after a storm, they can be found on the beach here about,' he explained.

'You mean someone, or something out there,' he nodded towards the sea, 'is carving these.'

'I doubt that,' said Bethran with a piercing stare, 'these were formed by the gods, they were once living things and have been petrified in the rocks.' Tyr began to shake his head.

'But they look like nothing that crawls the earth, or the seas for that matter.'

'Who knows what lives in the seas?' insisted Bethran.

'They are from the underworld,' cackled the old man, 'things that slither down there,' he smiled with a toothless grin, pointing to the floor.

'Well,' shrugged Bethran, 'I suppose that could be one explanation,' glancing over to Tyr and raising his brows. 'Either way, they are quite a curiosity, do you not agree?'

'Something like this makes a belief in the dark arts more acceptable,' agreed Tyr handing the rock back. They accepted the hospitality of the old man to warm and dry all their clothes, and Bethran shared bread with them. He tried to work out if they could still reach Tall Bridges before nightfall, but he was loath to leave the comfort of the fire. He passed it off as unimportant.

The man didn't offer a drink, but he regaled them with tales from the underworld and several stories of what the strange rocks from the sea were. Bethran added that he had scoured the beach on several occasions and found some interesting items.

'I once found a great tooth from some sea beast or other, it was as long as my hand with a sharp edge.' The old man nodded.

'Aye, young Gahead from the next hut found one this long,' and the old man pulled his twisted hands apart to show the length, 'and he used it as a knife on his boat, still has it as I remember.'

'I can understand that,' nodded Tyr, 'but the petrified beasts embedded in the stone are something I never thought to see.'

'There is more to see in this world than credit is given for lad,' grinned the toothless mouth of the old man.

Bethran thanked the man and as soon as their clothes were dry, they set off once more to try to reach Tall Bridges. The rain stopped soon after and made the going much easier, though it was wet underfoot. From the Lode River the land was much lower and several open plains could be seen with a few marshes dotted here and there, and after several easy but long climbs, the land levelled once more. As the sun set, Bethran realised they had not made good time, and though he had been thankful to the old man for the warmth of the fire, he now wished he was at Tall Bridges. As the light was lost, Bethran recognised the flat plain before the village and pointed towards the fast fading horizon.

'There is Tall Bridges.'

'What sort of settlement is it?' asked Tyr.

'It is a wealthy one,' admitted Bethran, 'with farming, metalworking and stone working. Some standing stones are worked here in a small quarry and there is a little fishing too.'

'Hospitable?' asked Tyr.

'Usually, you cannot see in the gloom, but the plains stretch right over into the mountains. There is so much grazing here that the people of Tall Bridges do not move up to summer pastures. There is a market here too.'

'And why is it named such?'

'Because the bridges are tall,' replied Bethran, and for a moment, Tyr thought the seer was smiling, but the light was fading fast and it could have been a grimace.

In the dark, Tyr could see very little of Tall Bridges, but he could at least see that to reach the settlement, they had to cross a wooden bridge. The structure wasn't tall as such, it was at ground level, but the rushing torrent of water below surged along a deep fissure in the rock. This made the river some distance below the bridge, which in Tyr's mind would mean certain death for anyone unlucky enough to fall in. The village looked sizable and had certain trades not seen in the smaller settlements. Bethran showed the way to a large hut that had a broom protruding from its gable. Tyr had heard of Ale Huts but had never until this moment come across one. Inside, the place was dimly lit and smoky from the fire, which was at one end. To the left was a large trestle that had mugs and jars of many types and sizes, where Bethran headed and asked for ale. The ale was poured by a burly man who seemed pleased to see Bethran, and the tables were also attended by a large, jovial woman who Tyr considered was probably the wife of the burly man. They sat at a small bench by the wall, and Tyr took in this new experience. The hut wasn't full but there were several men sitting and chatting quietly, mostly about crops or fishing, but some were discussing other stories or gossip, most of which could not be heard.

'I have never been to such a place,' put in Tyr quietly.

'Then do not get used to it for that is the first and

94

last ale I shall provide for you,' replied Bethran flatly.

'You said earlier, when the two warriors passed us on the road,' he paused and looked over to the seer, 'you said you would have to get me some clothes. You also told them I was your servant.'

'What of it?' replied Bethran, looking around the hut.

'Does that mean I can come with you?'

'Not at all,' insisted Bethran, 'it just means that we need to make you look less like a bandit and more like a servant,' replied Bethran, still looking at the other patrons.

'But, if you-'

'I have told you before,' growled Bethran, turning to him, 'do not try to see inside my mind, you will be wrong. You may come with me to the ferry, and then we part company. I have enough to pay my own fare only. As I said, you have to make your own way.' Tyr nodded slowly and sighed. If that was to be his fate, so be it, but he would learn all he could from the seer while he had the chance. The door suddenly opened and a small, grubby man came in. He smelled of fish.

'Arna, you want ale?' asked the burly man.

'Aye,' nodded the small man, 'there's a sea monster been washed up on the beach,' he announced with some excitement. The other people in the hut stopped their conversations and turned to face him.

'Whereabouts?' asked a clean-shaven younger man. The little man gulped down a mouthful of ale before he answered.

'North of the river, I think, the pot seller's

daughter walked down there looking for shells, she saw it and ran to tell us by the boats. It is too dark to see anything now.' The burly ale seller looked to the clean shaven man and said,

'We can get a team together just before dawn, it could be a blow fish.'

'Maybe,' said one of the others, 'not seen one for a few years though.' Most of the men continued drinking, but the talk now changed to sea monsters and other sea creatures, and there was some speculation of what the thing might be.

'What is a blow fish?' asked Tyr quietly. Bethran took a drink and turned to him.

'They are big fish, they come to the surface now and then and blow air through the tops of their heads, sometimes water.' Tyr didn't think he had ever set eyes on one, but when he was young he had seen a large fish out to sea.

'So why did he say it was a sea monster if it was just a fish?' asked Tyr. Bethran sighed a little.

'They do not fish deeper water here, they just scour the coast for smaller fish or crabs and lobsters, anything big will seem like a monster.'

'How big do they grow?' asked Tyr with genuine interest.

'Some, the size of a grown man, some, as big as this hut,' replied the seer looking around the building. Tyr didn't reply. He was too busy trying to imagine the size of the beast. 'Drink up,' added the seer, 'and then we will sleep. If this one is of a good size, we need to be there before anyone else gets to it.' Tyr did as he was told but was confused by the seer's comment.

Chapter 5 – Sea Monster

The early morning was unpleasant. It was that time known as the 'cold hours' where, for some unknown reason, the surrounding temperature both inside and outdoors, drops to an uncomfortable level. Tyr had been awake for some time. He was cold and had shivered constantly. Bethran however had slept well, Tyr had heard his snoring and on occasions a few words, but crouched in the lea of the smithy hut, he was so utterly miserable he considered going his own way. This habit of Bethran's of sleeping outdoors was understandable but infuriating given the situation. But then again, they didn't have the means for a hut or even a bed, and if Tyr had better clothing… well, it went without saying. Bethran had been correct. Tyr was not equipped for travel, and it was that fact that made him stand out. Who in their right mind would travel in a shirt, old leggings and poor shoes? He had never had good clothing, he had a blanket at Camma, but he had been forced to leave that behind. Most of his life he had at least had a roof over his head. True, as a drover, he had spent the summers out with the livestock, but even then, the cattle kept him warm, and on occasions he had even had a fire burning. The thought of a roaring fire crackled in his mind's eye, but the shivering would not allow it to warm him. He then heard movement and saw several people walking through the darkness in the village. He heard a few talking quietly, and it became obvious they were making towards the place where the sea monster had been seen. He decided to wake Bethran. It was worth risking his ire so that they might walk about to get warm. 'Humph, hey, what is it?' came Bethran's irritable voice.

'The villagers are making an early start, I think they are off to the beach.'

'The beach? What are you talking about?' growled Bethran.

'The sea monster?' added Tyr to remind the seer of the night previous.

'Oh, that,' grumbled Bethran sitting up and wiping his face. 'So why are we still sitting here?' he added equally harshly and stood, quickly rolling his blanket and forcing it into his pack.

The village was still in darkness, but Bethran could see two people walking towards the seashore.

'Where are you going?' snapped Bethran, still not recovered from his sleep.

'They have found Laman,' answered a woman's voice.

'Who is Laman?' asked Bethran.

'He is one of the fishermen, he did not return last

night but he has been found dead,' replied the other voice, also female. Bethran made a grunt and the two figures continued towards the beach. Bethran turned to Tyr and said,

'Come. Let us see what this is about,' and he picked up a few things from his pack and set off in the direction of the two women.

Down on the beach to the north of the river, several burning torches could be seen below the dunes, and a gathering crowd was evident. As they closed in, it was clear that this was the place where the sea monster had been reported, and Tyr was taken aback with the size of the dark shape on the beach. Closer inspection showed a body the size of a small long-hut with a smooth grey skin and there was a strong, sweet smell that was unpleasant. The main part of the crowd were gathered around what seemed to be the head of the beast, and as Bethran pushed through the assembled villagers, he saw a man's body. It was face down and one of his legs was in the beast's mouth.

'Bethran,' said a voice, 'I was told you had arrived.' The man was well groomed for a villager and it was clear he was one of the elders, though he wasn't particularly old. Bethran nodded to the man and asked,

'Who was he?' The other man looked down at the body.

'Laman, he was our most experienced fisherman.'

'When was he known to be missing?' asked Bethran.

'He was due to return on the late tide last night,

his wife,' the man looked around and nodded to a sobbing woman by the body, 'said that, when he had not returned, she and her brother sat on the shore in the dark until the tide began to turn.' The man looked back to Bethran. 'This morning they returned and found the boat on the shingle on the south beach. Thinking that her husband must have walked along the beach, they searched. When they came to this spot, they found Laman and alerted the village.' Bethran crouched by the body and looked down into the beast's mouth to where the leg was partly inside. He then stood and looked back to the elder. The man began,

'The beast must have surged up the shore to attack him.'

'I have never known a blow fish come into the shallows,' shrugged Bethran, 'unless it was dying.'

'That is what I said,' replied another man who could have equally been a fisherman, 'never seen one attack a man either,' he then added. Bethran began walking away and made his way outside the circle of people. In a whisper, he turned to Tyr.

'Here is my knife, sit in the dunes and when they have moved the body of the man, and the place is quiet,' he glanced back to the crowd lit by the torches, 'dig out a few of the teeth from the blow fish.' Tyr frowned. 'As many as you can without being seen,' he added.

'Why, what use are they?' asked the young man.

'They are good charms, people want such things and we can do well by them.'

'I see,' nodded Tyr, he was beginning to see how Bethran thought. Anything that he thought could be used in the future was taken.

'But do not be seen,' hissed the seer.

'You know enough about me to know that if I wish it, I cast no shadow and the moon will not even see me,' replied Tyr with a smile.

'Oh,' added Bethran, 'and be mindful, the blow fish sometimes erupt when they are dead.

'You have seen such a thing before?' asked Tyr in a whisper.

'Once, some years ago,' nodded Bethran and with an afterthought, 'and if I were you, I would take off your rags before you do the task.'

'Why?' frowned Tyr.

'The oil that comes from a dead blow fish is difficult to remove. Wash in the sea after you do the deed or you will reek for weeks.' Tyr frowned, he was now wishing he hadn't agreed to this.

'I will be safe, will I not?' he asked.

'If you do not get caught, yes,' nodded the seer.

'I meant from the sea, another blow fish hunting me,' explained Tyr.

'Of course, the beast did not kill the fisherman,' insisted Bethran.

'How do you know?'

'Because the leg inside the mouth was not bitten, the injury on the head is what killed him,' hissed Bethran. Tyr opened his eyes wide. If Bethran was correct, someone in the village must have committed the deed.

'But-' began Tyr, but Bethran cut him short.

'No more questions. Just do what I ask, and do

not get caught,' and he looked back to the crowd as it dispersed a little. 'I will meet you at the village later, I have things to do.' Bethran walked away towards the village and Tyr retreated to the dunes to keep an eye on the blow fish.

Bethran found himself back at the Ale Hut and was enjoying a pie and ale when a large man sat by his side. Bethran stopped chewing and glanced at the man.

'You are Bethran, are you not?' asked the man. Bethran continued chewing and swilled the food down with ale.

'I am, what of it?' and he took another bite of the pie.

'You were down at the beach this morning.' Bethran glanced at the man once more. He continued eating in silence. 'I told the elder-man that Laman was not killed by the beast.' Still chewing, Bethran raised his eyes but said nothing. 'I told him that after thirty summers of fishing these waters, Laman would never have been killed by anything that came from the sea. Maybe the sea herself, but not by any beast that swam in it.' Bethran finished the pie, swallowed more ale and shrugged. The man held up his arm and the pot boy brought a jug and filled both his own mug and that of Bethran. The seer nodded and ran his tongue around his mouth in an effort to rid it of food. 'I heard what you said down there,' continued the man with a nod to the side, 'I heard you tell the elder-man that blow fish do not hunt in shallow waters.'

'And that is true, if the fishermen I know are to

be believed.'

'Aye, it is true,' nodded the man with a serious face. 'I used to be a shield bearer for Lord Cullcoil, and in those times I stayed at Rysgle and often fished from there. The older fishermen told me that they sometimes hunted smaller blow fish in deeper waters. Oft times they brought back stories of the great beasts that swam the sea and about the biggest blow fish man had ever set eyes upon.'

'As interesting as this story is,' frowned Bethran lifting up his mug, 'what has it to do with me?' and he saluted the man with his ale then drank.

'I am just saying that I know my fish. I know about blow fish.' The man paused to join the seer in a drink. He wiped his mouth with his sleeve and continued. 'We both know that Laman was not killed by the beast, and I would like to know who did kill him.'

'I am guessing you are his wife's brother?' The man nodded to the question. 'Then as much as I would like to help, my *seeing* skills do not show such things, *my* skills lie in what might come to pass, not things that have already happened.' The man looked curiously at Bethran. It was at that point that Bethran's quick mind knew that there was something that the man was not telling him. He didn't want to get involved however, and so he ignored the reaction and drank from the pot once more.

'I understand,' nodded the man eventually, 'you do not wish to do this for nothing, I have little to pay you but I have a small gold brooch hidden away. It is yours if you find the killer.' Bethran's eyes lit up at the mention of the gold, but then he frowned. He was never sure why such a useless metal was coveted by other men, it was important for jewellery and other ornamentation, but at the side of other metals, it had no worth. Bethran knew, however, that gold could be exchanged for many other things.

'Gold or no gold, I tell the truth,' insisted Bethran, 'there is no method of seeing that I understand, that can tell of what has already passed. If I could perform such a miracle, I would surely do so and relieve you of your gold,' and he gave a slight grin. The man didn't return it. He just sat with a penetrating stare. He eventually frowned and said,

'So your servant is not telling me the truth?'

'My servant?' asked Bethran with surprise, and then he sighed. He realised the man must have been caught. He wondered why he hadn't seen him.

'He said that you hate injustice and find the truth in such matters.'

'Did he now?' frowned the seer, 'and where exactly is he? Where did *you* see him?'

'He was in the village near the smith,' answered the man.

'My servant, as you call him,' began Bethran, 'is a little struck by the moon. His wits left him some many summers ago. To take in what he speaks of is to be listening to the most romantic bard, a bard who tells tales of his dreams rather of what he sees.' Bethran finished the drink and stood. 'I shall find him and whip him for his lies, good health to you.' The man didn't reply. He simply stared at Bethran grudgingly. Bethran left the hut to find Tyr and headed towards the smith in the centre of the village.

The weather had improved and though it wasn't raining, the sky was full of cloud and the breeze from the east had returned. It took some time for Bethran to find Tyr, he eventually saw him in the small market in the centre. There stood a set of stalls and benches standing between the huts, selling all manner of items. Tyr was looking over a stall that seemed to have fabrics and clothing, and to Bethran's surprise, Tyr had a blanket wrapped around his shoulders. It wasn't a great blanket and there was at least one repair, but it was wool and when new, had been of a better quality. Bethran grabbed the young man roughly and spun him around, forcing him against the side of the stall. Both Tyr and the stall-holder were shocked.

'What have you been up to?' growled the seer.

'I, I er…' Tyr was momentarily stuck for words, 'nothing, I did as you told me why, what is wrong?'

'I have just had a visit from the brother of the recent widow,' explained Bethran with a savage look in his eye, his hand was still gripping Tyr by the throat.

'Oh, that?' gulped the young man, doing his best to think of an explanation. Bethran looked at the stall-holder who was becoming agitated. The seer let go of Tyr. Spun him again and pushed him along the side of the huts and to a stockade at the rear. Bethran threw the young man to the ground and several pigs scampered over to see what the fuss was about.

'I did not have much choice,' began Tyr, trying to

explain. He remained sprawled on the ground as he continued, 'I thought it was the easiest way to explain myself.'

'So you were caught after all?' barked Bethran. Tyr looked a little disappointed at this question.

'Of course not, I got the teeth as you said and then went to wash them, and myself,' he gave a little shudder. 'You were right about the smell.' Tyr sat up and brought his knees to his chest. 'I washed and washed, but I was then too cold to stay in the water, I moved into the dunes to dress. There I found an iron pot sticking out from the sand. It must have been washed up from the sea, but I thought it would be ideal to put the teeth in and bury it. The problem was, it was light by then and there were more people around the beach.' He looked up at Bethran. 'In the end I thought on what you had told me, to make my own way, so I buried the teeth in the sand and placed a small rock over the spot, so we could retrieve them later. I then looked at the pot. It was rusty but did not have a single hole in it. I took it, and tried to get what I could for it, and though it was not a very good pot, I managed to swap it for this,' and he tugged at his blanket. Bethran was now feeling a little guilty, but he still felt angry and began once more.

'I do not want to hear your life as one of the great sagas, just tell me why I had a visit from this brother of the widow?'

'I was getting to that,' explained Tyr, and he considered it was safe to stand. 'This big man asked me where I got the blanket as he recognised it as the one he had over the door of his hut. I explained I had traded it for an iron pot. He did not fully believe me and took me back to his hut to ask his wife. Once he knew the truth, and I had not stolen it, he asked me who I was.'

'And you, in your wisdom, told him you were my servant,' said Bethran, folding his arms.

'Yes,' nodded Tyr, 'after all, it was a legend you began.'

'Yes, but to get us out of a situation, to stop you being killed at the hands of those warriors. I said it as an expedient, not as a matter of fact,' frowned Bethran. Tyr had only just noticed how tall the seer was and how menacing he could be when angry.

'I could not tell him I was a beggar, could I?' Bethran didn't answer, though he knew it was the truth. When Tyr saw Bethran was thinking this over, he continued. 'He and his wife offered me bread, and I sat with them and we spoke.'

'What of?'

'Our journey mostly, I may have improved it in the telling,' added Tyr, raising his brows.

'And somewhere in the telling of this tale, you told them that I seek out injustice?' asked the seer, eventually unfolding his arms.

'I may have included something of that sort,' replied Tyr but he then looked slightly excited, 'after all, as you said, I have to make my own way.' Bethran glared at the young man and then sighed.

'What is done is done, we must ready to leave.' It was then he noticed a dark shadow pass over Tyr's pale face. 'What are you not telling me?' Bethran's frown was so deep, Tyr thought small animals could get caught up in the folds of skin.

'He er, I er…' there was a pause as Tyr looked to the floor. Bethran gave out a deep sigh.

'By the guardians of the underworld, what have you done now?'

'I mentioned…' there was another pause before he let out the whole story, 'I told him that we, you,' he amended, 'could find out who had killed the man. I told him you were good at rooting out evil and bringing men to justice.'

'You truly are moonstruck, what in the name of the great horse spirit were you thinking of?' Bethran was in a rage once more. He grabbed Tyr by the scruff of the neck and marched him away from the village. He didn't know why, he had no intention of harming him, but he just need to think. Once again he threw Tyr to the floor, but the lad jumped back up.

'Do not you see?' announced Tyr, 'this is something that could be good for you. You said that the new religion will ruin what you do, I just thought that this is something-'

'I make my own destiny,' bellowed Bethran. Tyr remained quiet to give the seer time to calm. It took some moments as he walked around and around thinking through the situation. 'Then I must leave, and now you will *not* be coming with me.'

'You are running away from your destiny, and you do not see that,' insisted Tyr expecting to feel the wrath of the seer.

'You would not recognise destiny if it appeared riding a flying horse and struck you with a bolt of fire from the sky,' raged Bethran, 'destiny is fixed, it cannot be changed.'

'I think it can,' replied Tyr, so calmly that Bethran ceased his rant. He looked into Tyr's face and thought back to something he considered some days previously. This young man questioned everything, and that left Bethran thinking that *he* had forgotten who he was. He suddenly saw a younger Bethran in this man, he saw himself standing in front of him with eager eyes and a hunger for knowledge. The seer gave a snort. On a colder day, steam may have issued from his nostrils. The sky had cleared and Bethran looked to the blue and wondered if Tyr had a point. He calmed his mind and looked for a sign, but he saw nothing. Were the gods allowing him to make his own decision? Did they not care if he turned from them? He looked again and in the copse of trees to his right, a blackbird sang out his sweet refrain.

'That thrush is singing sweet,' he said in a very steady voice. Tyr nodded, still expecting some kind of outburst. 'It is too late and too early for him to sing.'

'I er, I do not understand,' said Tyr softly.

'They sing at morning, they sing at evening, but never at noon,' explained Bethran looking back to the sky. He didn't think it was a convincing sign of sorts, but he could easily take it as a positive omen. He looked at Tyr and asked,

'How can you be sure that the killer of the fisherman can be found?'

'I cannot be sure, but if we combine our strengths, our will of mind, I am sure we could get to the bottom of it.'

'The big man offered me gold to find him,' continued Bethran looking over to the village.

'I told him your fee was not a trifle,' shrugged Tyr, 'but I never mentioned what it was.'

'I need ale,' sighed Bethran, and without another word he headed to the village. Tyr watched him go and then wrapped his blanket around himself once more and followed.

'What have I done?' he asked himself.

'Bethran was halfway down the second mug of ale when Tyr came into the hut. The young man sat and looked at the table.

'I think that I have made a big mistake,' he said quietly as the pot boy came over. Tyr shook his head and the pot boy left.

'Just one?' asked Bethran sullenly, 'I can think of many, compounded by my own very grave error of allowing you to walk with me.'

'That may well be, but I can solve the problem for you,' replied Tyr, 'I am going to leave you, It is not just about you, it is about the people who expect you to arrive each year. I have not considered this, and that is my mistake.'

'I will be the first to admit,' said Bethran, widening his eyes, 'my services have been important in the past.'

'They still are, I see the faces of the people who come to you.' Tyr spoke with a level tone. 'They need you, not just for what you bring to the village. You bring them hope as individuals.'

'Once maybe,' sighed the seer, 'not now and when Christianity comes north…' he trailed off and grasped his pot. Tyr stood and said,

'Farewell, Bethran.'

'Where will you go?' asked the seer.

'I do not really know. I may go back to Lliefoot. I will find some supplies and get off.' Bethran looked at him sullenly.

'Take the teeth with you, many will barter with you for monster teeth,' put in Bethran. Tyr nodded, thanked him and left. For some moments, Bethran thought through what had happened. The lad's idea hadn't been a bad one. Bethran had already noticed a few things about the site where the body was found. He knew Laman had been placed in the mouth of the blow fish. He sighed, he realised that it couldn't profit him anyway. So the man would give him a trifle of gold, how long would that last? He finished the dregs of the ale and was about to leave when the door opened and in came the elder from the village.

'Will you walk with me, Bethran?' he asked. The seer nodded and followed him outside. When they were out of earshot of other villagers, the elder said, 'I was told that you have some skill in divining felons as well as the weather.' Bethran took a deep breath.

'I use different methods,' he replied, 'I look, and sometimes the facts reveal themselves.'

'Then you '*see*' what happened?'

'Yes,' nodded Bethran, 'but I use my wits, nothing more. There are no bones to cast and no water to scry.'

'No magic?' asked the man glancing at him. Bethran shook his head slowly.

'And if the signs are not present, then I cannot see anything. There is no help from the gods in these matters, it is me alone.'

'You are telling me that there is no certainty of success?' asked the man.

'Indeed, which is why I cannot undertake such a task.'

'I was told by the brother of the widow that he could not afford to pay you what you needed.' There was a hint of humour in the voice of the man.

'Is that what he told you?' smiled Bethran. 'In some ways, he was correct. It takes time to follow such a procedure and I cannot make my living when engaged, so yes, my time has to be taken into consideration.'

'I can resolve your worries in that regard, but...' the elder broke off for a moment as they reached the dunes and he stopped. He turned to the seer and continued, 'I do not believe the man was killed in any other way than by the blow fish.'

'Then why come to me?' asked Bethran. The man looked around him and then back into Bethran's eyes.

'The position of an elder-man is a precarious one in these modern times,' he began, 'of the three of us on the council, I have the most enemies you might say. The man who died, Laman, was involved in some sort of feud with one of the other fishermen of the village. The brother of the widow thinks that I am doing nothing about his suspicions because I once had connections to this other man.'

'I see,' announced Bethran.

'So, in truth, I do not particularly care one way or the other if you find that some evil has been done. All I need, is to seem as if I am doing something positive. That I am financing you to look into it.'

'I see,' said Bethran once more.

'I think you do, I think you do,' he repeated. 'So, what do you need from me?' Bethran stared at the man, did he mean payment? The seer didn't know what he should ask for if that was it, so he decided to come from another angle.

'Well, to start with,' he began, 'I need to examine the site where the body was found.' The man nodded.

'Yes, of course, we have people cutting the great fish up. It will supply us for some time. I can have the beach cleared, anything else?'

'The body of the man, where is it?' asked the seer.

'The widow and her family will be with it but,' he paused, 'I can arrange for you to examine it, if you wish.' Bethran nodded at this and then he ran his hands through his beard as he thought.

'I will need somewhere to work.' What he meant was, he needed somewhere to stay, but the elder seemed happy enough with the request.

'The old forge would suit. The smith has moved out to the new forge in the village. It has room and is away from prying eyes just out of the main settlement.'

'Good,' nodded Bethran, 'that would suit,' then something struck him, something important. 'Oh, I need my servant here, I er...' he hesitated and then added, 'I sent him to Lliefoot on an errand. Can you send someone to stop him and turn him around? He cannot be far from the village.'

'Done,' replied the man, 'I will leave you to it then, if you need me, just ask in the village,' he turned and left Bethran wondering what the hell he was doing and where he should start. He decided he would begin at the ale hut, but this time just to eat. He had to think and as soon as Tyr returned, if indeed he did return, he would have to formulate a plan of attack. He wondered if he required anything for the forge, he would have to look over the place first.

He was mopping up the last of the stew with some bread when Tyr eventually walked in.

'I thought I would find you here,' he said with a frown. 'A runner stopped me on the road, said I was to return to Tall Bridges on pain of death.'

'Did he now? That is not the message I sent.'

'Well, it might not have been those very words, but he was insistent,' explained Tyr, 'but he said that my *master* required me at the village as soon as possible.'

'Yes, that is more of what I said,' smiled Bethran, raising his hand to the burly man serving ale. Tyr became uneasy, it was most unlike the seer to smile, and what did he want with him? A pie was dropped on the table in front of Tyr and a mug of ale soon after.

'Eat,' demanded Bethran, 'and when you are refreshed, come to see me, I will be at the old smithy on the edge of the village.' He stood and walked to the door, then turned to the young man, 'we have a mystery to unravel,' and then he left.

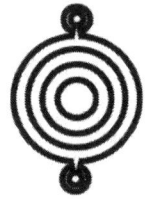

Chapter 6 – The Coming Storm

'So what are we looking for?' asked Tyr, watching Bethran examine the site of the blow fish.

'I have no idea,' admitted the seer crouching by the mouth of the beast. It was clear that other people had taken trophies from the jaw, as there were few teeth left. The body too had been cut in to, and a great deal of the animal had already been removed. The smell was overpowering. Bethran stood, but kept his gaze to the floor. 'There is nothing to see here, I have asked to see the body of the victim, but I think we are not going to find anything there either.'

'You said earlier that the man was killed by being struck on the head,' remembered Tyr, 'I assume that will be important,' he added. Bethran looked to him.

'It is not going to point to anything except the manner of his death though, is it?' insisted Bethran. 'Nothing of that nature is going to tell us who did it.' He sighed deeply. 'Come on,' he added, and began to walk to the village.

The two of them examined the body of Laman as his wife sat by it, staring into nothingness. The hut was small, probably one of the smallest, and was very dark. A single oil lamp lit the place, and even with the door open, it was difficult to see any detail. Bethran was silent as he looked at the wound on the skull and looked for other marks on the arms and legs. When he had finished, he turned to the woman and said,

'We have done here, I am sorry for your loss.' The woman fixed her swollen eyes on the far distance and in a feint voice said,

'What am I to do now?' There was no answer to give her. A widow of her age was too old to find a man, and she would have no means of making ends meet. In a few weeks she could be a beggar, or worse.

'Have you no children?' asked Tyr. Bethran glared at him. He didn't want them to get involved, then for the first time, the woman looked at his face.

'Our son was killed at sea in the storm two winters ago, and our daughter died in childbirth the year before that. I have no surviving children.' Her expression was one of stupefaction, as if all life was draining from her.

'Then your brother?' asked Tyr. The woman shook her head and considered this through her grief.

'They have little enough for themselves, he has four children surviving of his own.' Her voice seemed to drift off into the distance. The two men decided to retreat outside and walk back to the old smithy. On the way, they were quiet until Bethran broke the silence.

'I do not see how anyone can find out the truth after the event,' the frustration was evident in his voice.

'Then how would you approach a problem that had not yet happened?' asked Tyr.

'The bones, 'seeing' fire, scrying and several other methods,' explained Bethran, 'but they rarely work for things yet to happen, *never* for things that have already happened.'

'Then, it is clear,' nodded Tyr, 'that your methods have to change.' Bethran looked to Tyr as they walked.

'I sometimes think that you really are living in the fairy kingdom,' he scowled, 'this is what I know, this is what I do. I do not search places of death in the hope that some past memories will appear in my mind. That is necromancy and I do not believe it is a real art.'

'Necro...,' Tyr paused, 'what is that?' he asked with a puzzled expression.

'Contacting the dead spirit of someone and conversing with them,' explained Bethran, 'but in my experience, once a person is dead, they remain that way.'

'So you do not believe there is an underworld?' asked Tyr.

'No, I do not,' replied the seer with some vehemence, 'there are so many things to disprove it.'

'What things?' asked Tyr, but Bethran didn't want to get into a conversation about things he didn't think existed, just in case this quick-witted man got the better of him.

'It is not a subject for this moment, we have to

find who killed Laman, and to be quite honest, I have come to a complete stop.' As they reached the hut that was the old smithy, they entered and sat on a bench where they both gave some thought to the problem.

'Are you sure that the man was not killed by the beast on the beach?' asked Tyr.

'Yes,' barked Bethran, 'I have seen enough of the dead to know he was killed before he reached the beach.'

'How do you know that?' asked the young man. Bethran sighed and turned to Tyr.

'The wound on his head was old. Blood had soaked into his hair and had dried into a sticky mess close around it,' he explained as if speaking with a child, but saw a look in Tyr's face that made him think the lad didn't understand his point. He sighed again and tried to explain. 'When a severe wound such as that on the head of Laman bleeds, the blood always flows to the floor, does it not?' Tyr pushed out his lips and nodded casually. 'The blood on Laman's head had dried into a mat around the wound, there was no sign that the blood had run forward over his face, and there was no blood on the beach.' Bethran watched Tyr think this through.

'So,' he eventually said, but then paused, 'so,' he repeated, 'you think he was killed earlier and fell onto his back,' he paused again trying to work through the problem, 'so the blood would have pooled where he first fell,' he concluded and smiled. 'That makes perfect sense.' He nodded and folded his arms, the smile still playing on his features. Bethran looked away from him and stared into space.

'Not that it helps us,' he frowned.

'We need to find where the deed was done then,' insisted Tyr.

'That would prove nothing,' laughed Bethran sarcastically, 'blood can be found all over, and what if someone had been gutting fish?' Tyr nodded at this with his own frown.

'There must be something,' he sighed, 'something to tell us what happened.'

'Even if something is found,' insisted Bethran, 'no one will admit to it,' then a realisation came to him, 'even the elder-man is not interested in finding the truth of the matter.' Tyr spun around to Bethran.

'He is not interested...' began Tyr, but he broke off, 'then why is he willing to pay you for this venture? Does he know something already?'

'I suspect he does, but that means whatever is found will go no further.'

'But that makes no sense,' insisted Tyr.

'You are right,' nodded Bethran, 'but he is one of the people that runs the settlement. No one will turn against him even if *he* killed Laman himself.' Tyr frowned deeply. He knew it to be true. Only someone of Lord Cullcoil's stature could overturn an elder's decision, or the settlement themselves, of course.

'The really important issue,' continued Bethran, 'is that even if we find nothing, he will still pay us,' and he turned to Tyr again, 'he just wants to be seen by the village as acting for their good.' Tyr put more thought into that point as Bethran stood. 'I have to move on the day after next, whatever happens.'

'Why?' asked Tyr.

'I have to be at Southferry by the first full moon after the longest day,' he paused, 'and that is soon.'

'Your clothes?' asked Tyr, raising his brows. Bethran nodded and looked into his pack.

'Do you have food?' he asked. Tyr shook his head as Bethran broke off some bread and handed it to the young man. 'I am running short of supplies and the means to buy more.' Tyr thought that too many visits to the ale hut could be the reason, but he kept quiet. It wasn't his business.

'So we have two days to find something out,' was what he said instead.

'We can do a little prodding, tell the elder-man we have found nothing, take our payment and then move on,' nodded Bethran, biting into the hard bread. Tyr felt a little disappointed at that thought. He considered that there must be a way to find out more about the incident. A thought then struck him.

'Do you think you could carry a man the size of Laman and push him into the mouth of the blow fish?'

'I would think so,' nodded Bethran. 'Only the leg was in the mouth so, I think it could be done.'

'Hmm,' sighed Tyr.

'You were thinking he was not alone?' smiled Bethran. Tyr nodded.

'Well, if it makes you feel better, I do think there was at least another person involved,' added Bethran, sitting on a bench to finish his food.

'You do?' asked Tyr, his expression brightening.

'Yes,' nodded the seer, 'what happened to the other fishermen?'

122

'What other fishermen?'

'The ones who were with Laman,' replied Bethran. 'They would have seen something, and if they did but remain quiet, they must be involved.'

'Just explain,' frowned Tyr, 'what other fishermen?' Bethran wiped his mouth and began.

'Laman fished the shallow water around the bay. He did not fish for lobster and did not fish from a line very often. There is a method using a flax net with stones to weight it down, and wood to make the top float.'

'I have never seen this done, but I heard of nets placed across rivers,' explained Tyr.

'That depends on the season,' explained Bethran with a nod, 'the fishermen here work through most of the year. The way they fish is by suspending the net between two boats and then scooping up any fish that tangle in that net.'

'So there had to be at least two boats out that night,' nodded Tyr, raising his brows.

'And at least two men in each,' added Bethran, 'most of the time, there are two crew needed to haul in the nets and keep the boats in position.'

'How do you know these things?' asked Tyr.

'I have watched the operation many times and the boats at Tall Bridges are of a fine quality,' replied the seer.

'Then I would think that these men know something,' said Tyr, standing and pacing around the hut.

'It may be those same men that struck him down,' nodded Bethran, 'who knows what fishermen argue about and to what degree?' Tyr stopped pacing and thought for a moment.

'If they were all involved, they will keep quiet, I assume,' he said, 'but would it not be wise to at least ask them?' Bethran shook his head.

'Lies from any source will only cloud the waters,' Bethran insisted, 'we need facts, not rumours.' Tyr sat once more and leaned forward with his elbows on his thighs. For several moments both men sat silently until Tyr announced,

'I'll fetch water from the river, I need to drink,' then he picked up an old wooden pail from the floor and left. As soon as he had gone, it was Bethran's turn to pace the hut. He stopped by the door and opened it to let more light into the dingy room. He saw an upturned boat by the nearest hut at the edge of the village. It was small and looked like it was in need of repair, and then he had an idea. It wasn't going to be easy to test his theory, but it was the only direction he had.

Tyr filled the pail, but it leaked badly. He decided to drink and then refill the pail in the hope it would still have some water left by the time he reached the old smithy. As he returned, in his haste, he tripped and lost what water was in the pail onto the floor. As he sat looking at the now destroyed container, he noticed the elder of the village having, what seemed to be, a heated conversation with a red-haired man, carrying nets over his shoulder. Though Tyr couldn't hear any of what was said, the elder pointed to the sea and then shook a finger at the man, who turned almost crimson and then walked away in a hurry. Tyr didn't know what had happened, but he could see that, as the elder returned to the main settlement, he looked furious. Tyr thought it time to return to the smithy and inform Bethran. The seer was busy as the young man entered the hut. He had placed some boards on a trestle, with objects placed on the boards. He began to inform the seer of what he had just seen, but Bethran seemed deep in study, looking at the items on the trestle.

'What are you doing?' he asked, as the seer moved one of the objects a slight amount.

'Hmm, er what?' stuttered the seer not taking his eyes from the boards, 'doing? Well, er…' and he moved another of the objects to the edge of the table. For a moment he looked across to Tyr and asked,

'What were you saying, about the red-haired man I mean?'

'I'll tell you after you explain what you are doing,' insisted Tyr. Bethran sighed and looked back to the boards and then walked to the open door.

'I had a shock just now,' he began, 'working on an idea. I went around the back of the smithy to find some boards to make this.' He pointed across to the makeshift table. 'As I carried them in, an owl flew straight past me.'

'In the daylight?' asked Tyr raising his brows, 'not usual I admit but-'

'Not so *unusual* either,' interrupted Bethran, 'but the fact that it flew past me and so close, suggests it was an omen.' Tyr sighed. He was hoping the shock was something to do with the death of the fishermen, not one of his portents for the weather. 'That omen is a coming storm,' added Bethran.

'There is a cloudless sky, and it is not really storm season,' pointed out Tyr. For a moment, Bethran's eyes seem to flit around as if they were looking into his thoughts, then he announced,

'It is not a weather storm I am seeing, it is a storm of another kind,' his voice was calm and slow, but there was a hint of unease there too. 'A storm of troubles,' he eventually added, and then he walked back to the trestle and pointed to a small wooden log placed by the other objects. 'That is the blow fish,' he said conclusively. Tyr looked at the objects and at once saw what Bethran had done.

'So,' paused Tyr, pointing to each object as he spoke, 'the tooth is the dead man, the picture stones are the people on the beach,' he hesitated a moment, 'what is the knife?'

'The boat and the small wooden box is the other boat.'

'Which other boat?' asked Tyr.

'The one that would be needed to help Laman fish,' replied Bethran, looking directly at Tyr.

'But surely,' insisted Tyr pointing to the objects, 'this shows everything as it was at the time the body was found?'

'It does,' nodded Bethran, 'what I am trying to do is look back to the time that he was killed, I was using this to try to do that.' Tyr nodded, it was a good idea, but it was still guesswork to his mind.

'And how exactly are you going to do that?' he

asked. Bethran looked to him. For sure, there was something on his mind. He took a deep breath and swallowed.

'I think that the whole thing is based on the boat,' he announced with a less than convincing expression.

'I do not understand.'

'The boat was found on the shingle,' insisted Bethran, but saw that Tyr still didn't see the point, 'where it was supposed to be.' Tyr looked blankly. 'Why was the boat found on the shingle in the early morning, when the widow and the brother had been there the night before and not seen it?'

'Do you know that for sure?' asked Tyr after giving it some thought.

'By the elder-man's admission, she and her brother waited for her husband in the dark, I'm sure she would have known her husband's boat,' insisted Bethran holding out his arms, 'it is a particularly fine boat.'

'So you think it arrived at the shingle later?'

'No,' insisted Bethran, 'I think it had already arrived and it was taken back out again. By the early morning, it was back on the shingle where it should have been.' Tyr frowned deeply and looked down at the trestle table with its many items. He scratched his head and then asked,

'So you think that Laman had somewhere to go, and he left in his boat, only to meet his death?'

'I do not know,' shrugged Bethran and then folding his arms, 'but I cannot think of any other explanation that would fit.' Once again Tyr went into deep thought and considered how the story may have unfolded. He eventually nodded.

'It is certainly possible, but how to show that was the case to the elder?'

'It means nothing if we do not know where Laman went,' insisted the seer. He walked to the bench and sat. For a brief moment, Tyr had felt as if they were moving along, but after considering their options, he slumped down on the bench with Bethran. He then helped him stare gloomily into the dingy hut.

It was much later in the afternoon when the two men even discussed the task at hand. Tyr had been into the forest looking for suitable wood to make a fire in the old smithy when the sun went down. It was to be a rare comfort sleeping indoors, even if it was on the floor, but a good fire would make it all the better. Bethran, on the other hand, had been sitting on a rock at the shoreline. Many people had seen him and some had even nodded to him, but none had received any acknowledgment. It took a large man who was vaguely known to him to walk across his vision for Bethran to come out of his dream. The man was standing, looking straight at him.

'Did I hear right?' the man asked, 'has the elder-man asked you to look into the death of my sister's brother?' Bethran nodded, narrowing his eyes slightly. 'That is what I heard, but I doubted it was the truth,' added the man.

'Have you time to talk?' asked Bethran with a neutral expression. The man nodded, and the seer added, 'somewhere quiet.' They walked from the beach and to the landward side of the village where a shabby wooden hut stood with a stockade, and a small stall containing rough formed timber staves. They went around the rear and into the stockade. There were many wood shavings and various shaped staves and shafts littered around, and the man threw Bethran a brief explanation.

'I work wood, mainly repairs and tools,' he said with an almost apologetic air. 'No one will disturb us here,' he added with a slight growl. Bethran could imagine no one would disturb the woodworker if he didn't want it. 'What have you got to say?' he asked, sitting on a pile of timber. Bethran looked around for a seat but there was nothing suitable, so he leaned on the side of the stall where several planks looked like they were being finished, to make them flat and smooth.

'To have any chance of finding out who killed your sister's brother, I have to first find out what he did when he returned from his fishing trip.' The big man nodded. He could see that would be important.

'I spoke with Unust about that. He is the man who went fishing with Laman. He told me that they went out to fish with line, and later met with Perst and his boat to go deeper, to fish with a net.'

'Did anything happen?'

'Nothing that he thought to tell me,' shrugged the big man, 'he said they caught a reasonable amount of which most was kept in Laman's boat, and when it was time, they headed back to the beach.'

'It was dark when they returned, was it not?' asked Bethran.

'Aye, nodded the man, 'but they find their way back by the beacon on the hill, they arrange for someone to light it at dusk, the task pays well in fresh fish.'

'I understand,' nodded Bethran, 'so did Unust say anything else?'

'Nothing much. They pulled the boat onto the shingle and unloaded the fish.'

'Would the second boat be with them? Is that how they get the boats up the shingle?'

'Perst would be there with his brother, but if the boats land at the right time, they rest on the shingle just after the sea is turning. The next tide will then float it as it comes in.'

'And with the catch unloaded, it will float easier?' asked Bethran, though he knew this was the case. The big man nodded. 'And was the boat in that position?' The man nodded once more.

'Aye, in her usual spot, just below the high tide line.'

'So what happened to the catch?' Bethran then asked.

'I do not know that,' replied the man shaking his head slightly, 'Unust says that the fish were put in the fish crates ready for the morning but when he looked in them the following day, they were empty.'

'Interesting,' nodded Bethran, 'was Unust the regular crew of Laman?'

'Yes, Laman sometimes went out alone to fish with line, but when they were netting, Unust went with him.'

'And did Laman always net fish with Perst and his brother?' asked the seer, folding his arms.

'I do not know if that was the case, I doubt that there was a regular second boat though. People who have their own boats go as they wish or need,' explained the man. Bethran nodded, he looked around the yard and tried to picture the scene that night, nothing came to him, mainly because he didn't know Laman, and that was something he needed to see in his image. All he had was the dead face of the man in his mind.

'Was Laman popular?' asked Bethran.

'Not by me, but others liked him.'

'You did not see eye to eye with him?' asked the seer. The big man shook his head.

'You have seen the tiny hut that my sister lives in, Laman was doing well,' he insisted, 'he was a skilled fisherman, and he could almost smell the fishes. He always caught a large catch, even out of season, and it made him well off. Yet, though he built that boat, one of the finest boats on the coast, my sister still had to live in penury, I will not say anything good of him in that respect.'

'I see,' nodded Bethran, 'but as a fisherman, he was liked and respected?'

'For the most part,' nodded the man, 'he would buy them ale and would gift them fish when their trips failed, but...' the man trailed off, he seemed to be thinking through the past, he was seeing something he had not needed to consider previously. Bethran raised his brows and gave a questioning look.

'I need to know everything,' he insisted.

'I always had the feeling that underneath, no one really liked him,' explained the man at length. 'They put up with his boasting and they put up with his stories, just because one day, they might need his charity.' Bethran nodded, there was much more to this fisherman than met the eye. Here was someone who could, and would make enemies. Probably not the sort of enemy who would bash him on the head with a rock, but he wasn't going to be the target of any sympathy, that was for sure.

'Is this why most of the catch that night was landed into his boat?' asked Bethran, unfolding his arms and moving his stiffening body a little.

'Possibly,' shrugged the man, 'but I would have thought it was because the boat was bigger in the beam than most of the others. As I said, it was a special boat.'

'Who built it?' asked Bethran.

'Laman did, I helped him, but it was his doing,' explained the burly man, 'he did not want anyone else to steal the design. He thought if a boat builder made it, everyone would soon have such a boat.' Bethran nodded, he could see very well that this man could indeed cultivate jealousy and resentment. 'It took us the best part of a summer to finish it, he named it Boann' added the man.

'Boann? The water goddess, very fitting,' nodded Bethran. The big man narrowed his eyes. He wasn't surprised that a seer knew about such things. 'Is there anyone you think would have information for me?' asked Bethran. The big man thought for a moment.

'Everyone knew him. All could tell you something, I suppose.' He ended with a shrug. Bethran gave a slight nod and then said,

'Just one more question,' he looked once more around the yard and then directly into the man's dark brown eyes. 'Who do you think would want him dead?'

The big man looked beyond the seer, his eyes then flitted from side to side before he announced, 'there are a few who would wish him ill, but to kill him? Perst,' he announced with confidence. Bethran had already wondered if the issue was based in fishing, it seemed obvious, but he added to his question.

'Why do you think it was Perst?' The big man took no deliberation with his answer.

'We altered Perst's boat for him as he could not afford to have a new boat made, but we made some alterations to it. Perst was never happy about it. He said the boat was worse than before we altered it. That wasn't the case, but he continued to tell that to everyone. Perst and his brother are not well thought of, but it did not stop the gossip. Many assumed Laman had ruined Perst's boat to be rid of the competition. It was not the case.' Bethran nodded.

'Thank you,' he gave a slight smile, 'I may call on you again if that is acceptable?'

'Yes,' nodded the man, 'I'm Birse, son of Ulm. If you need anything more, just ask.'

Bethran walked slowly back to the smithy to give him time to sift through the story he had just heard, and memorise the pertinent, and store the unimportant. He hadn't realised how elucidating conversation could be. He already knew a great deal more than he had that morning, and how much more could he uncover with a few more of those conversations? He also remembered that the wife of Laman seemed cold towards the death of her husband, and more worried about what would happen to her. Did she also dislike the man? She wouldn't be in a minority if that was the case. But then again, if that fishing boat Laman had named Boann was the unique vessel he boasted, then, his widow would be able to trade it to make her position safer. That was, unless she wasn't the one who would own the boat after his death. Bethran now wished he had thought of that earlier, as it could make a difference to his next questions. He sighed and was so deep in thought. He didn't notice there was smoke issuing from the old smithy. He was still seeing the events of that fateful night on the shingle. The boats riding the surf making that unmistakable hissing sound on the pebbles, the feet of four men jumping down. The unloading of the fish onto the shore, and the conversations in the dark. What had happened to that night's catch? Why had it gone by the morning? For some reason, Bethran couldn't help thinking that it was important. Four men knew of that catch. One was dead. That left Unust, Perst and his brother. Bethran considered that Unust would be the next one to speak to just as he pushed open the door of the smithy. The smell of wood smoke took Bethran by surprise, and he looked up to see a fire in the hearth and the whole hut looked more homely. Tyr had been busy, and the trestle table with the objects upon it took pride of place by one of the walls.

'Is it not too warm for a fire?' asked Bethran with a glimmer of a frown.

'Yes, but I wondered if the hearth would work or if it would choke us. It seems it works well,' announced Tyr.

'Now, if you had not traded that iron pot,' began Bethran looking at the flames dancing in the hearth, 'we could have made something to eat.'

'Not without something to put in the pot,' explained Tyr.

'True,' nodded Bethran, turning to the trestle table and staring at it for some moments. He looked back to the fire and then to Tyr. He seemed to be looking at Tyr's clothing, or lack of it, and he began to rub his long grey beard through his hands.

'What is it?' asked Tyr, a little worried.

'Talking,' said Bethran before sitting on the shabby wooden barrel placed by the trestles.

'Talking, what do you mean?'

'Talking to people seems to get results,' he announced, 'and you talk a great deal, I, not so much,' and Bethran looked over Tyr again. The young man watched the seer's eyes take him in and move around his body. He knew exactly what the older man was thinking.

'And you think that no one will want to talk to me if I look like a beggar?'

'More or less,' agreed Bethran, 'and that is a great pity as I have found much by conversing. The problem is, we need more conversation.'

'I cannot help there,' shrugged Tyr, 'I have no means to improve my attire, and probably never will.'

'I have an idea, but...' Bethran paused to try to think his way through it before speaking, 'there is a stall within the market that has cloth and trimmings.'

'I know, that is where you decided to throw me about somewhat, as I remember,' replied Tyr, raising his brows.

'Yes,' sighed Bethran with a frown, 'yes, probably with good reason, but anyway,' he stood and reached for his pack and pulled out a small sack. It was the sack containing the picture stones. 'Take these...' he paused, handing the sack to Tyr, 'and this,' he added pulling out another small bag, 'and go to the cloth seller.' Tyr looked into the bag and saw several small beads. He pulled one out and held it up to the flames of the fire. The orange of the flames danced through it with many iridescent colours. As he turned it between his finger and thumb, the shapes moved and the colours changed.

'What are they?' asked Tyr.

'The beads are made from heating various sands, they call it glass,' explained Bethran staring at the baubles. 'I got these from a fort south of Fidach. A jewellery maker there makes fine glass.'

'I have never seen such things before,' said Tyr with a look of wonder on his face.

'Well, stop drooling and take them to the market. Try to get enough cloth to make a new shirt, a coat, and some breeches. Shoes will have to wait.'

'I cannot,' frowned Tyr with a look of rebellion about him, 'I will not take your things for my gain, as much as I crave better clothing I cannot-' Bethran cut him short.

'Look upon it as a loan then, but I need you looking less like a beggar or a bandit and more like a man of learning. In short,' Bethran paused, 'I need you to talk to people. And make it quick, it is late.' Tyr looked into Bethran's face, a rising of pleasure and excitement flooded him.

'Then I shall do it,' he eventually said with a serious expression, 'and I shall not forget this, I will pay you back and more,' he said and left the hut.

'If only you knew what was coming,' whispered Bethran, shaking his head with a worried frown.

Chapter 7 – Alone at last.

The woman looked distraught. Her husband was dead, killed for some reason or other, and now she faced the future with little hope of survival. That was the way of the world. It was the same in war, the widows of the soldiers soon became casualties themselves, but this wasn't a war. A man going about his business was slain and his body moved to try to make it look like a sea monster had killed him. Bethran didn't sit, there was only one other seat anyway, but he hadn't come with the intention of staying for long. She looked up to him with a look of desperation.

'You are the one who is trying to find who killed Laman?' she asked. Bethran nodded.

'Yes, but I need to ask you a few questions.' She just stared at him, not moving her head, or acknowledging she had even heard him. 'Did Laman have any enemies, anyone who would wish him ill?' Bethran looked around the tiny hut and remembered what her brother had said.

'I cannot say, he told me little,' was her brief answer.

'So you knew nothing about his fishing methods?' the seer asked. Her head moved the faintest amount in the negative.

'No, all I know is what my brother told me.' Bethran knew he was wasting his time, so he tried a different tack.

'You should be provided with by the sale of his boat, should you not?' Her eyes took on a look of pleading as she replied.

'That is the thing, the elder-man came to me and said that they would have to wait to see if Laman owed anything to anyone,' her weak voice was failing, 'he thinks there should be something but he doubts I will make much from it.' Bethran began to suspect the elder-man more than ever with this single piece of information.

'I see,' he said and then asked, 'do you have skill with a needle and thread?'

'I used to repair the sails for the boats, and of course I make and repair our...' she paused and amended the sentence, '*my* clothes.'

'Then I have a small task for you if it is something you can do. I cannot pay much, but it should keep you going for a while.'

'What is it?' she asked. Bethran opened the door and beckoned Tyr in. He was carrying cloth.

'Can you make clothes for this man?' There was little room for three in the hut and she had to peer around

139

Bethran to see the man, but she looked him up and down.

'Yes,' she said without emotion, 'that would be easy enough.'

'One other thing,' added the seer, 'was Unust a regular crewman for your husband?'

'I think he took Unust most of the time, but I do not know for sure if there were others,' she replied blankly.

'Do you know where I can find him?' asked Bethran, unsure she would know anything about this person.

'I have no recollection of where he lives,' she replied, at least this time she shook her head, 'but I do know he helped out at the quarry when he was not fishing.' Bethran thanked her and went outside while she looked over the cloth and spoke to Tyr. When Tyr had done, he came outside.

'It seems the elder-man is deep in this mystery,' whispered the seer, and he told the young man what the widow had said.

'So, we probably need to know who the red-haired man was,' replied Tyr with a nod.

'What red-haired man?' asked Bethran with a frown.

'The one the elder was speaking to,' sighed Tyr, wondering if the older man listened to anything he said. 'I told you when I went to fetch water from the river.'

'Ah, yes,' nodded Bethran, 'I recall, I was deep in thought at the time. What happened to the water by the way?' added Bethran as an afterthought.

'The pail failed on the return journey,' smiled Tyr. Bethran nodded and then looked around towards the village as if he was finding his bearings.

'We need to speak with this Unust, the widow says he helps at the quarry,' and the two of them made their way back to the smithy and down the track to the small quarry that lay on the south side.

There were two huts on the edge of the outcrop of rock that was crucial to the small industry that had grown there. There were a few workers driving iron chisels into the rock face and two large stones were visible, they had obviously been sheared off the face previously. Several other men were chipping away at neatly cut stones. The larger slab was attended by a vast, bald headed man whose massive arms were tapping away as gently as a child. He turned when he saw the two men approach.

'What can I do for you?' he asked, still holding the pointed iron tool and a large, round-headed mallet that looked so small in his large hands.

'We are looking for Unust,' replied Bethran.

'Good luck then,' replied the man, and he turned back to the stone. He was chipping away at a design on the stone drawn on with charcoal. The design was a double spiral, the symbol of Arianrhod, goddess of the sky and the keeper of the silver wheel. It was a statement to all who saw it that they were entering the Kingdom of Cat, and here at least, the religion was of that great goddess. Bethran also saw that at the top of the stone, several designs had already been cut and younger men, probably apprentices, were deepening the marks carved previously by the stone-cutter. They used other iron chisels and harder, shaped stones to deepen the design into a relief. They were improving the sign of the mirror, the symbol that showed magic was practiced. Still in charcoal was the design of the comb, the symbol of modernity and civilisation. The people of Cat were keen to show they were an advanced race, and this stone was being made to proclaim that.

'So, he is not here?' asked the seer.

'No,' insisted the man, and he stopped his work once more, 'he was supposed to be helping the others to move the slabs up here, I sent one of the men to find him but he is nowhere to be found.'

'Is that usual?' asked Bethran, but the answer was sharp and angry.

'Do I look like I employ boys who stay at home when there is work to do?' Bethran took the answer as a no, and to change the subject, he asked,

'Is this stone going to the border?' The stone-cutter looked at the slab that was resting in a large box of sand.

'Aye,' he nodded, then looked back to Bethran, 'Lord Cullcoil wants it to replace the one just north of the ferry. He says the old one is not grand enough.' He shrugged and added,

'I cannot see the point, but who knows the workings of a man's mind?' and he got back to his task. Bethran looked to Tyr and nodded towards the village, and they left with no further questions.

'Where is the border?' asked Tyr.

'Of Cat?' asked Bethran, 'just under a day's travel,' he added without waiting.

'And beyond that is Fidach?' Bethran nodded. 'Cat is bigger than I thought it was, all the way from the northern ocean and the islands of the Boar Kingdom, to the border of Fidach in the south.' He was shaking his head in wonder, he had been told often that the kingdom was large, but not until he had travelled it, did the greatness of it become real.

'And beyond that is Fortriu,' added Bethran, as Tyr looked towards the mountains in the west.

'The world is so big, and yet I have seen just one tiny part of it,' he sighed. 'How big is the world do you think?' he then asked, but Bethran shook his head and insisted that they needed to solve the problem at hand before they moved on to others. Bethran didn't want to get into a conversation he had been involved with some years previously with another learned man. They had almost come to blows on the possible size of the world, mainly because Bethran had differing views to most other people. That was for some other time, and now he had encountered another little problem with the task at hand.

'Why has Unust gone missing? That is our issue at the moment,' he added.

Bethran spent some time trying to track down the man called Unust, but it was almost if the man had left the area. Nothing had been seen of him that day, and the only clue to his whereabouts was that he was seen on the shore the evening before. Tyr had asked Bethran what the next step was in their search for the killer of the fisherman, but the seer was once again looking at the items on the trestle table.

'I am unsure what to do next,' he said.

'We could look over Laman's boat,' suggested Tyr.

'I have done that,' replied Bethran, moving the knife closer to the small box, 'there was nothing to find but fish scales and the smell of the sea.' Tyr sat and looked towards the open door. He too was stuck for ideas.

'We have not spoken to Perst yet,' he suggested, but Bethran look directly at him.

'Simply because,' insisted Bethran, 'I do not feel he will speak a single word of truth.'

'You think he is involved?' asked the younger man. Bethran looked down to the table and specifically the knife. He picked it up and moved it around in his hand.

'I think several people are involved, I just think questioning Perst or his brother, will just let them know we suspect them,' sighed Bethran. He held out the knife towards Tyr. 'This is the problem,' he insisted.

'The knife?'

'The boat,' corrected Bethran, as he placed it back on the table. 'Something bothered me about the boat and I could not fathom what it was until now.' The seer looked a little more animated as he moved the box and the knife around on the table. 'I had already explained how the boats were beached on the shingle just before the tide was at its highest, ready for the next tide to lift them off.' Tyr folded his arms and nodded. 'So, if the boat was taken back out to sea, why was it not beached lower than Perst's boat?'

'It might have been,' suggested Tyr.

'No, it was not. Birse told me the boats were both in their usual places.'

'So, now you are saying the boat did not go back out?' asked Tyr with a confused expression. Bethran raised his brows over closed eyes and replied,

'I do not know,' he allowed a gentle shake of the head and then sat on the old barrel. Once again, the two men were silent until Bethran said,

'Come, let us walk.'

They made their way to the settlement and through towards the bridge. From there they walked to the beach where the blow fish remains were. Dark smoke rose from the beach, and a rancid stench permeated the air. On the sand, several large cauldrons and kettles stood over fires, and the remains of the blow fish that was deemed no good for food, were being rendered down for oil, to keep the village in winter light. Very little of the body would be left to the gulls and the crows, most would be of some use to the people of Tall Bridges. Bethran hoped the wind didn't change direction or the village could become a place no one would wish to be. The two of them looked south along the beach and then back to the area where the ribs of the blow fish stuck up like an open-topped cage. Each time someone went near it, a cloud of birds took to the air. The tide was claiming parts of the animal too, and in a few days, there would be barely any sign that the sea monster had come to Tall Bridges. Bethran lead them back across the bridge and down to the southern shore where the boats usually stood. Perst's boat was out to sea, but Boann, Laman's boat was being hauled up the beach by several of the older fishermen.

'What are you doing?' asked Bethran. The man who seemed in charge of the task looked at the seer as if he was about to tell him it was none of his business, but he didn't.

'Orders of the elder-man, until it is decided who shall own it,' he said in a rough manner. Bethran counted the men hauling it, and he had an idea.

'I wonder, can you help me with something?' The man didn't speak. He stood upright and folded his arms as if he was daring Bethran to ask. 'This boat is not all that big, could two of you men pull it, or does it always take six of you?'

'No point in pulling our tripes out when there are six of us,' laughed one of the other men.

'No, but I just thought you men of the sea would be stronger.' To Tyr's mind, Bethran seemed to be goading them. He knew why he was doing it, but he would have used a different way to achieve the answer. The man in charge rolled up his sleeve to show his arms and slapped his right arm with the left.

'Pulling a net full of herring into the boat is more than a normal man can do, I could pull this boat myself if I had the mind.'

'Well, amuse me. If you can do it, I will buy you ale,' smiled Bethran folding his arms. The big man took

146

hold of the warp and pulled for all he was worth, but the shingle made him lose his footing over and over until he bawled.

'Damn shingle, no chance with this,' and he threw down the rope.

'Two of you then,' said Bethran, looking relaxed, with a hint of a smile on his face. 'My offer still stands.' The man in charge pointed to one of the other men, and the new man went to the stern end of the boat and readied to push. This time the boat moved, not easily, but they soon covered the ten paces remaining, and only when the boat was off the shingle and on the hard ground did more men join.

'You owe me and my friend here a mug of ale,' grinned the man.

'And you shall have it,' announced Bethran, 'tell them at the ale hut, Bethran will pay for it.' The two men walked off as Bethran turned to Tyr, raising his brows. When the others had left, the two of them leaned on the boat and Bethran whispered,

'It would not be easy, but two men could drag the boat to the high tide spot.' Tyr nodded as he had a thought.

'And the other boats are smaller, easier to pull up the shingle,' he said. Bethran nodded, though he wasn't sure what Tyr was driving at. They eventually left so that Bethran could make good his wager with the ale hut, and then they returned to the smithy.

'I have to leave in the morning,' announced Bethran as he sat.

'You are leaving, just when we are making some

147

headway?' replied Tyr slightly astonished.

'As I told you before, I have to be at the ferry by the full moon. I am not about to go back on my word.' Tyr sighed. He was hoping that Bethran had forgotten his new clothes. 'You will stay on and continue to keep your eyes open.'

'Me, alone?' asked Tyr with surprise, 'I would not know what to do.'

'Just watch, listen and wait for me to return,' shrugged Bethran, 'that is why it was important for you to have the new clothes. It will make your task easier.'

'But I have no means to eat, no means to find food.'

'Neither have I,' frowned Bethran, 'my reserves are gone and I still have to pay for my clothes at the ferry, and your new clothes being made by the widow.' Tyr reached into his coat and pulled out a small sack.

'You will need this then,' and he threw it to Bethran who looked inside.

'So, it looks like you made a good deal on the cloth,' he said as he looked at several picture stones and a single glass bead. Tyr nodded, he was good at talking. He had convinced the cloth trader that he was a great traveller who had been shipwrecked, and he was on the lookout for a famous pirate. The cloth trader hated pirates nearly as much as moths, so he had been sympathetic to the young man.

For the rest of the day, the two men went over what they knew and Bethran insisted that all Tyr need do was observe. It was dangerous to go too far, and he should wait for Bethran to return. Tyr had agreed, but in the back of both their minds, they knew Tyr was too inquisitive to do such a thing. Bethran said he should be back in three or four days depending on the weather. In the early morning, Bethran divided what food he had left, which was a lump of stale bread each, and gave a shallow nod to the lad.

'Is there no option to you leaving?' he asked. Bethran sighed. He leaned into his staff for support and began to explain.

'These clothes,' he announced with another sigh, 'are to be more than my winter clothes. I have planned their making for several summers and I cannot, in all faith, forget them. I instructed the seamstress some moons ago, and she has been industrious since then, making them to my design. They are not just winter clothes.'

'I don't understand,' frowned Tyr.

'In the past, I realised that the people expect...' Bethran paused, 'something particular in a seer,' he continued. 'I still adorn my beard with beads and feather, braid my hair with the rarest shells from the sea, and wear trinkets and other oddities. But there was once a time when I would paint my face with colour and cast scented powder into the air, or cause the fires to flare up. In more recent times,' he continued with a sigh, 'and certainly now that the Christians have come, I realise that the adornments are no more than a guise that the people will see through.'

'And these clothes will change that?' asked Tyr.

'I hope they will,' nodded Bethran, grasping his

staff tighter. 'These clothes are fine and decorative. Not only will they keep me from the hate of the weather, they, for a time at least, should make me stand out above ordinary men in a different way. You know yourself, important people dress in important clothing.' Tyr nodded slowly. He was beginning to understand how rational was Bethran's thinking. If he was to compete in the world of the Christians, he would need to elevate himself in the eyes of his patrons. Clothing could achieve that.

'I understand,' smiled Tyr and they parted company after a short silence. Bethran headed south and Tyr watched him go until he could see the man no longer and then went back to the old smithy and the lump of bread. He ate it almost immediately as his hunger was severe. He then looked at the items Bethran had left on the trestle. Just two picture stones and the glass bead remained and they, he hoped, would pay for the clothes. Or maybe he would try to secure some food instead.

During the late morning and afternoon, Tyr felt low. The smithy was silent, and he didn't feel much like watching anyone in the village. He was hungry, and he felt alone. He hadn't realised how much of a difference Bethran had made to his life. He had the consideration of setting off south to catch the seer up, but he resisted it. He knew he wouldn't have the means to pay the ferryman. He then considered Bethran's bronze disc. It occurred to him that he hadn't seen it all the time they had been together. It was probably buried deep in that mysterious pack he carried. It always looked full, even when he took things from it, the pack seemed to be stuffed with items. He then realised that Bethran's blanket went in there when he had little else to carry. That didn't explain him not seeing the bronze instrument, though. He had always thought that Bethran used it constantly, but that clearly wasn't the case. He even knew the full moon was upon them, and yet he hadn't confirmed it by the disc. Then again, an average set of eyes could see that, just by looking into the night sky. For the rest of the day he did little, when his body complained from lack of food, he began to walk the streets and even went down to the beach where the remains of the blow fish were now beginning to putrefy. That put him off the idea and he walked back to the settlement. He passed the ale hut and doubled back to the beach. He sat on the side of Laman's boat for a while until he realised that the sun was getting low in the sky. He watched the boats unload their fish and once again the hunger bit. He noticed one of the older fishermen keep casting an eye towards him, but paid it no heed. As the rest of the fishermen left to carry their catch to the fish boxes or the drying hut, the one who had been watching him came over.

'You are with Bethran are you not?' He spoke in a quiet voice, as if trying not to catch anyone's attention. Tyr nodded silently. 'I didn't know that was who he was until he got us to pull the boat.' He nodded to the vessel Tyr was sitting on, he just shrugged. The man leaned on the boat with his back to it, resting his elbows on the gunwale. Tyr thought he was too close and began to take more notice of him.

'What do you want?' he asked, feeling a little isolated. The man almost jumped at the question, Tyr then realised he was perfectly safe from such a timid man. The man settled again and seemed to lean in towards Tyr.

'It is just that...' he tailed off and looked about him as if he suspected people were watching him. Tyr heard him draw in a breath. 'I think I know where Unust is,' he whispered. Tyr turned quickly to the man.

'You do?'

'Tell Bethran to look at Rook Point,' he hissed and then in a louder voice said, 'Aye, she is a fine vessel that one,' and he slapped a hand on the gunwale as he began to walk away, 'I wish I had the means for such a boat.'

'Wait,' called Tyr with a renewed life-force, 'Do you know where I could buy fish? Me and my friend are a little hungry.' The man stopped, and once again looked around.

'I will see if I can find someone who will sell you some,' replied the man, and he moved off into the village. That wasn't quite what Tyr was meaning, but he thought it had been worth a try. Where, in the name of the gods, was Rook Point, and how would he find it without asking someone? He ought to wait for Bethran to return, but he would love to see the seer's face when he came back to find that Tyr had solved the riddle. His stomach complained again, and he decided to return to the smithy, taking a slow walk to keep his stomach quiet. Once again he passed the ale hut and went down the passage to the smithy. He would light a fire, if he couldn't eat he would at least be warm in the cooling air. As soon as he stepped inside the smithy, there was an obvious stench in there, not dissimilar to the blow fish reek on the beach. He looked over to the trestle and saw something near the log, which was still there. Closer inspection showed it to be a fish. He didn't know what sort of fish it was, but a fish nonetheless. It didn't seem all that fresh, but after a time over a blazing fire, it would be quite good eating. He smiled as he looked for the kindling.

By the time Bethran had reached the first settlement to the south, he was ready for a drink and asked the small community for water. They had utilised one of the stone towers built by the ancestors, but they had lowered the height of this one and added extra buildings around its base. It made a solid structure that was cool in the summer but snug in the winter, and Bethran had passed through there many times. There were many of these towers still in use, and Bethran used them as markers along the long road to the south.

As he set off once more he was becoming used to the quiet again. Not having Tyr around was like it used to be and he tried to think how long he had been on the road with the young man. It seemed like many days since Camma, so long that Tyr had become part of his way of life. The time at Tall Bridges had made the connection greater, and it began to occur to Bethran that he need not go back north. He could continue south and return to Seal Bay for the winter. There were many reasons he could give Tyr and the elders of Tall Bridges for his change of plan, and if he was truthful with himself, he had no desire to make that journey back north once he had gone so far south. The plain below the dark hills of the south of Cat spread out, and he knew he was close to Northferry, and the river-mouth he had to cross.

He arrived at Northferry before noon and spoke to the ferryman there. A negotiation was made after Bethran had eaten an oatcake offered by the ferryman's wife, and he set off in the boat to cross to the south bank. He then made his way to the small settlement just south of the ferry and arranged for a meal at one of the huts there. He waited all day for his clothes to arrive and though they were late, he was extremely pleased with them and duly paid the required fee. He had already given the seamstress enough to purchase the cloth, but now he paid her for her excellent work. It was a silver pin brooch that had laid in his pack for just this moment. He then considered his next stop. That was to be Flowfoot, a large village on the south bank of the River Flow. He would have to walk down the river for half a day to the bridge crossing and then another half a day to Flowfoot. It was too late to start that evening, and so he decided to stay in the little settlement where he was. He was now in the kingdom of Fidach and he was heading to its capital some five days travel, three if he really kept up a good pace. He would have to quicken his pace too, as he would struggle to acquire food and drink without the means to barter. He could probably cast bones for someone, but if no one was interested in knowing their future, or how well their crops would grow, then he would become hungry. He was well known in Flowfoot, and it was a busy place, so he was sure that there would be enough trade for him to eat well, and maybe manage a few extras. That night, he slept in an empty animal stall and watched the stars through the open front. He thought about his past few weeks and eventually drifted off to sleep.

He didn't sleep very well that night, and his dreams saw him plagued by restless spirits and white wraiths coming from the sea. He awoke constantly and always seemed to return to similar dreams. When the morning eventually arrived, he sat in the stall wrapped in his blanket and thought about what the dreams meant. He had seen many images of spirits, which he assumed meant the restless ghost of the fisherman called Laman. He had seen walking wraiths coming from the cold waters of the eastern ocean, but he put that down to the lack of decent food. Another troubling image was that of Tyr, he saw him in a small fishing boat, and the boat was leaking and dropping slowly beneath the waves. He began to feel guilty. He didn't believe *all* dreams meant anything in the real world, but he did believe that some dreams could be helpful, even messages from the gods. The inclusion of Tyr in the dreams could be the gods saying that Tyr was in trouble, or even in danger. He cast the blanket aside and stood. He ached, and he had convinced himself that he would be travelling south, not north, but he wondered if the gods were correct. Was the young man in trouble? He sighed, he shook his head, and he ran his hand through his grey beard. That quick-thinking man from Camma was at Tall Bridges expecting him to return. Bethran had said he would return in a few days, and here he was thinking of abandoning him to his fate. Over the past week, Bethran had gotten used to Tyr. He wouldn't go as far as saying he liked the man, but he was *used* to him now. Bethran didn't owe him anything. He had saved him from certain death. He had provided him with new clothes. He had done everything he could for the lad. He owed him nothing. So why was he hurriedly packing his things, ready for another long walk north?

Tyr was standing in the tiny hut of the widow looking at the clothes she had made from the cloth that Bethran had provided, and though she looked no better than the previous time he had seen her, she was thankful that they had given her work and something to exchange for food.

'Oh, and can you tell me?' asked Tyr just as he was about to leave, 'Where is Rook Point?' The woman looked at him with weak eyes and pointed to the south.

'Just down the coast beyond the village where the rocks are.' Tyr hurried back to the smithy, and with an eager smile he untied the twine from around the parcel of clothes. He examined each item and looked them over excitedly and pulled off his old shirt, ready for the new one. Hearing Bethran's voice in his head, he replaced the old shirt and went to the river to wash. It was quick and not particularly detailed, but he returned thinking he had made some sort of difference. Once the new clothes were on, he smiled to himself. The clothes were simple and plain, but as he stood there in that dilapidated forge, he felt like Lord Cullcoil himself, holding court in the great long-hut at Camma. As he exited the hut, he paraded around the settlement as if he owned it. He wasn't sure if people were looking at him, but he felt they would be. As he settled into the idea that he looked very different to how he had done when he arrived. He became aware of the untidy hair at his cheeks and chin. Back at Camma, his treasured possessions had been his shaving knife and his comb. The comb he had made himself, but the shaving knife had been a gift for help in rebuilding a hut. He had kept it sharp and had used it regularly, but now, the comb and the knife were back at Camma with his blanket. Wearing the new clothes, he now felt the untidy facial hair didn't look right, and he kept his eyes peeled for anything that would improve things. His craving for food had been satiated the previous evening by the mysterious fish, but now his stomach was beginning to complain once again, and as he walked down the shoreline towards the south, he decided that once he had returned from Rook Point, he would plan ahead.

As he climbed the rocks to where he assumed was Rook Point, he noticed that the sky to the west was leaden and looked as if rain was heading over. He looked to the east and realised the wind had changed direction and so, with one eye on the clouds, he climbed over the uneven rocks. When he was at the top of the point, he looked along the shore. The cliff wasn't anywhere as high as most of the shoreline of Cat, but he could see clearly both ways. There was no sign of life on the beach and shingle, and he wondered if there was a cave or similar where a man might hide. He climbed down and walked the sandy line below the shingle and looked for caves. The rocks were simply not high enough to support caves, and Tyr wondered if the fisherman had sent him on a fool's errand. Another thought struck him. What if this was an ambush? His heart began to race. He ran for the cover of the rocks and weaved into them. It would be ironic if Bethran was to return to find his battered body on the shore, dressed in his new clothes, not even worn for a full day. He tried not to imagine Bethran trying to get a good price for them at the market. He stopped and listened, but even though the tide was out, all he heard were the waves and the gulls. That was a surprise in some ways, as he expected that all self-respecting seagulls would be picking at the rotting remains of the blow fish. He snaked his way through the rocks to where the gulls had congregated, and as they took to the air, he saw the body. He looked around but saw no one, and so he approached. Lying on its side, was a body that looked as if it was once a young man. Probably a little younger than himself, but the face was severely damaged and beaten. The gulls and the crows had obviously been there for some time, and so there was little to show who this may have been. He carefully, but quickly climbed the rocks to retreat from the beach and made his way back to the village as calmly as he could. Once there, he walked through the main street and made his way to the house of Birse.

'What is it?' asked the wife, seeing that Tyr was pale and shocked.

'Is Birse around? I need to speak to him.' She put

158

down the thread she was spinning and said, shaking her head,

'No, he's helping one of the farmers on the plains with his roof.'

'Oh,' sighed Tyr. The wife looked at his clothing but said nothing about the new coat and shirt.

'Is there anything I can do for you?' she asked.

'Where can I find the elder-man, the one Birse spoke to?'

'He lives in the village, the long-hut that usually has a hand cart outside.' Tyr thanked her and walked off to the hut she had described.

The elder-man was taken aback for a moment. He didn't immediately recognise Tyr as the young servant of Bethran.

'Sit, he said, motioning to a bench in the long-hut, 'you seem much improved since I last saw you,' there was a hint of a smile at the corners of his mouth. Tyr remained impassive and stared calmly at the man. It was now he remembered that this person could know more about the killing of Laman than he admitted to. Tyr would have to be careful.

'You wished to speak with me, I understand.' Tyr nodded and took a deep breath to give him time to think. He thought of a story that would sound a little more plausible than the truth.

'Yes, and thank you for seeing me,' he began. 'I was looking for a few herbs this morning and was walking on the road to the south. I decided to rest on the rocks there, and heard many gulls on the shore,' he paused to try to gauge the elder. He showed nothing but a feint interest in the story. 'I scattered the birds and found a body lying there.' The elder raised his brows, but that was all. 'I thought I would tell you first, as I have no idea who it might be,' concluded Tyr, he was playing the concerned villager, not the tenacious inquirer.

'Well,' replied the elder calmly, 'I better send someone to have a look around,' and he stood. Tyr automatically stood with him, but the man waved his hand.

'Please, remain seated, I will send someone to the spot. To the south you say?' Tyr nodded as he slowly sat down once more. The elder called someone and returned, and he was soon followed into the hut by a thin, rodent looking man. The elder sat and spoke to the man.

'Our friend here has made a discovery to the south,' he held his hand towards Tyr, 'he says that a body has been found by the rocks on the shore.' Looking at the rodent, Tyr suddenly felt that he was in danger. What if they moved the body and said Tyr had imagined it? What if they took him to the rocks and smashed his head in? He suddenly felt like running for the door, but that would do him no good. He now wished Bethran was here, *he* would know what to do.

'Was that somewhere near Rook Point?' asked the rodent in a thin but clear voice. Tyr was about to nod, but he thought better of it.

'I could not say, I do not know the local names yet,' replied Tyr. He was happy with that explanation and the two men seemed fine with it too. The rodent turned to the elder and added,

'I will take a couple of men up there and have a look around.' The elder nodded and then looked at Tyr. The young man knew exactly what was coming.

'Take...' the elder pointed with his open hand as if expecting a name.

'Tyr,' he offered in a failing voice. The elder nodded and repeated his name.

'Take Tyr with you, it will be easier to find the spot,' and that was it, quicker than he could imagine, he was walking back south with the rodent and three rough looking individuals to the place he had found the body. All he had to do now was to decide the best moment to make a run for it. To make things worse, it looked like the clouds were going to let go of their water very soon. Then Tyr considered something that his fear had made him leave out of the equation. They were pushing the hand-cart. That surely meant they intended to bring the body back with them. Or would they transport both his and the other body somewhere to be better hidden? He decided he would stay, but remain vigilant and hope his fears were unfounded. Where the hell was the seer when you needed him?

Chapter 8 – Wind from the South

Bethran sniffed the air. For a moment, he thought he could smell rain as he watched the sky. The clouds were gathering in the west. His sense of smell had developed over the years on the road, and he was able to feel the rain or a squall approaching. The air seemed to take on a different weight too, as if the sky was pressing down, or lifting itself up in some cases. Lack of payment for the ferryman would mean missing out the ferry crossing and walking down the river to a crossing in the west. It would take longer, but he was using up his resources far too quickly. It could add half a day, or even a full one, if the clouds kept their promise to move towards him. He was heading to the Kingdom of Cat once more, and though it would cause him to leave out some of his customary visits in the south, he just couldn't leave Tyr at Tall Bridges. The journey upriver was frustrating, as heading west seemed such a waste of time. He would have to retrace his steps on the opposite bank too, once he had secured a safe crossing. It was made doubly infuriating, as all the way, the opposite bank and the place he needed to be was always in view. He wasn't sure how far west he would need to walk to secure a safe crossing, but he was well aware that the estuary supported several bogs and marshes that were just under the water at high tide.

It didn't take all that long to find a place that looked reasonable to cross, but the land above the marsh was still tricky to negotiate, and he felt himself sink a little as he waded. As he neared the opposite bank, he saw another man looking towards him.

'Are you in trouble there?' called the man, but Bethran shook his head rather than waste breath shouting. As he struggled up the soft bank, the man had come to help him and was covered in mud for his trouble.

'Thank you for your help, but I could manage easily enough,' nodded Bethran, with a slight smile.

'I just thought you may be in trouble,' insisted the man who spoke with a strange accent, 'I tried to cross there but decided to go further west.'

'You have come from the south?' asked Bethran, sitting to scrape mud from his legs.

'Yes,' nodded the man, I have travelled from Seal Bay in Fidach, do you know it?' Bethran smiled.

'Yes, I know it well, I will be going back there soon,' he replied as he replaced his boots over his soaked leggings. 'But you do not sound as if you are from there at all.'

'No, that is true,' replied the man casting his eyes down a little, 'I was from a settlement in Northanhymbra but I have not been back there for many years.'

'I see,' said Bethran, but he wasn't sure he did.

'I should explain,' nodded the man returning his gaze to Bethran. He pulled back his hood and removed his cap. 'My name is Osfrith. I am a monk of the Benedictine order.' Bethran gave him a shallow nod and a suspicious eye as he replied,

'Bethran, of Seal Bay, and I am...' he trailed off. Did he need to tell the monk exactly who he was yet? He decided against it and then added, 'I am currently making my way north to Tall Bridges to help the elders there.' The monk was about Bethran's age, he thought with a pleasant face and very little hair left on his head, and what remained was almost white. His eyes were bright blue and were kindly yet confident.

'Then, should we walk together for a while, I can tell you my story as we continue,' smiled the monk. Bethran nodded, and they set out. The accent was now known to him. It had a hint of what he considered was the Angle's tongue, yet it was peppered with odd phrases that Bethran had not heard before. The monk replaced his cap as he walked, but left off the hood. Bethran was now aware of the black habit under his cloak and should have realised he was of the order, due to his lack of personal items.

'I was born in Northanhymbra and was fostered as oblate to the order there, but by the time I was a young man I accompanied another brother into Gododdin and spent several years there doing God's work.' Bethran had heard the phrase before, but no one had really explained what 'God's work' was. 'When I returned to my home monastery, I found there was a plague in the area, and my Abbot forbade any of us to return until the plague had ended.' In a softer voice he added, 'many people perished in that terrible time.' He paused for a moment and then continued in a more cheery voice. 'I was told to go back north, and soon after, found myself travelling further with a delegation into the kingdom of Fortriu and then into Fidach. We established several churches in those kingdoms and I decided to stay in Fidach when our initial work was complete.' He glanced to Bethran to assess his mood, but as usual, Bethran was unreadable. 'That is where I now work, at the monastery established on the Red Isthmus.'

'So now you are heading north to try to convert the kingdom of Cat?' asked Bethran with a less than friendly tone. The monk just laughed and shook his head.

'No, not at all. If only I were capable of such a feat. I am to travel into the kingdom and see how the people live. I will try to bring them the word and work of God but as to converting them, I leave that to God himself.'

'But others will come, I have seen it before,' replied Bethran. 'A wind that blows from the south, bending all before it, until it sweeps across the land, felling everything in its path.'

'That is not how we see it,' insisted the monk, 'we see it as an education in the world. We bring light into darkness and teach, rather than force people into submission. We bring lessons we have learned, we pray, we nurture and we sow the seeds of purity.'

'The problem is,' frowned Bethran, 'something is always reaped from sowing. There will be wheat, there will be chaff, and after all this farming is done, another kingdom will be conquered and subjugated.'

'I am not sure where your knowledge of Christianity comes from, but I assure you, there is no conquering, no subjugation,' insisted the monk.

'It comes from talking to monks and seeing it with my own eyes,' insisted Bethran.

'Conversatio murum, is our mantra,' announced the monk, and he was about to explain, but Bethran interrupted.

'Conversion of life, I know,' he scowled.

'You know Latin?' asked the monk with surprise.

'A little,' nodded Bethran, the language of the church at any rate, not that of the Romans.'

'Indeed, there is a difference,' nodded the monk sagely, 'it seems that you are not the usual sort of traveller that I meet.'

'Neither are you,' replied Bethran, glancing towards him, 'I did not expect to see the scouts of the army of the White Christ treading tracks this far north.' The monk shook his head with an ironic smile on his lips.

'You ought to try to see God's words as more of a teaching than an invasion,' he explained.

'But as I have said,' replied Bethran quickly, 'it is exactly that, an invasion.' The monk stopped and looked up to the darkening sky.

'Take those clouds,' began the monk, 'would you say they are an invasion? They pass over, they bring their water to raise the crops and then leave, their work done.' He looked at Bethran and continued, 'and some other time, they will return to refresh what they had begun. That is how I see our work. That is how I see God's work.' Bethran looked at the clouds, pulled his hood from his pack and placed it over his cap. He then sighed and looked directly at the monk.

'And we are left feeling uncomfortable while it rains, and are glad to see it gone so we can have the sunshine returned,' he said flatly, and continued on his way. The monk looked at Bethran, frowned, and then nodded twice.

'Did you study the art of rhetoric?' asked the monk, hurrying to catch up, 'or have you taught yourself?'

'You started it,' replied Bethran, 'I just returned the favour.'

'Your talents could be of use to our monastery,' smiled the monk.

'So you would have me take the holy orders now?' asked the seer, raising the pace of his footsteps.

'There are worse things in life,' replied the monk, the smile still playing on his face. 'Teaching is honourable, and it is the backbone of our work, and my particular order is extremely forgiving in the nature of the life there.' Bethran felt mischievous.

'Could I drink heather ale?' he asked, looking over to the monk. The monk smiled.

'Not only do we promulgate the art of oenology,

167

we refine it,' he replied.

'Oenology?' said Bethran, raising his brows, 'if you have a name for it, you must take it seriously, we just call it brewing.'

'Most, if not all our monasteries either makes wine or ale.'

'That is good,' nodded Bethran with a blank expression, 'what about wenching? Is that allowed?'

'Well,' nodded the monk, thinking through his answer, 'it happens, but most of us would prefer to use that time for our calling. I am sure that our abbot would be annoyed if I was calling on Achtland of Lofton each and every night.' Bethran gave out an audible chuckle,

'I see,' he smiled.

'It amuses you that it is so?'

'No,' replied Bethran, still smiling, 'the fact that you used the name of an Irish goddess amuses me,' then he paused for a moment. 'And the fact that Achtland does not live in Lofton, but I suppose you know that, and the fact that in legend she could not be satisfied by any man.' Now it was the monk's turn to smile, as he felt the first spots of rain on his head. Twenty or so paces later, Bethran added, 'What about the service to God?' The monk pulled his hood around him as he thought on the question.

'The order does have those who are not monks,' he replied, 'and I suspect that a few do not see as deeply into God's benevolence as do we, but they teach all the same. I know of one that tends our gardens and yet rarely attends mass. I suspect he only attends vespers for his supper.' Bethran had listened but had reached into his shirt for something that hung around his neck.

'So I would be able to light a fire, sprinkle petals around it wearing nothing but this?' and he pulled the item from his shirt for the monk to see. It was a perfectly smooth stone that was carved with a delicate image of an owl.

'It is pretty, what is it?'

'The mark of Blodeuedd, a maiden made of the blossom of the Oak, the Broom and the Meadowsweet. A face so sweet that they called her after the petals that always surrounded her.' The monk looked at the stone in detail, and as Bethran placed it back inside his shirt, he replied,

'I doubt the abbot would sanction...' he paused for a moment, trying to think of a word that would not upset his walking partner. 'Rites in praise of a non-Christian belief,' he added when he had found it, and he smiled, 'though, what is in a man's heart can only be judged by a higher authority,' he added. 'And we mere mortals cannot assuage belief to any great degree.' Bethran glanced at the man with a little surprise. Was this the way most of these monks thought, or just this one?

'Then I must refuse your offer,' laughed Bethran, 'for I have never removed it these last twenty summers, I could not bear to part with it now.' He was thinking that this man may be a good companion on his trek north just as the rain fell in anger. The monk strode off to shelter under a tree, and Bethran turned to watch.

'Does God tell you that you cannot walk in the rain?' he smiled.

169

'No, this is one of the decisions I make on my own,' smiled back the monk.

'So be it,' and Bethran paused, trying to remember the name of the monk. 'I on the other hand, am well-travelled in this land and can tell by *my* gods, that the rain will not cease until dark. I must continue. May *your* god keep you safe, Brother Osfrith,' replied Bethran with a slight bow of the head, and he turned and continued north as the rain became torrential. Bethran heard the monk reply, but he couldn't hear it correctly due to the deluge striking his hood.

In a very short time, the rudimentary water proofing of his hood and coat had failed, and the water began to cling to his skin and the cold was seeping through too. People would say that there was a limit to how wet you could be, that once soaked, there was nothing more the water could do. Bethran knew this to be wrong, for rain cooled the hot skin to begin with, but eventually, the skin turned cold and the wet became overpowering, intensifying the dropping of the temperature until shivering began. This he knew well, and so he quickened his pace, the more to try to warm his core. For a while, this would work, but eventually, the cold would bite and his pace would drop. There would come a time later in the day, when rest, food and the drying his clothes would become crucial to his survival on the road. Now he had a decision to make. Should he stop at one of the small communities, or should he continue on to Tall Bridges? At the moment, he considered the latter, as he knew he could be there before dark. There would be a warm fire in the smithy and he could dry his clothes and sleep in relative comfort. He knew well, however, by the time he saw smoke from a fire at the first hut, he would be willing to sell his soul to the Christians for a warm hearth, and some food.

By the time they were entering the settlement, the sky had turned from the colour of oat gruel to something more akin to the back stones of a hearth, and rain had begun to fall. Tyr knew his new clothes would suffer at the unforgiving attentions of the weather, but without a hood or a cape, there was no escape. The body on the handcart was taken to the tiny square in the centre of Tall Bridges, where someone decided to cover it from the rain, which looked like it would increase. The elder-man came out of his hut and cast a quick glance at the body, then said,

'Does anyone know him?'

'Aye, it looks like Unust,' said a small thin man. Others nodded to confirm this.

'It looks as if he fell from the rocks at Rook Point,' said the rodent, but just for a brief moment, Tyr saw something in the elder-man's face. It could have been disbelief, but it could also have been anger. Either way, the elder nodded gravely and said that the body would be taken for burial in the settlement's burial ground. Tyr had seen many burials in his time at Camma, but he knew this man would have a simple grave, containing the washed body, wrapped in a linen sheet, and empty, save for a few flat stones on the base. Maybe not even that if he had no relatives or friends. He would be buried east to west, his head to the west, and once the grave was covered, there would be nothing to show where the body had been placed. In Camma, if Unust had been old, he may have even been left out in the open on the hill, his body decomposing or being picked clean by the birds. His bones would later be collected and placed in a cairn close by. Here at Tall Bridges, most of the surrounding land was flat and used for farming, so the burial ground was the usual place for the dead. Tyr doubted that Unust had fallen from the rocks, unless he was an unusually clumsy individual, and he doubted that, seeing he was a fisherman and needed good balance due to the gyrating motions of a small vessel. Before he could check himself, he had asked the question.

'Had anyone seen him go up there?' The few people that remained looked blankly at Tyr. He wasn't sure why, maybe it was a surprise, that anyone cared what had happened to him. Even the elder-man gave a frown after he gathered in the reasoning behind the question. Just one person supported Tyr's inquiry.

'It is a point,' said a well-dressed man who had pulled a cloak over his fine coat, 'Unust was a young man, and it does not follow that he would fall from the rocks up there.'

'Some of those rocks are slimy,' insisted the rodent, 'I nearly went arse over noggin fetching him out of there.' Tyr had noted the rocks were slippery, but he hadn't seen the rodent slip. That made his statement over defensive. The well-dressed man saw the elder stare towards him. He shrugged, turned and walked away. Tyr decided to follow the man discretely. He walked through the rear part of the settlement and entered a hut with a covered area to the front of it. Stone jars and pottery jugs were collected to one side. He also noticed more containers just inside the door as the man entered the hut. As the well-dressed man turned to close the door, he noticed Tyr looking at him.

'You are the one who found Unust, are you not?'

'I am,' nodded Tyr. 'I am servant to Bethran the seer,' he added, becoming more comfortable with the nomenclature. It made him sound a little more socially elevated than 'beggar' or 'worthless traveller'. The man's eyes seem to look down and to the left as he nodded, and he looked as if he were considering something. Tyr noticed him look both ways up and down the street before he said,

'Come in please, we are about to eat, and the weather is terrible.' Tyr was about to refuse, but the rain was strengthening, and he *was* hungry. The man closed the door and guided him past a great many jars and jugs, into a second room where a young woman was cooking over a hearth. The second room was as large as most huts, and Tyr considered that this man, who was probably some kind of merchant, must be reasonably wealthy. The man motioned for Tyr to sit by the table, and then he sat himself.

'I am Bolder, this is my daughter Coblaith,' the man explained with a friendly smile. The young woman turned and Tyr saw she was a very pretty girl, but then again, the man was handsome too. It was fitting that she would take after him. 'My wife died some years ago, so we both run my little business here.'

'You are a trader?'

'Yes,' nodded the man, 'I used to own my own ship, we traded all along the coast but a storm cost us everything and I had to start all over again.'

'I'm sorry,' said Tyr with honesty.

'It is what the gods chose, I do not feel aggrieved, and it was partly my fault. She was bringing a cargo from the Western Isles and was probably overloaded. She was lost near the Boar Islands in a storm. Just two of the crew survived.'

'Many say the straights there are treacherous.'

'Indeed,' nodded the man. 'So you are the servant of Bethran,' he added, changing the subject quickly.

'Yes,' smiled Tyr, 'I have not travelled with him for long.' Tyr then thought it was his turn to change the subject lest the man delve more deeply. 'What do you trade?'

'Pottery, mainly larger items. The blow fish landing on the beach has been profitable. The villages needed many pots to collect the oil, so I will soon need to find more for the business.'

'You do not make them?'

'No,' he replied shaking his head, 'I leave that to the artisans, I collect anything I think will sell from the larger settlements up and down the coast. I am to travel north to Broadbay soon.' Tyr nodded and saw the daughter readying bowls for the table. She then brought a large shallow bowl of water and placed it on the table with a cloth, and what looked like a block of tallow. The man reached for the tallow and began to wash his hands with it. Once he was done, he handed the tallow to Tyr,

174

who followed suit. Tyr knew that many people washed often, he knew Bethran did the same, but in Camma, he had never seen anyone wash their hands before they ate. He then noticed Bolder's hands. They were spotlessly clean, and his nails were short and neat. The girl's hands were the same, and as Tyr dried his hands on the cloth, she removed the bowl. He noticed her clothes too. The bottom of her coat reached to the floor as most women's did, but in her case, the bottom edge had not been replaced. That meant that she had more than one set of clothes. Most women had to replace the bottom edge of their gowns, as being so long they would drag in the dirt and the wet. Coblaith probably had another gown that she would wear for the outdoors and that set her above most ordinary women. Her hair seemed brown but twinkled in the light from the fire of a golden hue. It was long and wound with a comb in a circle before cascading over her shoulder. She was impressive, and Bolder saw him watching her as she brought the food to the table. To distract him, Tyr asked,

'You seemed to agree that Unust did not fall from the rocks.' The man glanced down to the food and then back up to Tyr, lifting his spoon but hesitating. The girl sat with them and when she was settled, Bolder said,

'Unust, from what I knew of him, was a lively lad. He was a fisherman and was always busy. I cannot even see him going to Rook Point unless there was work for him to do,' he hesitated, 'and there is nothing up there but rocks and sand.' He began to eat and so Tyr followed suit. The food was a stew made from fish with peas and oats. There were delicate tastes from herbs, and the unmistakable sweetness of crummock within the dish, and Tyr was impressed with the taste. There was bread too, a large golden loaf that had fruit within it.

'The place where I found him was lacking of any high rocks. It occurred to me at the time that if he had fallen, he must have been very unlucky,' said Tyr, trying to sound as casual as he could. He caught the eye of the girl and added, 'this stew is excellent.' She smiled and then let her eyes drop to the bowl.

'It is just fish stew,' she said quietly, 'if I had known we were to have visitors, I would have served something else.' Her eyes flashed to him again and then back to her bowl.

'She is the only person I have known that could equal her mother's talent for making salted fish taste like it ever came from the sea,' laughed Bolder, breaking a lump of bread from the loaf. The girl looked to her father and smiled. Tyr was beginning to think she was the prettiest thing he had ever seen, and he did his best to keep an impression that he was socially her equal. He didn't know why. They all knew he wasn't.

'You and the seer are trying to find who killed Laman?' she asked. Her voice was quiet, yet clear and had a tinkling quality, almost musical. Tyr nodded, finishing a mouthful of the stew.

'Yes,' he eventually said, 'Bethran is away for a few days and I am left with the whole puzzle.' He wasn't sure if he should admit Bethran had left, but he felt safe here, and it was likely everyone knew the seer had left by now. 'Do you have any interest in the affair?' he added.

'I was the one who first saw the monster on the beach,' she said calmly. Of course, Tyr remembered that a young woman had seen the beast and fled to the village. He now needed more information.

'It must have been fearful. What do you remember about it?'

'Everything,' she replied, widening her eyes considering it was a strange question. 'I had been collecting shells from the long beach to the north. I noticed it was becoming late, so I headed back along the path. It was still light enough to see the village, and as I looked to the left, I saw something on the beach in the surf.' She had placed her spoon in her dish, yet she had not finished eating. 'I thought it was a ship that had grounded, and so I walked to the beach and over the dunes. There was just enough light to make it out. I had never seen anything like it and it seemed to be moving.'

'It was still alive?' asked Tyr, intrigued by the story.

'Yes, I think so,' she said, 'the waves were crashing over it so it was hard to tell in the twilight.'

'Did you see Laman or anyone else on the beach?'

'No,' she replied, shaking her head, 'but by then it was difficult to see very much.'

'And I assume you wanted to raise the alarm?' Once again, she shook her head.

'No, I just wanted to get away from there,' she smiled, 'telling someone was an afterthought, I went past the shoreline where the fishing boats land, and spoke to the men there.'

'Did you recognise anyone there?' he asked.

'Yes,' she said, the smile now gone, 'I saw the one called Perst, and his brother, and there was another man there who I recognised. I do not recall his name though.'

'And Laman?' asked Tyr. This time she shook her head more confidently.

'No, I did not see him or Unust there.' Tyr nodded. He sensed that he was asking too many questions, so he decided to ask his final one.

'What did they do? How did they react?'

'They just nodded, they said they would look at it when it was light.' She thought for a moment. 'I suppose that made perfect sense, it was dark by then.' Tyr then made a few comments on how frightening it all must have been, but beyond that he dropped the subject and finished his meal.

By the time he left their company, the rain had slowed considerably, and he headed back to the smithy and with a good meal inside him, he felt much improved. He couldn't get the image of Coblaith from his memory however. She was quite different to most young women he had seen. She was more like the wives of noblemen or great warriors, women who had grown to command the same respect as their men. His thoughts of the girl left him as he reached the smithy. The flimsy door lay broken and smashed on the floor, and inside, the trestle bench had been upturned and broken too. There hadn't been much in the smithy, but what could be broken, had been. The place was a mess. The tatty roof was also

178

damaged and larger holes than previously could be seen where the rain was dripping through. He suddenly became afraid. They had come for him, they had come to do him harm, but he hadn't been there. He needed to get out of there. He needed to hide, but where? It was still raining, and he really didn't have much of an option. If he stayed in the smithy, they could return. If he fled to the woods, he wouldn't know when Bethran returned. He hurried outside and began to walk north down the path and over the bridge. He then made his way into the woods and looked for the best protection from the rain, which came underneath a large oak. He then wondered if they would track him there, but suddenly, he realised he didn't know who *they* were. They had to be men under the control of the elder. He had found the body of Unust and now they would make him suffer for tracking it down. No, that couldn't be the case. The body wasn't even hidden, so why would anyone punish him for that? Was it the person who had killed Laman, trying to stop him and Bethran finding out their identity? He now wished Bethran was here again. He didn't know what to do. He had found Unust, he had found the woman who had first seen the sea monster, but he was no further forward in finding out the name of the man who had slain Laman. Had the people who had gone to the smithy followed Bethran? Was his body now lying at the side of the track with its head smashed in? He didn't think anyone would get the better of Bethran, but then again, he was a seer, not a warrior.

Under the oak tree, Tyr had a little shelter, but rogue raindrops still made their way along the branches and the leaves of the tree to fall onto him below. He crouched and hugged his legs as the damp began to cool him slightly. He thought long and hard about what he should do, and the images of that fateful night at Camma came back to him. The prospect of being thrown off the cliffs had not driven into his soul as much as he expected when faced with death, so why did he feel nervous now? He realised it was because then, he was protecting his lover. He was making sure that she was safe and therefore, thoughts of his own safety were put aside. At the appointed time he had been afraid, not about death, more about the shock and pain he would feel as he fell and bounced down the rocks. But the rest of the time he had felt calm. The vast number of thoughts that had rushed through his mind had done that, the focus on what he had to do, had taken away the fear. He tried the same tactic as he sat under that oak tree, and he began to speak to the tree as if it were Bethran. The tree was a god, after all.

'I must forget the fear, I have something I have to do, I must continue,' he began. 'If I am to become a better man, I must come to terms with my fate, I must think like Bethran and understand that, what will be, will be.' He just didn't believe that, and so he stood and turned to the tree, putting his hand gently on the trunk. The bark felt warm to him, like a heart was beating under that grey skin, like blood, not sap ran through its body. He looked up at the canopy above him and closed his eyes as the random raindrops struck his face. He breathed in deeply and then out slowly. He looked at his hand on the tree and felt strength entering his body. The fear left, and he saw what he was. He was a man, a man that could shape his own destiny. A man that could become whatever he wanted to be. He had seen so many wonders on the road with Bethran, and all in a very short time. He knew there must be a great deal more to come. It was as if the gods were promising him that. He dropped his hand from the tree and turned to face the direction of Tall Bridges and set off back to the track in the light drizzle.

Chapter 9 – Silver

The rain had slowed by the time Tyr reached the old smithy, and he set about making the place a little better by sorting out what might still have use, and breaking up what didn't. One thing the intruders had provided was firewood, and the door, being of no use for blocking the doorway any longer, was relegated to the firewood pile. The heap of wood was now the most prominent feature of the hut, and even the old barrel was in pieces. Tyr found one of the slimmer barrel staves that might be used as a weapon and threw the remainder on the pile. Tyr was no fighter, but his years as a drover in the lonely hills had taught him to defend himself from the wild beasts that roamed there. He would just consider that any assailants would be the wild beasts of Tall Bridges, and he grasped the curved wooden club and swung it a few times. He was about to light the fire and he knew smoke might attract attention, but he would give as good as he got. To his annoyance, since the hut had lost more of its ability to provide shelter, the kindling and the wood for starting the fire had become wet, and so he looked around for options. He eventually found his blanket in the debris and his old clothes. The shirt he tore apart and wrapped strips of it around the oak barrel stave. He then found an old copper nail and carefully hammered it through part of the cloth, but the oak was tough, and the nail bent under the attention of the small rock he was hammering it with. Making a torch wasn't easy. His idea had been to walk to the beach, dip the end in some oil, and light it on fires used to render down the flesh of the blow fish. He would then bring it back to light *his* fire. It would only work if he could make a torch, but scouring the rest of the hut provided nothing more he could use to secure the cloth to the stave. Instead, he shook the dust from the blanket and hung it over the doorway. It wasn't a good fit and each time the wind blew, the rag danced around as if someone was playing a tune on a whistle. Though his activity had warmed him somewhat, his clothes were still wet, and he had run out of ideas for lighting the fire. He then noticed an old bird's nest in the thatch. It looked like it was dry, and so he climbed up and pulled the thing down. The nest was duly deconstructed, and the straw mass was placed under the driest wood in the hearth. He then chose a small, dry twig and went outside looking for flames.

The village was quiet, with most people staying under cover if they didn't *have* to brave the rain, but Tyr was very cautious and his eyes flitted from one sign of movement to another. Twice, he stopped to allow people to move off ahead of him and then he saw flame. It was the new smithy and a hot fire could be seen just inside.

He asked if he could use the fire, and to his surprise, the smithy offered him a tallow lantern to get his fire going. This he took willingly and promised to return it as soon as he had flames. The lantern was a small iron cage, the sides of which allowed light to spill out, but protected the flame from breezes. It had a handle on one side so that it could be carried easily. As he returned to the hut, he once again kept his eyes peeled as he did his best to protect the lantern from the breeze and the drizzle.

It was later in the afternoon when Tyr had dried to a comfortable degree after returning the lantern. He had been sitting by the fire, gently steaming in the warmth until he considered he was safe enough to remove his gown. His shirt still needed the finishing touches, however, and so he returned to the fireside and took up the oak stave. For some reason, the longer he sat alone, the more fearful he became. The earlier feeling of bravado had gradually left him and the isolation was making him keep his eyes on the blanket, gently shimmering in the light breeze. The rain had stopped, but the sky, which could be seen in several places without leaving the hut, looked heavy and ready to release more water. Tyr wondered if it was readying itself for a coming storm. Bethran had mentioned a storm and had said he was not talking about the weather. What exactly had he meant? Tyr then began to doubt that the seer would return. True, he had said it would be a few days, and Tyr had no idea how far south the ferry was, but here, alone… He shrugged. Of course he would come back. The little he knew of Bethran was that he would not forget the promised payment from the elder-man. But then again, if the elder-man was involved, as Tyr suspected, there would be no payment. Had Bethran realised this and left Tyr to his own fate. Tyr didn't believe in fate and so he dismissed the idea with his hand, brushing away some unseen item as if it were smoke or dust. He leaned the stave back against the hearth and threw a log on the fire. It was the same log Bethran had used to represent the monster on the beach. There was so little firewood left and the rickety bench he was using as a seat would soon be needed. Maybe he shouldn't have kept such a roaring fire going. He looked back up to the sky. It was becoming darker, but not just because of the clouds. Night was coming. He turned his position so he could see the doorway. If anyone was going to return, they would probably come after dark.

By the time the dark had fallen enough for the fire to be the only illumination in the hut, Tyr had stood and looked at the bench. He could have a seat or a fire. There were no other options under the circumstances. He had long since replaced all his clothing and he was plenty warm enough, but the fire had been some sort of comfort to him. He pulled back the blanket over the door and looked outside. It wasn't quite as dark out there as it seemed, but very soon it would be night. In the season of the big sun, night never truly came to the Kingdom of Cat, but with a thick canopy of cloud, it was already difficult to see detail. The wind had dropped though, and there was a lovely smell of earth and undergrowth, it was the kind of night Tyr remembered from his youth. He dropped the blanket and returned to the last dancing flames of the fire. He had decided to leave the bench and let the fire die, and he wondered if it was worth trying to find firewood outside. He knew the chances of finding anything dry enough were remote, and so he sat and watched the final surge of the flames. He was now hungry again. The realisation of the hardship on the road was now beginning to make him consider his past life once more. He had been hungry before. Oh yes, he knew hunger, but in the past, half a day of work for someone would provide a reasonable meal. How could he get food here? He then thought about the old fisherman who must have brought him the fish. For a moment, his thoughts went back to the information he had provided to find the body of Unust. How did he know where to find Unust, and was he part of the reason the young man was dead? He didn't know, and his hunger once more made him think of the fish. Maybe it wasn't a good idea to go and find the man, particularly in the dark. He stood once more and paced the hut, reaching for the stave as he passed the hearth. To make himself feel more comfortable and ready for a fight, he began to brandish the club as if it were a sword. He had never held anything other than an axe for chopping wood, but for a moment he thought of the stave as a fine sword. He chopped and swung the weapon in the dying light of the fire, seeing assailants coming from this direction and that, and every time, he was accurate and fast, or so he thought. It felt quick, and it felt good, but he knew it would be very different if someone came through that door, and he shot a glance to see a figure there, just

186

visible as a dark shape against the slightly lighter background. His heart almost stopped as he realised they had come for him, but he wasn't going to fall easily and he held the club in both hands towards the figure.

'Put that down before you do yourself an injury,' said the irate voice. Bethran walked in and looked around the hut. 'Well, it is not what I would call an improvement,' he added as he walked to the hearth. Tyr's jaw was only just returning to its proper position, and he copied Bethran by glancing around the darkening hut, and eventually dropping his arms by his side. Bethran warmed his hands on the stones of the hearth as he sat on the bench. 'So I am thinking,' continued the seer, 'you burned everything in the hut to make such a furnace in the hearth, that you then poked holes in the thatch to cool it down.' He then reached out and took the stave from Tyr and placed it carefully on the embers. Gradually, the shock left Tyr, and he stuttered back to life.

'Er, no,' he looked around the hut once more, 'we had a visit this morning.'

'A visit?' asked Bethran with his arms still outstretched.

'Yes,' nodded Tyr, 'I didn't see them, but they broke everything up, including the door.' He pointed to where the blanket still hung. Bethran looked to the door too and frowned deeply. A trace of steam came from his arms, and Tyr could smell that Bethran was still wet. He must have walked all day through the rain. Bethran looked to be thinking through the situation.

'And you came back here?' asked Bethran with

surprise. Tyr shuffled his feet and then with lack of anywhere else to sit, he crouched by the hearth, Bethran still sitting on the bench.

'Yes,' he admitted, 'but at first I did run, but where would I go?' He watched the stave smoking and then a small flame took hold. 'I did find a few more things out though, and there has been another death.' Bethran's frown grew deeper.

'Are you going to explain?' began Bethran with a penetrating look, 'or shall I get my bones out?'

'Unust,' replied Tyr quickly, 'I was told where to find him and I did, his body that is.' Bethran held his hand up at this, and once again seemed deep in thought.

'Who told you?' asked Bethran.

'I do not know his name, one of the fishermen I think, though I have not seen him in a boat.'

'Then we better move,' he suddenly said, raising his tired body to its feet, 'and quickly.' He pulled his pack over his shoulder and headed for the door. Tyr didn't need any further explanation. He followed the seer outside, pulling the old blanket from the doorway as he went.

For the remaining hours of darkness, Tyr explained everything that had happened whilst Bethran had been away, including the meeting with the merchant and his daughter. Bethran spoke little, replying with a grunt here or a humourless laugh there. He had taken them to the woodworking yard of Birse, and in a corner they had crouched in the darkness until Bethran had fallen asleep, and Tyr soon followed.

With the dawn, they were both awake, but Bethran waited until it was fully light and the village was coming to life before he moved. Tyr didn't know what the older man was thinking. He had still told him nothing of their plans, if indeed there were any plans. Birse arrived in the yard just as they were leaving, and except for a few words to explain why they were there, Bethran was quiet.

'So what are we doing?' asked Tyr, a little annoyed over the silence.

'Getting our reward from the elder-man,' grunted Bethran.

'So you know who killed Laman?'

'No, but the elder will pay us nonetheless,' insisted Bethran. For a few steps, Tyr was quiet and then he couldn't hold it back any longer.

'So we are to leave it at that? Take the reward and just go?' he asked.

'You said it yourself,' grumbled Bethran, pausing as a villager walked past, 'if the elder is involved…' and he trailed off. It was clear to both of them, there was no happy ending if they went to the elder and told him, they knew he was the one who had killed Laman, and he had hired them to move any blame from himself. They could both end up buried at the side of Unust and Laman, or at best, driven from the village without the reward. No, Bethran was thinking hard on the problem and thought he knew what to do.

'It just feels wrong when we are so close,' sighed Tyr.

'So close,' admitted Bethran turning to the man,

'that someone came looking for you to prevent you going any further.' They were near to the elder-man's hut now, as Tyr said,

'But does that not show that we are proving-?' but Bethran stopped and turned on Tyr. Quietly, but with a hiss in his tone, he said,

'Proving what? We are no closer to knowing who killed Laman now than the first day we arrived. We do not even know *why* he was killed.' With this, Bethran walked briskly towards the hut.

'Bethran, hello again,' called a voice. Bethran stopped and looked to his right. There stood the Benedictine monk with a broad smile on his face. He noticed that the villagers were staring at the monk, dressed in his black habit, his cloak open and his head uncovered. 'Indeed, your god was correct, it did rain until dark.'

'Brother Osfrith,' nodded Bethran, 'it seems that your god should teach himself some weather lore, maybe it would be useful to his flock.' The monk laughed heartily as he walked towards the seer. 'How does the morning find you?' asked Bethran.

'Damp, but well, and you?'

'As well as can be expected given the hunger of my insides.' Bethran allowed a slight smile, he noticed that quite a number of villagers were looking at the unlikely man dressed in black.

'Without hunger,' smiled back the monk, 'we can never truly know the goodness of simple food.'

'And without a brisk walk in a rainstorm,' replied Bethran, squinting his eyes a little, 'we can never truly appreciate the warmth of a simple fireside.' The monk laughed as the two of them gripped arms as if they were old friends, rather than fellow travellers for a very short time. Both men had found something to be appreciated in the other.

'Are you sure you will not come and teach rhetoric, you are the master of it. You could help our initiates in *ars praedicandi*,' Tyr didn't know what rhetoric was, and he certainly didn't understand when the stranger spoke a foreign language. He didn't know who the man dressed in black was either, but he could see there was a connection between Bethran and the man. He came closer and examined this new arrival.

'As I have already said,' replied Bethran, tilting his head to one side, 'my grasp of the Roman tongue is limited.' The monk smiled genially and asked,

'Is your business in the village concluded by any chance?' Bethran gave a slight nod as he said,

'Soon to be concluded, yes.'

'Then could I ask you for a kindness before you leave?'

'I will try, what is it?' replied Bethran with a serious expression.

'You said you were helping the elders,' he said this in a quieter tone, fully aware that villagers were watching. 'I wondered, could you introduce me to them?'

'I could, that is where I am going at the moment,' Bethran paused, 'but there is only one of consequence. I have been lead to believe that the two others are either too old or too lazy to be of any benefit.'

'I'm not looking for benefit,' said the monk, raising his brows slightly, 'just permission to stay and talk with the people for a while.'

'Then follow me,' he replied and turned to leave, but Tyr interrupted.

'Bethran, can we speak first?' Bethran turned to him and then saw the monk smiling at the man.

'This is Tyr,' began Bethran, 'he is…' Bethran paused, searching for the words.

'His servant,' added Tyr with a smile to the monk.

'He is not my servant,' insisted Bethran, 'he is simply someone who will not cease following me,' and he gave Tyr a frown before adding, 'and someone who keeps interfering with my thoughts and plans.' Tyr just shrugged and smiled once more to the monk. This Benedictine was clever enough to see that Tyr and Bethran had formed some sort of bond, even though the outward image was quite different.

'Apprentice?' said the monk with a bow of the head.

'He does not like the idea of such,' smiled Tyr, 'he thinks that I would become much better than he, so he tells everyone I am his servant.' The monk laughed, but Bethran was turning a light shade of purple.

'Shall we go?' insisted the seer, spinning on his heel, not before giving Tyr an ugly sneer.

Inside the long hut, the elder-man was sitting to a large bench studying some counters on a painted board.

'Ah Bethran,' he said looking up, 'do you play?'

he asked motioning to the table. Bethran looked at the board and shook his head. 'Ah, a pity. What can I do for you?'

'I have come to present Brother Osfrith of Northanhymbra, he is travelling to the north and wishes to be known to you.

'A Christian?' asked the elder, raising his brows. Tyr glanced to the monk. So that was what a Christian looked like, very much a disappointment. Tyr had considered that Christians would look more exotic, with odd coloured skin or a different shape to normal men. This Osfrith looked like any other sort of man. He looked older than his years, and he spoke differently to others, but essentially, he was the same.

'Indeed,' bowed the smiling face of the monk, 'but I am here as a mere traveller.' Bethran was beginning to like the monk even more. He was clever, he was crafty, and if other Christians were like this monk, he was starting to see why the religion was growing.

'So you have not come to steal all our children in the night?' laughed the elder, but the laugh was false, and Bethran saw that the elder-man didn't like the idea of the monk being in Tall Bridges. Why would he? If the elder was using the village as his own personal kingdom, he wouldn't want a Christian upsetting the status quo.

'How long are you here for?' asked the elder with a more serious face.

'If it pleases you, just two nights,' smiled the monk, 'I have want of nothing, I will rest and then continue north.'

'So be it,' nodded the elder, 'now if you will

forgive me, I have business with our seer.' The fact that the elder had said 'our seer' surprised Bethran. Was this man making it clear that the village had its religious support and didn't need any other? Or was there another, not altogether honourable reason? Either way, the monk bowed to the elder and then to Bethran and left. 'What can I do for you, Bethran?' asked the man after the monk had left. His tone was much harsher than normal.

'We have concluded our search for Laman's killer, but I can find nothing to suggest that anyone in particular is responsible.'

'So it was the blow fish as I suspected?' nodded the man a little less abruptly.

'I did not say that,' insisted Bethran, raising his brows.

'Either way,' frowned the man, 'you will confirm to the village that is the case so we can have an end to the matter?' and he stood. He walked to the rear of the hut and opened the lid of a small iron chest.

'With respect, you are the one to make speeches to the populace, not I.' The elder pulled a small linen pouch from the top of the chest and walked back, placing it on the table.

'I appreciate your help,' he said as he sat once again and looked to the pouch. 'I always reward those that help me Bethran, and I am aware that much of your time has been taken up with this.' He paused, 'but in one final action, I require that it is you that explains the situation. As I told you previously,' his frown deepened, 'I merely required you to be seen to be investigating the matter.'

'And my part of the contract is completed,' nodded Bethran. The elder looked at him for some moments without any expression. Tyr felt uneasy in that silence.

'I believe you have been away for some time.' Bethran knew it was the elder's way of letting the seer know, he had his informers.

'That is true,' nodded the seer, 'but it can be the case that rats do not come out to eat whilst the cat is in the grain store.' The man glared up at Bethran for a moment, but Bethran looked down with a neutral look in his eye. The elder put his hand on the pouch, and once again stared at Bethran.

'So you will not do as I ask?' he said in a brusque tone.

'I cannot stand up and tell people what I do not believe,' insisted Bethran. 'The blow fish did not kill Laman, that was done by someone in the village as we both know. All I can tell anyone is that I have not found proof of any particular person involved.' As his sentence drew to a close, his tone darkened too. Tyr was now uncomfortable, and he felt his palms sweat. After a few more moments of staring, the elder pushed the pouch towards the seer and Bethran picked it up. He tried to guess what was in it and it certainly had weight to it.

'I assume you will be continuing south now?' asked the elder, but it was more like a statement than a question.

'Yes,' nodded Bethran, still holding the reward, 'we have supplies to gather first,' and he motioned to the pouch and turned. He didn't move, however, and Tyr could see something in Bethran's eyes, a sort of fire, a glow, his spirit shining out of them. He turned back to the elder. 'The widow of Laman?' he suddenly asked.

'What of her?' frowned the elder far too harshly.

'Is she provided for?' Bethran placed the pouch in his gown.

'No, why should she be?'

'Does she not now own Laman's boat?' asked the seer.

'The boat?' sighed the elder, 'Laman was a gambler,' there was an impatience and an anger in the elder's voice. 'He would bet on anything and it seems his debts far outweighed what the boat was worth.' For a moment, the elder looked as if he would say more, but he checked himself. His anger was clear now.

'Oh,' said Bethran with surprise, then he nodded as he stared at the floor. 'Then his debts would be considerable,' continued Bethran, looking up to the man. 'Seeing as the boat is one of the best on the coast,' concluded the seer and he turned and left the hut.

'What was all that about?' asked Tyr, as quietly as his excitement would allow, but Bethran said nothing. He walked to the centre of the village and into the tiny market. He slowly scanned the stalls until he stood at the front of the cloth vendor, who mentally rubbed his hands at the sight of a previous customer in Tyr. Bethran felt at a scarlet cloth and then lifted a larger piece of linen to the sky as if looking at the weave. His back was turned to both Tyr and the merchant.

'Lovely bit of linen that,' said the merchant, 'I can do a deal on that and throw in some trim for the neck.' Tyr glared at the man and then moved to Bethran's shoulder.

'So this is it?' he whispered, 'you have your reward and you are buying cloth?' When Tyr got no response he added, 'you do not even know what he has given you.'

'Silver,' replied Bethran unhesitatingly.

'Silver? How do you know, you have not even glanced inside the pouch?'

'The weight, the feel, there is something about silver,' he replied, lowering his arms and glancing to Tyr. 'Too open for a winter shirt,' replied the seer placing the linen on the stall. The merchant tried his best to show him something else, but Bethran had moved on to the bakery. He negotiated two loaves of bread for a small bronze figurine drawn from his pack and placed the loaves inside. The pack now looked very full. Tyr wondered why Bethran hadn't used the silver to pay for the bread, but there was another, more pressing question.

'So we are leaving?' he Tyr with some impatience. As Bethran walked from the bakery, he allowed Tyr to catch him up, and then spoke in a low voice.

'It seems the elder-man wants to know what we are doing, do not turn, we are being followed.' Tyr was impatient to turn around now he had been told, but he resisted, just.

'How do you know?' he asked instead.

'I looked back when I was looking at the cloth, that is what I was about, and he has followed since.'

'Why would he do that now you are rewarded?'

asked the younger man.

'I am not all together sure why. It could be one or several reasons,' replied Bethran, as he gave a quick examination of some very basic wooden bowls. 'It could be because he knows *we* know. It could be because he wants to see us leave. Then again…' paused Bethran, walking on, 'he may be curious to where we would go next.' Bethran paused yet again, this time to examine some ironware, the use of which was unknown to Tyr. 'He could of course just want his silver back,' and he shot Tyr a pair of raised brows. Tyr swallowed hard as he followed on.

'But would not that throw suspicion onto him once more?' said Tyr.

'That could be, but since I refused to play the rest of his political game out,' replied Bethran, 'he will still be seen to have done little to solve the puzzle of Laman's death.'

'The village must know we have been working on that though.'

'I suspect they do,' agreed the seer, 'but he clearly needed me to tell them that it was the blow fish that killed the man.' Bethran turned back towards the market in a casual manner and looked at the other stalls, few of them open and the ones that were, had little on them.

'So what now?' asked a confused Tyr.

'We have known all along that this venture of his was an exercise, a political move to allow the people of the village to see him as a caring man, getting to the bottom of an outrage.'

'Yes, but…' then the puzzled face of Tyr showed some enlightenment, 'I think I see what you mean,' he said with another pause, 'and as it stands, not a soul knows he has rewarded you.' Bethran nodded. 'He wanted you to stand in front of the village as the trusted seer and tell them that you agreed with him.' Bethran nodded once more. 'But you refused,' concluded Tyr.

'Not just refused,' added Bethran, taking another stroll along the market, 'but told him that I may know who was responsible, I just do not have proof.' Tyr frowned as another thought entered his mind.

'But that is not good for us, surely,' he said, opening his eyes wide. The ramifications of being two travellers with a purse of silver was serious. He now saw that the elder-man had options for any eventuality, and Bethran had seen this too. He looked around for whoever might be the man following them, but no one stood out. Bethran stopped and pointed to a stall that held jewellery made from shells and coloured twine. He said something so quietly that Tyr had to lean closer.

'Sorry, I did not hear what you asked.'

'When I ask you the next question,' whispered Bethran, 'your answer must be, *yes, and fresh fish*. Nothing more, nothing less.' Tyr had no idea what was going on in the seer's muddled mind, but he decided he would do what he was asked. It was some moments later, as they walked, that Bethran spoke in a normal voice.

'You want fish?' Tyr looked at his questioning face.

'Yes,' he nodded, 'and fresh fish,' then Bethran looked as if he was thinking it over, and then shrugged.

'Then fresh fish it is,' and he walked towards the shore with Tyr following on, beginning to understand what Bethran was up to.

On the shoreline at the edge of the village, a small stall stood, which for most of the time provided fish for any who would want it or could afford it. What didn't sell was taken to the smokehouse, a few paces away. There was no fresh fish on the stall that day as it happened, but plenty of dried and salted fish and a few crabs. The two men looked at the items on offer as if interested, and then Bethran looked down to the shingle to see all the boats were out, except for Laman's boat, which was on the hard ground above the beach. Several nets were hung across it.

'Can you see anything of the man who told you where to find Unust?' asked Bethran in a quiet voice. Tyr looked, but after a moment shook his head. There were few people about, so the odds of the man being there were low. 'Then we will wait until he shows, we need to talk to the man,' he insisted.

'I am doubtful the man will speak,' announced Tyr, 'he seemed very nervous even talking to me before.'

'We will see,' replied Bethran and then added, 'come, we will wait over here, anyone following would stand out in this deserted spot,' but as Tyr looked back at the fish hanging on hooks, he was aware of just how hungry he was.

The weather had brightened and the promise of another squall had gone. The sky looked blue with large white clouds, slowly traversing the kingdom to the rim of the sea. Two empty fish boxes lay by the shore hut, Bethran righted them and sat. Tyr followed suit, and the seer pulled out the bread and broke off two lumps for them to eat. When they had done, Bethran looked around to make sure there was no one close, and then he pulled out the linen pouch and looked inside. Tyr watched his face change from surprise, to deep doubt in an instant.

'What is it?' asked Tyr, wondering if the pouch contained nothing more than beach pebbles. Bethran looked around once more and then emptied the contents into his hand. There were several silver lumps that shone as the light struck them. Tyr looked into Bethran's face. 'It... it is silver, is it not?' stuttered Tyr. Bethran nodded and then said,

'Silver yes, recently cut from a larger piece too,' and he emptied them back into the pouch all except for one, which he began to study. Tyr was puzzled.

'Where...?' he paused, 'why...?' he paused again.

'Why silver?' asked Bethran, tired of waiting for Tyr to ask. 'Silver is valuable, sometimes cut into pieces to buy small items. Most of it came from the Romans long ago, coins and trinkets, melted down but still valuable.'

'Then why has he given you these?' asked Tyr, thinking that the reward was large for such a task.

'He wanted to pay me well for solving a big problem, but...' now it was Bethran's turn to pause, 'I think we are in a great deal of trouble now I refused to go along with his plan,' he concluded.

Chapter 10 – The Method

'So what are we to do?' asked Tyr. For a moment, Bethran didn't answer. He looked around, then said,

'We needed to speak with the fisherman of yours, but as he is not here…' he trailed off as he looked around once more.

'Are we still being followed?' asked Tyr.

'Probably,' nodded Bethran, 'we should speak with Birse too, it may be that he can enlighten us on a few things.' The two men walked directly towards the woodworking yard of the widow's brother and found him whittling some wood down with the help of a boy. Birse saw them arrived and nodded, passing the tool to the boy and telling him to leave.

'Have you time to talk?' asked Bethran cautiously. The big man wiped his hands on his shirt and nodded, but he said nothing. He then motioned to the shelter that covered the wood. He leaned on the frame and waited for Bethran to speak. 'I should warn you, we are being watched,' began Bethran.

'They have been watching me since I first kicked up a fuss about this,' growled the man.

'Do you know who is watching you?' asked Bethran. The man gave a single curt nod.

'Aye, that little rat, Cinoch, he sometimes does work for the elder-man.' The mention of 'rat' conjured an image of the rodent looking man Tyr had seen.

'What does he look like?' asked Tyr. The big man looked at Tyr as if seeing him for the first time.

'A small man with a pinched face, hardly any hair and what he does have, looks like straw,' replied Birse. Tyr looked at Bethran and nodded.

'He sounds like the one who took the handcart to bring back the body of Unust,' he explained.

'Aye, that is him,' nodded Birse, 'I saw you all arrive with the body,' confirmed Birse and then he added, 'no better than his brother.'

'And who is his brother?' asked Bethran.

'Perst,' replied the man, almost spitting out the name. 'If I could ever get them alone in the dark, I would smash them to tiny bits.' Bethran and Tyr were in no doubt he could do it, and so neither commented on the statement.

'So they work for the elder-man?' asked Tyr, beginning to understand the situation.

'Not as such,' replied Birse, 'Perst and the elder do not often see eye to eye, but Cinoch is usually doing his bidding when not fishing with his brother.'

'So if any of them are involved,' began Tyr, glancing to Bethran for support, 'they would probably all know about it?' Birse shook his head with a doubtful expression.

'I do not know, I know nothing of them, I just know that they are all no good.'

'I heard that Laman was a gambler,' interrupted Bethran seeing Tyr's question was going nowhere.

'Aye, he was that,' replied Birse a little more relaxed, 'he would bet on anything, how many fish in a box, what the weather would do, they even raced snails in the summer.'

'Did he lose money in that way?' asked Bethran.

'Laman?' asked the big man with a stifled laugh, 'not him, he had the luck of a fairy charm maker. He used to say if he brought in a good catch, his luck was in.'

'So you would not expect him to be in a great deal of debt?' inquired Bethran.

'I cannot know for sure, but I doubt it,' replied Birse with a shrug, 'he had mentioned having a second boat built, and finding someone to crew it not long ago.'

'That does not sound like a man in debt,' offered Tyr.

'No,' replied Birse with a frown, 'that is why I disliked him, he could have kept a better place for my sister and I never forgave him for that.'

'So it is likely you did not know his dealings or his gambling in any detail?' asked Bethran, thinking something through.

'No, he told me little,' admitted Birse, 'we put up

with each other for my sister's sake, we had little to say other than when he needed my skills.'

'Did he pay you well?' asked Bethran.

'I am not a man taken to greed. He gave me what I asked for my work. He paid Unust well too when they were fishing. As far as I could tell, he paid his dues if that is what you are getting at.' Bethran nodded casually at this answer.

'So you would be surprised if someone had said he was deep in debt due to gambling?' he then asked.

'If you heard it through the elder-man,' growled the big man, 'it is probably a lie, the man is a snake. If it were left to me, I would tie him to a horse and drag him through the streets.' The man spit to his side and then added, 'Elder-man my arse.'

'There are three elders, are there not?' asked the seer while they were on the subject.

'Aye, but the other two are spineless, Comat pays them off to do as he asks, that is the only reason he keeps his position.'

'So why does the village allow it?' asked Tyr, genuinely interested. In Camma, such a thing could not have happened. The big man looked at Tyr for a moment and wondered what his experience of life could be.

'Here in Tall Bridges, there is much industry, the traders make a good living,' Birse began. 'They want to keep that alive and so they close their eyes to what goes on around them. They hold the sway, they have the power to change things but they do not want change.'

'The pot merchant seems to want change?' put in Tyr.

'He was not born here, he is an outsider. There used to be others, the smith for instance. Comat shut him up by having a new smithy built. Then there was Almon, one of the fishermen,' continued Birse, 'he spoke up but woke one morning to find his boat full of holes. He lost his means to make a living overnight.'

'I see,' nodded Tyr thoughtfully, assuming now that Comat was the name of the elder-man.

'If only others saw,' growled Birse with venom.

'Have you been threatened?' asked Bethran. The man creased his face like a demon.

'If they come to threaten me, it will be the last thing they do,' he concluded.

'Is Almon an older man?' asked Tyr. 'Short in stature with little hair?'

'Yes,' nodded Birse, 'helps out on the shore for scraps of fish these days, the elders will not allow any more fishing boats to work from the village.'

'They cannot set a limit, has anyone petitioned Lord Cullcoil?' asked Bethran, concerned.

'We do not have the ear of the lord,' laughed Birse, 'as long as the tithe is paid, nothing will change.' Bethran sighed, the man was correct. For someone like the seer, someone who was well-travelled and known to all, people like Cullcoil would see him differently. Not as quite an equal, but almost. But to a few villagers, they were just like property, like the lord's cattle. Elders were the people appointed to raise the tithe, and fighting men if the need arose, but as for speaking directly to Lord Cullcoil, that was not a possibility. Bethran knew *he* could do it, but the thought of yet another trek north was not appealing.

'I see your point,' was all Bethran said, but it had given him an idea.

'Without the merchants putting pressure on Comat,' continued Birse, 'nothing will change.'

'And what of Unust, did he come into the story in any way?' Bethran elaborated on the question, 'I mean, was there a reason to have him killed?'

'That I doubt, unless he knew more about the death of Laman,' shrugged the big man, 'he was a fairly quiet lad. Hard working and honest, as far as I could tell. He had no family and so Laman gave him work helping him with the fishing.'

'And the stone cutter I believe?' added Bethran.

'Aye, many gave him work, the wood turner let him stay at his hut for help too.'

As Bethran and Tyr walked back through the village, Tyr asked a question, but his frustration was showing.

'Can this *be* solved? I mean, how can we act on this if the elder-man has this power over the people?'

'I do not know,' replied Bethran, shaking his head. 'I am beginning to think that there is little we can achieve, but at the same time, I feel that if we leave the village, we too will be in danger.' Tyr cast him a glance, he had already considered that the reason they had been followed, and probably were still being followed, was so that they could be got rid of as soon as they were out of sight.

'Then we have a problem,' he said. Bethran had

been giving some thought to the matter, but he needed a little time.

'I have to see someone,' he eventually said, 'but I need you to see the pot merchant. Find out how he feels about the situation and if there are any other merchants willing to support him.' Tyr was quite happy to call on the merchant again, particularly if his daughter was there, but he felt it would be a fool's errand.

'I will try, but I think he is under too much pressure. As I said, he sold many urns to collect the oil from the blow fish, and I think that was to keep him quiet.' Nevertheless, he set off to see the merchant.

By the time Bethran had done what he needed to do and returned to the pot merchant, it was dusk, but the merchant invited Bethran to supper. It seemed Tyr had spent a good deal of time telling the man and his daughter a few stories about the seer. As they sat to eat, the merchant spoke.

'Tyr has explained to us about the situation here, but I doubt that anyone will help. Without the support of the elders there would be little trade for us, and most are afraid that much worse could be our fate.'

'I understand that,' nodded Bethran, 'but if there were enough to put some pressure on the elder, it would give us more time to delve deeper into the issues here.'

'You must understand Bethran,' frowned the merchant, 'we have no means to protect ourselves,' he looked to his daughter and reached for her hand, 'and I suspect the others would not risk all for no good reason. We do well, we have to play by the rules laid down here, but we do well.' Bethran nodded, but the look on his face gave away how he really felt. They were sheep, just like the animals kept on the plain below the village, grazing happily until the farmer came with his knife. One thing that Bethran hated more than the likes of the elder-man, were people like the merchant, those who grew fat while they watched the others die. That's why he travelled. He disliked villages and settlements, or rather the people in them. He could see that Tyr was comfortable having the confidence of the man and more particularly the daughter, but he wanted nothing to do with them. Tyr had found out very little, and it was time to leave. Bethran was polite enough to thank his host, but with a glare towards Tyr he said it was time to leave.

'I see you are becoming used to life besides a hearth,' said Bethran as they walked back through the darkening village.

'It has more charm in there than the leaky old smithy,' replied Tyr, as upbeat as he could.

'It will be the wood yard tonight,' insisted Bethran as he turned down the lane. Tyr sighed, he knew the smithy was a poor domicile, but he had to admit, under the current circumstances, the wood yard would probably be safer.

The morning was bright and pleasant as Tyr awoke, but he noticed Bethran had gone. Tyr wrapped up his old blanket and slung it around his shoulders and set off to look for the seer. He found him close by, at the side of the track, sitting on a pile of unused stones.

'What is it?' he asked. The seer seemed to be

deep in thought.

'Eh, what?' exclaimed Bethran, taken a little by surprise. 'Oh, so you finally woke from your dreams of the pot seller's daughter then?' Tyr was beginning to think that his travelling partner had something against the merchant. Tyr said nothing. He already knew Bethran enough to know he was in some kind of dark mood, and nothing could change that. He turned and walked back in the direction of the village. 'So where are you going?'

'To try to find the man who slayed Laman,' replied Tyr without looking back.

'And how will you achieve that?'

'I do not know,' replied the young man, he stopped and turned to the seer, 'what I do know is that your...' he stopped, 'our methods are just not working.'

'Methods?' asked Bethran, 'we do not have methods. I am a seer, a ceremony leader, I read weather lore and sometimes I advise the nobles. What we are doing here does not even have a name.'

'Then we need to find a name for it and teach ourselves how to do it,' called Tyr, for the first time becoming angry.

'But that is it, I do not need to do this, you are nothing but a fornicating labourer, I have a calling,' spat Bethran rising to Tyr's ire. The younger man glared at Bethran for a moment. He knew he was overstepping the mark as he slowly paced towards the seer. In a quieter voice, yet still brimming with anger, he said,

'You *had* a calling, you have seen the black cloaked Christian, they are coming, and they are close. Your time is finished, old man. Who will want to know

210

the future when the Christians can promise eternal life? Who will be interested in what the weather will bring when the Christians bring their gold?' Bethran stood, Tyr was once again aware of the old man's size. He seemed to have grown as he rose up.

'Oh, yes, you are right,' said Bethran, clearly but calmly, 'they are coming, they bring their promise of eternal life, they bring their gold. But I have seen it all. That gold will be their undoing. The men from across the eastern sea will come on their dragon boats, and they will take that gold, and they will kill our people.' He stopped to glare deeply at Tyr who was beginning to see that Bethran believed in what he had seen. 'And what is clear to me, is that the Christians will not be able to stop them, we will need a king to do that.' Bethran turned and lifted his pack. He slung it over his shoulder and walked back to the village. Tyr didn't turn to watch him. He looked up to the blue sky and sighed. After a few moments, he sat on the stone pile where Bethran had been sitting previously, and leaned on his knees, glaring at the ground. By the time he finally looked up, Bethran had gone from sight and had wound his way into the village. Tyr looked up the track to the north and then back south to the village. He didn't know what to do now. He had exhausted everything he could, and his only recourse was to head back to Lliedale and try to pick up some work there. At least he had better clothes and looked less like a beggar than he had done, but he couldn't help thinking that there was a way to solve the riddle. Any riddle. He saw a bird feather on the floor and picked it up. Where did it come from and how would he work that out? Well, it was obvious, it was a feather from a blackbird, but had the bird pulled it out, or had the bird died before that? That was a puzzle. How would he work that out? No matter how much thought he put into that simple problem, nothing came to him. Was it as Bethran had said, could such a puzzle or a riddle not be worked out? He stood and decided to go back to the smithy. He didn't know why, but he soon found himself back there, looking around the deserted hut, trying to recall what he and Bethran had spoken of there. He remembered Bethran placing the objects on the trestle table and how he explained what he was doing. He had been trying to turn back the days, trying to go back to the day that Laman had been killed and before. Was that it? Was that the way to solve it? He then walked to the shore but moved south of where the fishing boats were unloaded, and as he did, he saw someone. It was the red-haired man he had seen talking to the elder-man, the one who seemed to have been arguing with him. He quickly slipped behind the net hut and watched the man readying his boat for the sea. He was loading line and nets into the boat and then a large stone with a hole through it. A stout line was tied through the stone, and Tyr wondered if that was what allowed the boat to remain still in the water as they fished. After a short time, another man walked to the boat, it was the rodent, and then it struck him. This was Perst. It was Perst and his brother, the rodent. As he watched the two men drag the vessel into the surf, he saw that there was ill feeling between the two. They didn't speak, they didn't even acknowledge each other. They jumped into the boat and made their way out to sea as if each man was doing his best to ignore the other. He then had an idea. When the boat was out of sight, he walked south along the shore and found an area where he could sit. He then drew out a representation of the village in the sand and tried the same method as Bethran had done with the objects on the trestle table. They had more information now and some of it made sense. The problem was, so much still made no sense whatsoever. He eventually gave up and went to find the hut where the wood turner lived, maybe he could find something out there.

The small hut that held a decorative sign in wood, announcing the trade of the occupier, was just off the area of the market. The door was open, and inside there was a smell of wood sap and other wood related odours. The man was well built and wore a leather apron over his stained shirt. He had a kindly face, but was surprised to see Tyr walk in.

'What can I do for you?' he asked as he stopped his bow that was turning the wood. Tyr looked quickly down and was so fascinated by the equipment the man was using, he almost forgot what he was going to ask.

'Er, sorry for the interruption,' he said quietly, 'but I heard that Unust lived here, and sometimes helped you with your trade.' The man lifted his arm and rested it behind his head. He was actually going to scratch but stopped and then folded his arms with a questioning look on his face.

'You are the lad with Bethran, are you not?'

'I am,' replied Tyr, but he was hesitant to say more on the subject.

'Well, I told him all I know, he is next door,' and he motioned to the left with his thumb.

'Oh,' frowned Tyr, not expecting that at all, 'yes, I will,' and he exited the hut to see the smaller building on the side of the hut. The roof was low and the room tiny, but inside Tyr found Bethran standing motionless against the rear wall. He looked around to Tyr and then down to the rough wooden cot on the earth floor.

'I was under the impression you were leaving,' said Tyr in a neutral tone.

'I am,' said Bethran, still looking down at the cot, 'but when I decide, and as yet, I have not decided.'

'So have you found anything?' asked Tyr, as if he was passing the time of day with a stranger.

'A chair, a cot and a wooden whistle,' replied Bethran, knowing it wasn't what Tyr had meant. The younger man looked around the small space. He couldn't get in any further as there wasn't the room but as Bethran had said, there was little to see. The wooden whistle was on the floor, under the cot and against the wall. Unust must have played it when he had the time. Tyr looked at Bethran who was still looking at the cot and then he suddenly looked at his own feet. He then looked up at Tyr. He lifted his right foot and then placed it back down with a thump. Tyr was beginning to wonder if the old man had lost his wits as a small cloud of dust scattered. Tyr felt uncomfortable. He sighed and folded his arms. It was then Bethran looked across to him and asked,

'So what do you see?'

'The same as you, chair, cot, whistle.'

214

'And what is not here?' asked the seer.

'Everything else,' shrugged Tyr, not quite understanding. Bethran widened his eyes a little, and it worried Tyr. It wasn't an angry stare, but there was something behind those eyes that sent a shiver down his back.

'It is called *The Method*,' he said calmly.

'What is?' asked the still puzzled Tyr.

'You said I needed to find a name for it,' replied Bethran, still glaring, 'when I said we had no method, and it did not have a name,' he added.

'So you decided it would just be called, the method?' asked Tyr, thinking it wasn't very inventive. Bethran didn't answer. He continued to glare for a moment, then said,

'It works, and I know why it works.' Tyr was even more puzzled now. He sometimes wished that Bethran made his explanations a little less complicated. He decided to shrug and hope the seer would inform him exactly of what he was talking. After a moment, he dropped his gaze from Tyr and had one last look around the room and exited, almost pushing Tyr out of the way. He then turned, thrust his head back into the tiny hut and said,

'The secret is in what you do not see, not in what is obvious,' and he left Tyr in the room. Tyr wondered if Bethran had been in the ale hut spending his silver. He couldn't quite grasp what the old man was talking about. He eventually bent to pick up the whistle, and as he did so, he saw something. Tiny pieces of straw, and he picked one up. He looked at the whistle closely and then back to the straw. It didn't mean much, but then it struck him. He looked outside and saw Bethran leaning on the wall of the hut.

'The bedroll, it is not here,' he said, though he couldn't see the significance.

'Well done,' nodded Bethran, folding his arms, 'and the wood turner has not removed it.'

'There could be many reasons for it not being here,' insisted Tyr.

'So that is all you found?'

'Yes,' replied Tyr, holding up the obvious whistle.

'Then look again,' insisted Bethran, 'and look at the floor.' Tyr wasn't sure what he was getting at but he returned inside and looked down. It was an earth floor like most other huts, bits of loose straw from the bedroll, the cot, dust, footprints... He looked closer at the footprints. Earth floors were usually solid after years of feet walking over them. In this hut the ground was loose. He bent down and ran the dust through his fingers. It was sandy, like most of the ground around the settlement. He brushed it away with his hand, and underneath found the hard floor that would have been usual. It was stained, a large stain that certainly looked like blood. A voice broke in behind him.

'Cover it back up before you come out,' said Bethran, realising Tyr had found it, 'we do not want anyone knowing we have found that stain.' Tyr quickly scattered the dust back over the stain and walked outside. Quietly, he said to Bethran,

'So Unust was killed in there, and the body was

216

probably wrapped in his bedroll to get him out.' Bethran said nothing. He refolded his arms and leaned on the wall where he had previously been. 'So what next?' asked Tyr. Bethran casually looked around and then glanced to Tyr.

'We still need to find the fisherman that told you where to find his body,' he replied.

'I have not seen him and neither do I know his name for sure,' shrugged Tyr.

'It could be the case that the man is lying somewhere, he too suffering the damage caused by a heavy rock,' said Bethran.

'But how do we find him if that is not the case?' asked Tyr, not sure what to suggest.

'It will have to wait,' frowned Bethran, unfolding his arms and looking at the sky. 'We can do no more than look around the village, and I have to meet someone in the ale hut.' Tyr wondered what the seer was about. One moment he is for leaving, the next he is back on the hunt. Now he is going for ale.

'So what shall I do?' he asked. Bethran shrugged.

'Walk around the village and see if you can spot the fisherman, just do not make it obvious and stay where there are other people. If you see the man, follow him and see where he lives.' Bethran then walked off in the direction of the ale hut.

Tyr ambled around the settlement for some time. He looked at every man that could be possible, but no one looked at all like the man who had told him about Rook Point. Then he had an idea. He wondered if the pot

217

merchant may know who the fisherman was.

'And you say he was older?' asked the merchant.

'Yes,' nodded Tyr as he spoke to the merchant at the front of his hut. He had been stacking some new pots by the door. The daughter wasn't there.

'There are several older fishermen,' replied the merchant, squinting in the sun, 'I do not know their names, but usually they help out when the catch comes in.' The merchant looked up suddenly and smiled. Tyr turned and saw the daughter, Coblaith.

'Hello Tyr,' she said with a smile, 'hello father.'

'You are back early,' replied Bolder, returning the smile.

'Yes, it is such a pleasant day I thought I would return and help you stack the pots.'

'Well, Tyr has helped me with these larger ones,' smiled the merchant. Coblaith also smiled at Tyr again.

'That is most kind of you,' she beamed shyly.

'It was as much as I could do to reward your kindness,' replied Tyr with a slight bow. He was suddenly very conscious of the growth on his chin again. He thought of asking her about the fisherman, but decided he didn't wish to talk of such things with her there. Then, for some reason, an idea, or rather a memory, jumped into the front of his mind. He waited for Coblaith to retreat inside before he brought up the subject.

'I collected flowers from the wood,' she said, holding up several blooms that Tyr recognised as Anemones and Corncockles. 'I will place them in water

218

before they droop,' and she entered the hut. Tyr watched her go, wishing he had the power to enchant her. She was a delicate beauty, just like the blooms in her hand. He came out of his dream and looked to Bolder.

'I wonder, do you know the name Almon?'

'I have heard the name. Could he be your fisherman?' Tyr nodded.

'I could be him, I was told his boat was damaged and he no longer fishes,' explained Tyr.

'Yes,' nodded Bolder, sitting on a large pot, 'I do remember that. Many think it was one of the other fishermen who put him out of business.'

'Do you know where he could be found?' asked Tyr.

'I do not know him personally, but if you ask in the ale hut, I think the brewer knows the man.' Tyr nodded, but for a few moments he waited to see if the daughter would return. When Tyr considered he had stood around for an embarrassingly long period, he left to find Bethran.

'The seer was sitting near the open door of the hut sharing a mug of ale with another man. The other man was sitting at the same table, a stocky, powerful man of a similar age to Bethran, though in truth, he looked younger. Not having the beard, but rather a fashionable moustache, his short hair seemed to make him look 'fresher'. Bethran watched Tyr enter and ceased his talking to the man to turn and signal to the pot-boy.

'Sit, Tyr,' he said, pointing to a spare seat. 'This

219

is my friend Callin. He was once a warrior…' he looked at his friend with a grin, 'of sorts,' and Callin laughed, 'who was with the retinue of Lord Cullcoil.' In Tyr's mind, that made him a true warrior, but both Bethran and Callin knew that a true warrior is one that survives a battle. 'This is Tyr of…' Bethran was going to say Camma, but as the lad had been expelled, he paused and then continued with, 'well, we do not quite know where he is of now.' The pot boy placed ale for Tyr and he lifted the mug and drank.

'Pleased to meet you Callin,' he said, wiping his mouth with his hand. Callin nodded with a smile.

'I sent a messenger this morning to fetch Callin, if he had the time,' he glanced at the man before continuing, 'as I thought we could do with some little help.' Tyr nodded as Callin said,

'You know I would be here as soon as I could anyway, no matter the cost,' and Tyr became interested that the irritable Bethran could find such a close friend as this man seemed to be. It made him think that one day, Bethran may see Tyr as such a friend. At the moment, however, he was becoming annoyed with the seer, for not telling him exactly what he was planning.

'Can I have a word with you?' he asked. Bethran nodded. 'In private,' he then added with a glare.

'If it cannot be said in front of Callin, it cannot be said,' frowned Bethran, 'he is here to help, he is here as a friend too.'

'Very well,' nodded Tyr and then began in a voice that Bethran had not heard in the young man previously. It was annoyed and harsh. 'If we are to continue in this endeavour, I need to know what you are about, I need to know what you are thinking. From one day to the next, you change your mind, your ideas, and honestly, I am becoming sick of it.' Callin began a ripple of laughter that annoyed Tyr even further until the man looked at Bethran and said,

'I like this man, he is the only man other than myself that has ever had the balls to stand up to you,' and he continued laughing and slapped Tyr on the shoulder. Bethran remained impassive.

'Well?' snapped Tyr.

'Well, what?' frowned Bethran with Callin still laughing.

'Do I get to know what you are planning or not?'

'I have kept nothing from you,' growled Bethran.

'You mean,' insisted Tyr with his own growl this time, 'that you spoke to me about sending for the help of one of your friends? Well, it is either I that cannot recall it, or you, that forgot to tell me. I knew nothing of this and it makes me wonder what else I do not know about.' Callin had reduced the laugh to a grin as he said,

'He is in the right of it, old friend, you cannot keep things from your partner.'

'He is not my partner,' insisted Bethran glaring at Callin.

'And that is another thing,' spat Tyr, 'I am finished with the idea that I am your servant, or whatever the moment takes your fancy to call me.'

'Oh, he is angry now,' grinned Callin but Tyr game him such a scowl, he went silent, yet the smile still hung on his lips.

221

'He is right, I am angry and we either finally set out what I am doing here, or I leave and take the information I have with me.' Bethran continued to frown, but he looked deep into Tyr's eyes.

'I accept, I did not mention the messenger I sent to Callin,' nodded Bethran, taking a gulp of ale.

'Anything else?' asked Tyr, raising his brows.

'There…' Bethran paused as his eyes flitted around the room, 'there maybe something else I did not mention.' Tyr did not speak, he tilted his head as his brows raised and his eyes widened. 'I gave the silver to Osfrith the monk.' Tyr's expression changed to shock. 'I sent him north with a message for Lord Cullcoil.' Tyr looked dumbfounded. He wasn't sure what Bethran was thinking about. They would hardly be able to continue without the means to acquire food. There was silence from the stricken Tyr. It was Callin who broke it.

'Well, let me refill our pots,' he said, 'and Bethran can explain why he gave several lumps of perfectly good silver to a Christian, for I cannot.'

Chapter 11 – Catching a Mouse

Bethran lifted the freshly filled pot to his mouth but paused, and then said in almost a whisper,

'It is very simple, if we are to achieve anything here, we need authority.'

'What do you mean, authority?' asked a bemused Tyr, trying to keep his voice down.

'Let me explain,' replied Bethran, and then he drank several gulps of ale. 'When the elder-man paid me for my services, he took the silver from an iron chest in his hut. The small pouch that he gave me was just sitting on the top of whatever was in the chest.'

'So you think the chest is full?' asked Callin.

'It is full of something, I am not saying that it is all silver, because I also saw pewter and fine pottery in the hut,' replied the seer, glancing to his friend.

'But either way,' nodded Callin, 'this man seems to have more wealth than an elder-man ought to have.'

Bethran didn't reply. He gave Callin a questioning look and then a shrug. 'But that is what you suspect, and if indeed the box is full of silver, it is likely that he got it through underhanded means?' Callin put it as a question to try to pry more information from the seer.

'Either that, or he found an old Roman stockpile somewhere,' hinted Bethran taking another drink.

'But there is nothing we can do about that, is there?' put in Tyr, 'it is hardly our business.'

'For what seems on the surface a bright lad,' frowned Bethran, 'you can be pretty slow at grasping a situation.'

'I think what this old goat is trying to say is,' began Callin, pointing his thumb to the seer, 'to fight this battle on equal terms, we have to gather weapons first,' and he turned to Bethran and continued. 'Which is probably why you asked me to come?' Bethran nodded.

'Partly,' he admitted, 'we are very much outnumbered here and unless we can keep ourselves safe, there is no route forward. If we can put pressure on the elder-man in some way, he will forget that we are still trying to chase the killer of Laman. That is why we need authority.' Bethran noticed two more men enter the hut, and so he motioned for the others to drink up. They exited the hut and stood outside for a moment.

'So where does the silver, and the monk come in?' asked Tyr, still not convinced of the reasoning.

'I asked the monk for a favour. In return, I gave him something he needed.'

'I was under the impression that monks did not need earthly goods,' frowned the young man.

224

'Not the silver,' replied Bethran, turning slightly and looking around the village, 'an introduction to Lord Cullcoil. The monk wishes to travel the Kingdom of Cat, talking to people, I just gave him that introduction by giving him a message to deliver to the lord.'

'And he gives a message to Lord Cullcoil that one of his elders has a pile of silver but is sending no tribute to his lordship,' smiled Callin, pointing to Bethran. 'Very clever.'

'Does he have to do that?' asked Tyr.

'Yes, of course,' nodded Callin, 'any large finds of treasure have to be reported to the lord, he owns them after all.'

'What if that is not the case and there is no silver?' asked Tyr with a worried expression.

'Then, I am simply doing my duty,' grinned Bethran, 'and Cullcoil gets a small purse of silver for his trouble.'

'And the monk gets his introduction, but have you considered?' asked Tyr, still with a look of surprise, 'that you are helping the Christian religion grow by introducing the monk?'

'As I keep telling you,' shrugged Bethran, 'they will come anyway,' and he turned to watch as a man hurriedly made his way to the hut. He looked in distress, and at first, Bethran thought he was heading towards him. He passed by, however, and ran straight into the ale hut. Bethran raised his brows to the others and then followed back into the hut to see what the hurry was.

'What is it?' asked the burly brewer.

'We need ale, one of the fishing boats has

returned, he has lost his crewman,' panted the man before picking up a newly filled mug of ale and making off.

'Which boat?' called the brewer as the man left.

'Perst,' replied the man, hurrying away. Tyr and Bethran looked to each other and turned quickly, Callin wasn't sure what it was about, but he turned too, and set off after the two men.

There was a small crowd around Perst's boat and the red-haired man was still sitting in the vessel, wet and downcast, drinking the remains of the ale the fisherman had brought.

'So then what happened?' asked one of the villagers.

'I am not sure,' replied Perst, still looking down into the boat. 'Whatever it was, it pulled at the net with such a force that it nearly took both of us with it. I managed to free myself, but my brother…' and he paused, shaking his head. 'I think his foot must have snagged in the nets.'

'We should scour the rocks for his body,' said another man.

'There is no point,' replied the dejected Perst, 'I stayed there for some time, the nets did not surface and neither did his body.' Tyr frowned deeply. He looked inside the boat, it was true, there was no net, but there was nothing else either. No fish, and no equipment for fishing. This puzzled him and he looked at Bethran, but he could see that the seer was also unsure about the story. He caught the gaze of Tyr and nodded slightly in the direction of the settlement. The three men quietly slipped away and headed towards the privacy of the old smithy.

'So what do you make of that?' asked Tyr, 'another man goes missing,' but he could see that Bethran was deep in thought.

'I am not sure. Could it be the truth, was it an accident?' asked the seer as if to himself.

'You are surely not suggesting that he killed his own brother?' asked Tyr, but then, he too thought of something, 'though…' he went quiet.

'What?' asked Bethran, coming out of his own dream.

'Well, I saw them readying their boat,' frowned Tyr. He tried to remember exactly what he *had* seen.

'Is that it?' snapped Bethran.

'No, no, that is not it,' replied Tyr testily, 'I was thinking back through what I saw.' He paused again and then said, 'I saw Perst, the red-haired man loading his boat. He dropped nets and a large stone with a rope through it.' He looked at Bethran as they walked and then added, 'I do not know what it is called, but I believe it keeps the boat in place on the sea floor.'

'An anchor,' suggested Callin bringing himself into the conversation.

'Well, whatever it is called,' shrugged Tyr, 'neither it, nor the net, was in the boat just now.' Bethran stopped suddenly, and though the other two carried on for a pace or two, they stopped and looked back to him.

'No, you are in the right of it. There was no anchor, nor anything else. Interesting.'

'It would not be the first time someone has killed his own brother,' said Callin.

'No,' agreed Bethran, 'but if that is the case, there is a much greater story to this little mystery.' He then continued to the smithy.

'Nice place you have here,' scoffed Callin, looking for somewhere to sit. He eventually slumped by a wall and stretched his legs out. Bethran was looking at the empty hearth as if there was a fire blazing away. There were certainly sparks in his eyes. He eventually looked around to Tyr and said,

'Come with me, we need to gather a few pebbles and stones, I want to rebuild the plan we had on the trestle table.'

'I will wait here,' said Callin, removing one of his boots to sooth his feet. The other two found a few items close to the hut and then returned and began to place them around the floor. Bethran then took his knife and scored a rudimentary map of the coastline and the village onto the earth floor. Callin shook his head several times but said nothing. When the whole picture was to Bethran's satisfaction, he began to place objects around the map. He stood and then said to Tyr,

'So what would make a man kill his own brother?' Tyr began to consider it but then Bethran added, 'And a brother who had previously been at least close enough for them to fish together?' Even with this, Tyr still didn't know why. Fortunately, Callin provided a probable answer.

'Jealousy, greed or a woman,' he offered,

'nothing as sure as one of those things to cause a family rift.'

'Or some information that the elder brother did not want releasing?' put in Bethran.

'I do not see that,' replied Callin, shaking his head, 'that would have to suppose that they were never close. If the brothers did not trust each other, yes, but you say they were on good terms at one stage.'

'There is something else,' said Tyr suddenly, staring into space for a moment.

'Like what?' frowned Bethran. Tyr flashed a glance to Bethran and then crouched down by the map. 'I know that Perst's brother was working on occasions for the elder-man, I also know that they were not alike, either to look at or in character.'

'Half-brothers?' suggested Callin.

'That I do not know, but the younger brother has the confidence of the elder-man, the elder brother is at loggerheads with the same man.'

'It has possibilities,' shrugged Bethran, 'but we have to remember that the first killing was Laman, and he has no real connection with a family feud between Perst and his brother.'

'As far as we know he does not,' said Tyr widening his eyes, 'we know from the elder-man's own lips that Laman had an issue with another fisherman, and we now know that was with Perst. Did his brother side with Laman?'

'He has a point,' nodded Callin as he watched Tyr moving the objects around on the map.

'So,' began Bethran watching Tyr, 'Perst flies

into a rage over the feud with Laman and bashes his head in. His brother is there and sees it happen, he helps him to take the body to the blow fish. And then we have a problem.'

'Problem?' asked Tyr.

'Why does the elder-man have little interest in finding out who killed Laman?' asked Bethran, 'if he is looking for a chance to get rid of Perst, finding out that he had killed Laman would surely do the job.' There was a sudden silence in the room until Callin offered,

'Because the young brother wanted to protect the elder brother?' he announced but then held up his hand and added, 'no forget that, it does not make sense.'

'Then why would Perst kill his brother for that loyalty?' asked Tyr. Callin nodded then replaced his boots.

'Unless, as I suggested earlier,' added Bethran, 'it was an accident. A large blow fish tangles their net and pulls one of them over the side.'

'I still feel that there was some aggression between them as they left in the boat.' Again the hut went silent. After some moments, Tyr stood and leaned on the stones of the hearth, Bethran paced the room and then crouched close to Callin.

'There is still the matter of the elder-man having a chest that may contain a hoard of silver,' he said.

'We do not know that for sure. It could contain documents,' suggest Tyr.

'Yes, it could,' nodded Bethran, 'but other than that, I am at a loss. There is a piece of this still missing.' More silence.

'If the younger brother,' began Callin, 'was in league with the elder-man and not his brother, would it not be an idea to watch the elder?'

'That seems a good idea,' nodded Tyr standing.

'It may put him under some pressure, it may be worth it,' agreed Bethran.

'I'll do it,' suggested Callin standing, 'he does not know me and I need to stretch my legs, what does he look like?' They described the man to Callin, and where to find him before Callin left for the settlement. For some time after, Bethran moved the objects around on the floor until Tyr became bored and went for a walk himself.

For some reason he could not fathom, he found himself close to the hut of the merchant called Bolder. At the back of his mind, he was wondering if he might catch a glimpse of his daughter. He leaned on a building at the opposite side of the street, watching the front of the merchant's hut until a voice from his rear said,

'Hello Tyr.'

'Oh, er... hello, er...' it was the daughter, Coblaith. In the sunlight, he could see her hair was much fairer than he recalled.

'Are you waiting to see my father?' she asked in her soft silky voice.

'Er no, I mean yes, well...'

'He has travelled north to Lliefoot, he has some business there.' She smiled. 'He should be back before sundown.'

'Oh, er, right,' he stuttered again, 'I will see him when he returns then, it is nothing important,' he added.

'Or is there something I can help with?' she offered. Tyr gulped heavily, so heavily he was sure she would notice it. He tried to calm himself, but he felt both sick and hot at the same time.

'Er well, I do not...' he tried to settle himself again. 'I, er, I-I am not sure,' he knew his embarrassment was as obvious as the untidy facial hair on his face. 'I think I had better speak to him myself,' he said, mainly to give him time to think of a good lie. She smiled again.

'Fine, I will tell him you called.'

'Oh, yes... thank you,' and she walked towards the hut. He watched her long dress swing from side to side, matching the rhythm of her long hair, as if she was controlled by the tides and the waves of the sea. It was a motion that thrilled him, and he wanted so much to be her equal in society. As it was, he would probably be whipped for even talking to her, if they really knew his background. She stopped before she entered the hut and looked back to him. She cast him the loveliest smile he had ever seen and then stepped elegantly into the darkness of the hut. He knew exactly what he needed to do. He returned to the smithy, where Bethran was still puzzling over the items scattered across the floor.

'I need to find someone who can shave me,' announced Tyr. It was normal for Bethran to ignore people, but this time he heard perfectly well.

'In my opinion, I would not allow anyone in Tall Bridges near my throat with a knife at the moment.'

'Then I need to find a shaving knife,' he insisted.

'It would be a waste of your time and effort. She will never become close to you,' he replied without taking his gaze from the floor.

'What are you talking about?' demanded Tyr, 'I just find the need to shave.'

'I'm talking about the pot seller's daughter,' announced Bethran, looking up to the lad.

'What has shaving to do with Coblaith?'

'Is that her name?' asked Bethran with a nod, 'she is a merchant's daughter. She has no use for a man such as you. Her father will choose her a merchant for a husband.'

'Then why is she not spoken for already?' asked Tyr with a deep frown. Bethran stood and stretched his legs to return the feeling to them.

'So what has shaving to do with the pot seller's daughter?' shrugged Bethran as a parody of Tyr's own words. Tyr shook his head.

'I just wish to look more presentable, you said yourself that I need to improve the way I looked.'

'Then shave,' nodded Bethran, 'I just wished to point out that you are wasting your efforts with this girl,' and he thought about her, 'though she is a very pretty bauble, I will give you that.' He looked down to the floor once more and rested his hands on his hips. 'What was the information you had?'

'Information?' asked Tyr, unsure what he meant.

'Back in the ale hut, when you were telling me exactly what you thought about me,' frowned Bethran, remembering Tyr's rage, 'you said, if I did not tell you everything, you would leave without giving me the information you had found.' Tyr thought for a moment, then he remembered.

233

'Oh, yes, it had slipped my mind with everything that has happened.' He looked into Bethran's face as he recalled the altercation, but the seer had let the frown drop. 'I think I know the name of the fisherman who told me where to find Unust's body.'

'Do you know how to find him?' asked Bethran.

'I was told the brewer at the ale hut knows him, his name is Almon.'

'Then we need to question the brewer, so we can find this fisherman,' and he paused this time and looked into Tyr's eyes, 'before anyone else can get to him, I think we will know a great deal more about this twisting tale once we have what he knows.' Bethran looked down to the objects on the floor for a moment and then scattered them with his foot.

'Then you have found nothing from this?' asked Tyr, pointing to the map on the floor that Bethran was destroying.

'On the contrary,' replied Bethran, picking up his pack and slinging it across his back. 'I have made a great deal of progress with it, we just now need to hear what the fisherman has to say,' and he headed out from the hut with Tyr following closely, giving a final, quick glance at the destroyed map.

The two men had been to fetch Callin from his position watching the elder-man's hut, but the burly man had said he had seen nothing unusual. This wasn't what Bethran had wanted to hear, but in the larger scheme of things, it didn't matter all that much. As they walked, Bethran explained what Tyr had found out, and they were heading back to the ale hut to question the brewer. Bethran wanted Callin to stay outside, just in case they were interrupted by anyone. The ale hut was quiet, mainly due to the news about Perst and his brother, and many were still by the seashore. The brewer was placing mugs on a rack as they entered, and he gave a quick smile as Bethran and Tyr closed in on his table. Bethran nodded to the man and looked around the hut at the other customers.

'Can we speak, privately?' The brewer pursed his lips and nodded.

'Boy,' he called, and the pot-boy came from behind a screen at the back of the hut. 'Watch the shop for a while,' he added, and led Bethran and Tyr behind the screen and into a stall where the ale was kept. 'What can I do for you, Bethran?' asked the brewer, leaning on a wooden barrel.

'You know the man, Almon?' he asked.

'I know him,' nodded the brewer, 'he comes here when he has the means to purchase ale.'

'Where can we find him?' asked the seer. The brewer shook his head vaguely and shrugged.

'I could not say, he bides on the waterfront usually, but he no longer has a boat. I think he helps the others now and then.' Bethran could see a worried look underneath the seemingly carefree expression.

'He could be in danger,' insisted Bethran, 'we need to talk to him, he has information that is going to get him killed.'

'We were told you knew him,' added Tyr, seeing the man was hiding something.

'He's a customer on occasions,' nodded the man, 'but I have not seen him much of late.'

'Hello Bethran,' came the jovial woman's voice from behind them. She was passing through the small passage, but when she saw the collection of men in the ale room, she stopped and dropped the smile. 'What is it?' she asked, 'is the hut so full we have to serve in here?'

'No, er, no my dear,' stuttered the man seeming to be a little upset that she was there, 'they are just asking me a few questions in private, nothing to fuss about.' Bethran saw the defensiveness overcome the man and he went for the kill.

'We were asking him about one of your customers,' began Bethran, 'Almon, the old fisherman.'

'Oh him,' she sighed, but Bethran saw the brewer's shoulders sag a little.

'Have you seen him of late?' he then asked.

'Not as much as in the past, but I think it was two nights ago?' she concluded, looking to her husband for confirmation.

'I do not recall,' replied the brewer, shaking his head, 'I thought it was longer ago.' Now Bethran knew the man was lying, but he didn't know why.

'As I said,' confirmed Bethran, 'we think his life is in danger and if we do not find him soon, I fear there will be nothing we can do for him.'

'Then you had better help them husband, he is not our best customer, but he is harmless enough.' When the brewer began to shake his head, the woman interceded. 'Now, I know you know him well,' she insisted to the brewer, and it was obvious she was probably in charge of the business and the household, 'and I know he gets you cheap fish, but if he is in some danger, you'd better say. This is Bethran,' she added as if the seer was some kind of demigod, 'he is not going to make things up,' and the man began to crumble to his wife's insistence.

'He has gone into hiding,' nodded the man eventually capitulating to the pressure, 'he seemed to think he was being watched and he told me he had to leave.'

'Do you know where he has gone?' asked Tyr.

'I do not know where he is hiding,' replied the man, shaking his head, 'but I may be able to get a message to him.'

'That will not do,' insisted Bethran, 'it may scare him and then we will never find him. How would you message him?' The man cast his eyes down and began to pick at a loose shard of wood on one of the barrels. He looked up at Bethran, then over to his wife. She merely glared at him. 'He asked me to tell no one and I-'

'Would you rather his pursuers find him?' hissed Bethran. The man shrugged.

'I leave him a little food and messages most nights by the Kissing Stone in the woods,' he eventually said. Bethran looked to Tyr, but the young man shook his head.

'Where is the Kissing Stone?' Bethran asked, but it was the brewer's wife who answered.

'It is in the woods, four or five hundred paces past the old smithy.'

'We will find it,' nodded Bethran, then he turned back to the brewer, 'you may just have saved the man's life,' and he turned to leave.

They had no real plan for finding the old fisherman, they would just have to leave a little food at the Kissing Stone and wait for him to show. It took a short time to find the stone in the woods, a leaning rock, half of the height of a man with two indentations near the top. Tyr couldn't see why it would have been given the name, but he suspected it was a meeting place for young lovers, away from prying eyes. They placed the food on the stone and sat in the trees, waiting for the old man to arrive. Callin was at one side, and Bethran and Tyr at the other. All could just about see the stone, but as darkness fell, it became more difficult to see anything within the trees. As the visible distance decreased, Bethran quietly crept towards Tyr.

'Can you see anything from here?' he whispered.

'Not much,' replied Tyr in a similar manner, 'but I can just about make out the bread on the top of the stone.' Bethran said nothing more. He slowly curled up on the floor in the undergrowth and waited. Tyr had been thinking a great deal about what Bethran had said in the old smithy, just before they had left. He had said that he had made a great deal of progress from the map he had drawn on the floor of the smithy. Tyr recalled the way he has scattered the pebbles and stones as if he had done with them completely.

'So what did you learn in the smithy?' he whispered. Even in the fading light he could see Bethran frowning. 'You said you had learned a great deal from the map on the floor,' he added. Bethran nodded as if he understood. 'So, what did you find?' asked Tyr again. Bethran sat up and leaned over to Tyr.

'I managed to work out a series of events for how Laman was killed. With everything else we now know it makes sense.'

'So are you going to explain?' whispered Tyr a little too loudly for Bethran's liking.

'This is not the time, nor the place,' insisted the seer, and Tyr admitted it was difficult to communicate, and so he left it at that. Bethran tried to get comfortable and Tyr stretched out his legs for a moment before crouching and looking towards the Kissing Stone.

They heard owls, two sets of scurrying footsteps from small animals and the sounds of Tyr's stomach making some very loud complaining noises, but no sound of the little fisherman coming for his food. Bethran had thought that the man would come early in the evening, so that he could ensure the beasts of the woods would not carry off any offerings on the stone. That hadn't been the case, and now he was wondering if the man had been caught by whoever had been watching him. As he thought through what they were doing, he likened the process to catching a mouse. The little fisherman had been described as a small timid man with large dark eyes, and here they were, setting a trap with a half loaf of bread to catch the wood mouse. For a moment, he smiled. Luckily, in the darkness of the undergrowth, Tyr didn't see it. Bethran was beginning to like the young man, but he wasn't going to tell him that.

He would continue to build the legend, that he would prefer it if the man went his own way. What if he did? Would Bethran try to convince him to stay? No, he didn't think he would, but he was becoming acclimatised to the fact that Tyr was almost always around. In some ways, he could sense a part of him becoming fatherly to the lad. Tyr's life was not unlike Bethran's. He had also once sought the attentions of a married woman. Luckily, he hadn't been caught and the whole affair had fallen apart before anyone could be damaged or offended by it. He would never tell Tyr the story though. That *was* a secret he would keep. The thoughts caused Bethran to think about the women he had known. Like Tyr, there had been one who had shown him the workings of the world. She hadn't been a lover. She had taken him in and taught him many things, including how to read the bones and divination by other means. She had been more like a mother and in times of dark thoughts, he used her memory to calm himself still. He felt in his shirt for the stone that hung around his neck. He wore it still, the stone she had given him when she called him her 'Little Owl'. She had told him the story of Blodeuedd, the most beautiful woman that had ever been, and he decided that she would be a talisman thereafter. He was thinking of the time that he first tied the stone around his neck when there was a shout and a further commotion from over by the Kissing Stone. He was up on his feet quicker than Tyr, but Tyr shot past him soon after. Callin had the fisherman pinned to the floor and his large hand over the man's mouth. In the near darkness, they could see the terrified face of the little fisherman.

'We are not here to hurt you, we are here to help you,' insisted Bethran in a calm voice. Tyr moved closer to the man's face.

'It is I, the one you told about Unust.' He watched the man's eyes soften at the recognition. 'If we let you up, will you stay calm?' he then asked. The man nodded under the restraint of Callin's hand, and Tyr nodded to him to release the fisherman. Slowly, Callin released his hand, and in a single tug, brought the man to his feet. The man still looked shocked, and Bethran saw that indeed he had some similarities to a mouse.

'You are known as Almon?' he asked. The man nodded franticly and swallowed hard. Bethran reached down for the half loaf that was now on the floor and gave it to Almon. The man looked dumbfounded still, taking the bread and then looking back up to Bethran who towered above him. 'Eat,' he said, 'and then we will move.' The man looked at their faces and then shook his head, pointing back into the wood, the way he had come.

'I have a safe place in the woods,' he still looked shocked, 'we can go there.' Bethran looked into the woods and considered that there may be some logic in staying in there for the night. He nodded to the man and he lead them back to the place he was hiding.

The little fisherman's lair was organised and well hidden. In the woods was a fissure in the rocks where an overhang jutted out and was covered over by trees. As they entered his small camp, they saw a few other supplies, a small cooking pot and a campfire. The fire wasn't ablaze, but the stone circle showed recent ash. There was even a rudimentary bedroll made from

241

bracken and straw, and a small pot of water stood on a rock ledge. It was a well-organised bolthole.

'When I was young,' explained the man, 'myself, and my brother would stay here when we were...' he didn't finish, so Bethran helped.

'Poaching?' he asked. The man shook his head slowly.

'No, not quite,' he paused, unsure if he should say anything. He looked at Bethran and decided that there wasn't a problem. 'We were in a small gang that stole cattle.'

'I am surprised you have admitted to that,' frowned Tyr, but Bethran interrupted.

'In some parts of the four kingdoms, cattle theft is more of a sport than a crime, it is not always frowned upon as it is at Camma.' He then turned to Almon. 'This is a nice little hide, I must say,' and he allowed a brief smile as he sat on a convenient stone. They may have caught themselves a mouse, but he was a very industrious mouse indeed.

Chapter 12 – Distant Thunder

The little mouse of a man was so industrious, that as soon as the others were sitting, he produced dry wood to light a fire and began about the work. Bethran looked over to Tyr who nodded as if he were saying 'let him continue.' It certainly seemed that the man felt easier when he was actually doing something.

'We need to talk Almon,' Bethran said, there was a calm reassurance in his voice. The little man looked up as soon as he had flame.

'Yes, talk,' he said and bent to blow the tinder into life. Several twigs were placed on the small flame and he put other wood around it. He blew the flames gently and then sat back on his haunches. 'Yes, talk,' he repeated. 'I do not know much though.'

'How did you know that Unust's body was at Rook Point?' asked Tyr, a little too eagerly. The old man blinked at him and looked into the growing fire.

'Since I lost my boat,' he swallowed, 'I managed

to scrape by doing small jobs for the other fishermen, loading their catch, lighting the beacon at night,' he explained, 'but it was little enough and that was not regular, so I took to catching crabs and sometimes lobsters within the rocks up at Rook Point. No one ever went there and so I had the shore to myself.' He looked over to the bread that had been brought from the Kissing Stone. 'I was down there one afternoon when I saw two men dragging a sack or something down to the area of the rocks. I hid, but when they had dumped what they were pulling behind them, I went to see what they had been about. I saw Unust, he was dead.' The man stopped and reached for the bread and took a bite.

'Did you recognise the men?' asked Bethran. The little fisherman nodded.

'Perst and his brother.' he said as he chewed. Tyr looked to Bethran, who was frowning once again.

'So, why did you not report the find yourself?' asked Bethran. The man stopped chewing and stared wide eyed.

'Because I am not stupid. It would not take them too long to work out that I had seen them up there would it?' He finished chewing and swallowed, then reached for his mug of water. 'I knew you were looking for the people who killed Laman, so I wanted to try to help.' He put the mug down then added, 'and Unust was a fine lad, it is just cruel that they did for him, just cruel.' He looked back to the flames as he shook his head.

'Do you know why they killed him?' asked Bethran softly.

'Because he had worked out what had happened,

244

he knew Perst had killed Laman, most of us did. I think Unust pushed it a bit too far though. He kept saying that it was wrong, that the elder-man had not done anything about it. He then started saying that Perst and the elder-man were in it together, and that was enough for Perst to do for him.'

'So why did Perst kill Laman?' asked Bethran. The old man looked at Bethran as if it was the most obvious thing in the world.

'Because of the bet, I thought you knew,' said Almon eventually.

'Bet? What bet?' asked the frowning seer. Almon shifted uneasily on the rock he was seated on, as if the ground were becoming hot. His confidence in the seer, as an all-knowing being, was severely tested, and he wondered if what he was hearing was correct.

'The bet that Laman and Perst had over the boat,' the man said, as if he were waiting for Bethran to say, 'oh, that bet'. But he didn't, so the man took another drink and continued. 'Laman had grown tired of Perst saying that he had ruined Perst's boat, and one morning when the day's catch was landed, Laman told Perst that if the boat was so terrible, he would race Perst to find out for sure. He told Perst that whoever won the race would take both boats. To make it fair, he said he would sail Perst's boat and Perst would take Boaan.' He stopped and drew breath. 'Boann was what Laman called his boat,' explained the man. Bethran nodded knowingly, which went a little way to placate Almon. Then he continued with the story. 'Foolishly, Perst accepted, so another boat went out and anchored off the shore. They would sail out and around the anchored boat, and the first one to return and touch shingle took all.'

'You say foolishly, why so?' asked Tyr. The mousey man blinked, seeing that it wasn't just Bethran who was slow.

'Because Laman was a good sailor, it was even said that he had learned his trade on a pirate ship,' explained the man. 'But, there was also the fact that Laman could easily sail Perst's boat, but Perst had never sailed anything like Boaan.' Bethran nodded at this as the man continued. 'Laman took the lead straight away and by the time they rounded the anchored boat, Perst was lagging behind. By the time he got to grips with Boaan, it was too late, Laman won easily.'

'So Perst's boat belonged to Laman, and he had made a fool of Perst into the bargain?' asked Tyr. The man nodded and took another bite of bread.

'And Perst did not like the idea of being in debt to Laman for his boat, and so he killed him,' added Bethran, and Almon nodded once more.

'I may be missing something here,' began Callin for the first time in the conversation, 'but why did not the elder-man do anything about it?'

'I do not know for sure,' shrugged Almon, 'but Unust said that Perst knew something about him that he had got from his brother, though Unust did not like Perst or his brother. It may not have been the whole truth.'

'I think it was,' sighed Bethran, 'and I think I have an idea *what* it was.' He looked over to Tyr and then said, 'we had better eat and get some sleep, I think tomorrow will be a very busy day.'

246

Dawn broke, a blackbird was the first to announce it, followed by many of his cousins, and Tyr awoke from a surprisingly restful sleep to see a grey sky through the canopy of trees. He stretched and saw that Bethran was awake and speaking quietly with the old fisherman, sharing some bread he had left. When Almon saw Tyr was awake, he stood and walked to the fire.

'I can make a reasonable pottage here if you want something hot.' Tyr was certainly hungry, but he looked to Bethran for encouragement as he yawned.

'We must move soon,' said Bethran, in anticipation of Tyr's unspoken question. 'There is still bread and we can get more food later.'

'Where is Callin?' asked Tyr looking around for the man.

'I sent him ahead,' replied the seer, 'I need to know what is happening in the settlement.' Tyr nodded at this and stood to stretch his legs.

'So what is first?' he asked after a short yawn.

'A great deal depends on the answer to a question I sent with the monk,' replied Bethran. He wore a distant look on his face. 'If I get no reply,' he paused for some moments, 'well, I just hope there is a reply or we may just have to head south.' Tyr said nothing to this. He was beginning to realise that Bethran had been correct. Without authority, there was nothing they could do.

'Have you worked out why Perst killed his brother?' he eventually asked reaching for a small lump of the bread, 'if he indeed did?'

'I cannot be sure, but...' Bethran paused before he gave his full reply. He was thinking it through, and he didn't feel confident about the answer. 'I think it comes down to the first theory I had some days ago. Laman's boat has been central to this all along, and I think the boat is still the issue here.' Tyr nodded, he knew there was no point in pushing any harder for a more complete answer. When Bethran was ready, he would tell him. He ate the bread and when they were finished, the two men stood and set off to the village, leaving Almon to remain in the wood. Bethran knew the safety of the mousey fisherman was important if they ever needed proof of the crime. As they walked, Tyr asked another question.

'So, do you think it was Perst who originally damaged Almon's boat to put him out of business?'

'I spoke to Almon at length this morning,' began Bethran, 'he told me quite a story. He and his brother were cattle thieves as he had said, but the gangs began to get savage with each other, and rather than just stealing cattle, people were getting killed in minor skirmishes. They decided that was not for them and took their profits to buy an old fishing boat in Tall Bridges. The brother got bored with fishing and went back to the cattle stealing trade. Unfortunately, he was killed in a fight.' The seer paused as they ducked under some small trees. 'Almon continued fishing, but he and a few others were outspoken about the elders of the settlement.'

'So he thinks the elder-man smashed his boat?' asked Tyr.

'No,' replied Bethran shaking his head, 'he thinks that Laman or Perst did it, he says they wanted less boats in competition, and one of them holed his boat before spreading the rumour that the elders had done it.'

'It is possible, I suppose,' shrugged Tyr.

'Anything is possible in this village,' replied Bethran, just as they walked clear of the woods.

'So where are we going now?' asked Tyr.

'We need to wait,' shrugged Bethran, 'if no reply comes today, then, we move on.'

'And the reply you are expecting is from Lord Cullcoil?'

'Yes,' nodded Bethran as they passed the old smithy, 'I have sent him the information about the elder, if he chooses to ignore it, then so be it. If he sends a warden down, then we will assist.'

'Do you think that a warden will come just for a little extra silver?' asked Tyr with surprise in his voice.

'Never underestimate the power of gold or silver, young Tyr.' The lad was surprised by the use of 'young Tyr', it was an affectionate term of endearment and Tyr raised his brows to himself. Was the old seer becoming warm to him, or was he so deep in thought that he had forgotten to berate him in some way?

'So,' asked Tyr, but paused to see if the seer was listening. After a glance to him, he saw he was. 'Where are we going to wait?'

'We shall take a turn around the market to pick up Callin, and then we shall take food at the ale hut. After that, we will see.'

As the day wore on and no reply was forthcoming, the three of them ate at the ale hut and drank a mug of ale each. Bethran then went to speak to Birse about some information they had, and to confirm a few details, leaving Callin and Tyr with little to do. Callin asked Tyr about his previous life as they took a stroll towards the waterfront and Callin told Tyr a little about himself and his connection to Bethran.

'So you were a warrior?' asked Tyr, very interested.

'Trained as such yes, though Bethran will tell you that the levy soldiers of Lord Cullcoil are not true warriors,' and he laughed remembering Bethran's remarks. 'He always says that a true warrior has scars from battle, he has suffered hunger, thirst and deprivation at the hands of the weather, as well as the enemy.'

'Yes, I can almost hear his voice,' replied Tyr, raising his brows. 'So, you said you and Bethran travelled together?'

'Yes,' nodded Callin as he stopped and sat on the shingle above the south beach. 'We were escorting a noble's daughter to be married. It was easy enough, and we enjoyed each other's company. Bethran was an advisor for the mission. He knows about our customs and the correct procedures like no other man. I was just one of the soldiers guarding the girl, but we struck up a friendship that has endured.'

'But now you farm? Why the change?' asked Tyr, sitting beside the man.

'As Bethran himself will tell you, age catches up with us,' shrugged the man, 'soldiers have to keep up a quick pace, on the march and the battlefield. I think I just got too slow.' He picked up a pebble and examined it. 'I thought farming would be an obvious choice, but it is difficult and there is a great deal of pressure to provide for the community through the harsh winters.' He threw the pebble towards the sea, which was some way out. 'I have become bored with it too,' he added with a depressed tone.

'I can see that it must come as a shock after soldiering,' nodded Tyr.

'I have done it long and tirelessly,' he explained, 'Some seasons were better than others, but each one becomes more difficult to manage. In the summer, the work is hard and long, in the winter, there is little to do.' He picked up another pebble and felt its smoothness before casting that one away too. 'And, I never get used to the deaths in the small settlements. It is sometimes worse than war, for the young and old are the hardest hit.' Tyr could see the man becoming low. He was thinking of a way to raise his spirits when he thought of a question.

'In the time you have known him,' he began, 'has Bethran ever taken a woman?' Callin opened his eyes wide, and slowly turned his head to Tyr.

'I am not sure it is my place to say,' he replied, but there was a hint of a smile on his face.

'I just wondered,' shrugged Tyr, 'I have told you everything about my idiotic past, and I just thought that Bethran may have something...' he trailed off, not sure what to say. Callin looked out to sea and leaned over to one side.

'There have been women in Bethran's life, but for the time I was with him, there was no one. He has told me a few stories about his past,' he paused, 'but I will leave it for him to tell you about them.' Tyr nodded, he thought about changing the subject but before he could, Callin was on his feet and walking back towards the village.

'I do not like this waiting around, I think I may go and get some sleep,' he said as Tyr caught up and so, once they were in the settlement, they parted company. Callin went back to the smithy and Tyr took a turn through the market to look for a shaving knife. The market wasn't very busy again, but he searched around the stalls. He didn't have the means to purchase one if he found it, but then he saw something much more precious. It was Coblaith, and she was alone, looking at the linen seller's wares. Tyr stood and watched her as she moved across the display of cloth, feeling and stroking the fabric with her delicate hand. Twice she looked up, but Tyr turned away and she didn't see him. Eventually, when he had watched her move on, he moved towards her, trying to make it look like an accident.

'Oh, hello,' she said. Tyr looked at her with surprise, he wasn't good at keeping his feelings at bay but he thought she didn't realise he had already seen her.

'Oh, what a surprise, are you looking for something in particular?' he asked.

'No,' she smiled, 'just looking if there is something new.' She looked at the closest stall, which had jewellery on it. 'Are you?' she asked.

'No, just trying to pass the time really,' he said, thinking back to what Bethran had said before they parted. They could soon be leaving Tall Bridges, and that was now weighing heavily on his mind.

'Did you speak to my father?' she asked.

'Er, no I did not,' he then realised he hadn't yet thought of a reason why he wanted to see Bolder. 'I managed to find the information I wanted, so…' he trailed off with an embarrassed smile. As he looked into her delicate features, he had to wonder why she had not been married off yet. He would have thought she would have a trail of men following her every whim. He so wanted to ask her why, but he didn't think he was ready to hear what she may tell him. She spotted a trader with vegetables and she pointed to it.

'Oh, I must see what is there,' and so Tyr followed on and examined the produce with her. She looked around but soon moved on with Tyr following.

'There is nothing very good there, I think it is too early for good vegetables,' she said. Tyr knew if Bethran had said the same thing, he would have not answered as the subject matter would be of little interest, but from Coblaith, he was transfixed by the subject. Still, he couldn't think of a suitable reply and just said,

'Yes, that is true,' and she walked on a little further. As she reached the end of the small market, she turned to him and said,

'I do not know if you would be interested, but would you like to come for supper, I could make something a little better than my fish stew?' In all his life, Tyr had never been so stuck for words. He had never felt so utterly drained, not even when the prospect of being thrown from a high cliff was on offer. But what could he say? He so wanted to say yes, but they could be about to depart. Did he have to go with Bethran, no he didn't. He could very happily stay in Tall Bridges with Coblaith and… And what? As Bethran had made clear, Tyr had nothing to offer a merchant's daughter. He didn't even have the means to shave. Even his clothes looked plain and drab, now he was used to them.

'Yes, yes, I would like nothing better,' he found himself saying before he had time to consider other options. She smiled at him and said something else, but he had no idea what it was. The mix of emotions that were flooding through his head stripped him of the power to hear. Even when they had parted company and Tyr was staggering back towards the smithy, he felt as if he had been punched. He leaned on the nearest building and looked to the sky. He sighed so deeply, it felt as if all the air and the blood had departed his body. For several moments he just stood with his back to the building and recovered his senses before he returned to the hut. How was he going to tell Bethran? What would he say? He knew it would vex the old seer a great deal, but he had no intension of going back on his word. As his body settled to the idea and his light-headedness gave way to a stupid smile, he made his way back to the smithy.

As he turned the corner to the track where the smithy stood, he heard a noise. At first he thought it was thunder, but looking at the sky, even that had brightened somewhat, so he thought of other causes. It was constant too. A low rumble, and then he saw something too. From the north came several riders. More horses than he had seen in a long time, and they were galloping to the village. As they closed in on the wooden bridge, they slowed to a walk and Tyr could see there were five of them and he thought he recognised the first one in the group. They walked noisily over the wooden planks of the bridge and headed into the settlement.

'Riders have arrived from the north,' called Tyr into the old smithy. Both Callin and Bethran were there, discussing something or other, but they came out to see.

'Where?' asked Bethran.

'They have entered the village now. They cannot be seen, but I think it is Lord Cullcoil at their head.'

'Lord Cullcoil?' asked Bethran with surprise, 'are you sure it was not his warden?'

'I think the warden is there but I know the sight of the Lord well enough, I am sure it is he,' insisted Tyr. Bethran knew that Tyr would see the lord coming and going at Camma, and so he accepted what the lad had seen.

'Come then, we had better go and find him,' he said, and after picking up his pack, they walked into the settlement.

Five fully equipped horses stood by the ale hut with two horsemen watching over them, and many villagers beginning to gather around. Bethran thought that they were the two they had seen heading north some weeks ago, but he wasn't sure. One of them barred his way to the hut.

'I am Bethran of Seal Bay,' he said, 'I am here to see the lord.'

'He is expecting you. You may enter, Bethran,' and he walked inside, but Tyr and Callin were held back.

Cullcoil was seated with another man who Bethran vaguely recognised as his bodyguard. The Lord was eating and had a pot of ale in his fist, with the brewer and his wife fussing around them. All other villagers had been cleared out and as he saw Bethran, he smiled and dismissed the brewer and his wife.

'Bethran, old friend, sit please,' and he motioned to the seat. Bethran sat and said,

'My lord, I hope I find you well.'

'Well enough, and it sounds like you have a pretty tale to tell,' he lifted a large jug and poured ale into another mug and pushed it to the seer. 'Tell me about it.' Cullcoil continued to eat as Bethran spoke.

'As I told the monk, I have no proof that the man is doing anything wrong, but...'

'I trust your instinct Bethran,' he said between mouthfuls, 'even if you do not.' Bethran took a gulp of ale before he continued.

'I think he has means above the normal for an elder-man and the other elders of the council have little or no say in the day-to-day running of the settlement.'

'Indeed,' nodded the lord wiping his face with a cloth, 'the silver you sent me was of a fine quality, I would be interested to know where he came by it, if nothing else,' and he took a drink of ale.

'I suspect him of abusing his authority too,' frowned Bethran, unsure if he had chosen the correct words.

'How mean you?' asked Cullcoil, placing the mug on the table.

'To my certain knowledge,' began Bethran,

'elders organise the workings of the settlement, they dispense local justice in your name and if anything is more important, they send for you or your warden.'

'Correct,' nodded Cullcoil, 'but I give most of them a free hand in that respect. The larger and wealthier villages I have more interest in, but rarely get involved.'

'Here at Tall Bridges, I suspect the elder-man has been running it as his own kingdom and seems to have the wealth to do that.'

'I see,' nodded the lord, 'we will soon know, I plan to visit him.'

'If he has not fled due to your arrival,' added Bethran.

'I thought of that,' smiled Cullcoil, 'I have sent over the warden to keep him there.' Bethran nodded. 'Drink with me,' continued the lord, 'have you eaten?' Bethran nodded but took another drink. 'Now tell me about the death of the fisherman, the monk mentioned something of what you had told him.' Bethran tried to outline the story as briefly as he could and to the best of his knowledge, and Lord Cullcoil seemed interested in the way they had gone about it. He stopped and asked questions in certain places and nodded attentively at other points of interest.

'There seem to have been quite a few deaths here,' frowned Cullcoil, 'have you pieced the full story together yet?'

'No, there is just one part missing and I hope that once you have spoken to the elder-man, that final part will give me a complete answer.' The lord nodded at this and drained his mug.

'You have been busy, I can see that,' nodded Cullcoil, 'but I will have to see what the elder-man says about this wealth he has not admitted to.'

'As I have said, I could be wrong,' insisted Bethran.

'I will find out soon enough,' said the lord with a serious look on his face, 'in some ways I hope you are correct, I could do with a large windfall of silver at the moment.'

'For war preparations?' smiled Bethran, but secretly he was wondering what the lord had been doing north of Camma. Bethran expected the lord to either tell him he was as bad as the populace or laugh with him, but he did neither. He seemed deep in thought for a moment and then said,

'Since the battle of Dun Nectain, that wondrous victory by the Great King just six summers ago, we have been seen by the people of Northanhymbre as powerful and wealthy. There will not be another attack from them.' Bethran nodded in agreement. 'But what people forget is that just four summers before that, King Bridei almost destroyed the Boar Kingdom and though the rift was settled, Dalmar has never forgotten that his family had their power removed.'

'So you expect an attack from the islands?' asked Bethran with surprise.

'It is possible and likely, especially if King Bridei attacks the Irish.'

'I was under the impression that a war with the Irish would not happen.'

'It may not,' admitted the lord, raising his brows,

'but I wish to be ready. The Great King has made it quite clear that he favours the Roman church over the Irish church.' Bethran nodded.

'And I understand the reasoning behind it,' he replied, 'the Angles and most of the other kingdoms across the water have moved to the Roman church. It is politically and financially beneficial. But would he go to war over which Christian church he sides with?'

'That I cannot know,' shrugged Cullcoil, 'I do know however, that we need to prepare and to that end, I need silver aplenty if we are to repel any attack from the islands.' He sighed and then stood, calling for the brewer.

'Make sure Bethran and his friends have ale,' the brewer nodded. 'I will go and speak with the elder-man now,' said Cullcoil, turning to the seer. 'I will send for you when I have made a decision about the elder-man.' He turned and left but the seer heard him speaking jovially with Callin at the door. Tyr and Callin then entered the hut and sat by Bethran.

'What did he say?' asked Tyr as soon as he was seated. The brewer placed new pots down for them and poured.

'He is looking into it,' shrugged Bethran, 'and he will send for me when he finds something out.' Bethran was saying little, particularly as the hut suddenly became full with people trying to find out what had been happening. It wasn't every day the lord arrived with a small retinue and took over the ale hut. The brewer was equally non-committal, particularly as he knew nothing of what had passed between Bethran and Cullcoil.

'So we still know nothing?' frowned Tyr. Bethran gave a quick glance around the room and then said,

'I'll tell you when we have drunk this,' and he lifted his mug, 'courtesy of his lordship, and returned to the smithy.' He drank, and the other two joined him, inquisitive glances and whispered talk surrounding them. 'But for now,' added Bethran, placing his mug back on the table, 'we have to make plans. Whatever the lord decides, I will be returning south in the morning.' Tyr considered his meeting that evening, he had no idea what would come of it but he knew he had to attend. 'Are you coming with me?' Bethran asked, looking at Callin.

'I will,' sighed Callin as he raised his brows, 'but I think this will be my last year there.'

'What will you do?' asked Tyr.

'I do not know yet but that life...' he paused and looked down to his mug, 'best not to talk about it yet, I still do not have many options to be honest.'

'We all have to make our way in the world my friend,' nodded Bethran, 'we none of us, can decide to just stop doing what we do. There has to be an alternative.' Callin nodded, then he drank the ale greedily but said nothing more on the subject.

'I suppose you will return to Seal Bay for the winter?' he asked. Bethran nodded and then said,

'Eventually, there are two more events I must attend, but I may also spend a little time in Flowfoot,' he smiled a little, 'I too have to make my way, and Flowfoot may be the place to accomplish that.'

'What about you Tyr?' asked Callin. The young man looked from him to Bethran and then back to Callin.

260

'I had hoped to travel with Bethran but he seems not to want my company,' he replied.

'Our friend,' began Bethran nodding to Tyr but looking at Callin, 'has taken a fancy to the daughter of a merchant, and he thinks he has a chance with her.' He then turned to Tyr and with a penetrating stare continued, 'this life is not for someone with such notions.' Turning back to Callin he concluded with, 'Let him remain and chase the sun, it matters nought to me.'

'What do you mean by that?' asked Tyr.

'To chase the sun,' smiled Callin, 'is to pursue something that it is not possible to capture.' Tyr looked at Bethran, and before he could control his temper, he had already said it.

'I am to take supper with her tonight.' Callin made a whistling sound, but Bethran just held his gaze. 'So you have nothing to say?' asked Tyr, thinking the seer was stuck for words.

'There is nothing *to* say, I am correct, you do not have the temperament for a life on the path,' was the seer's reply.

'When you get to know this old goat better,' laughed Callin, pointing to Bethran with his thumb, 'you will know, he has a way of leaving you with two options. He then tells you why each option is the wrong one to choose. That way, he is always right.' Tyr thought about this, Callin was correct. At one stage he had told Tyr he had no chance of getting close to the girl. Then, he said that Tyr would not cope with a life on the road. Whichever turns out to be the case, he can say, 'I told you so'. It was clever and something he hadn't seen in the man previously. Tyr looked at Bethran, but the older man had dropped his gaze and was looking around the hut. Tyr scratched his neck in frustrations and then said,

'To answer your original question, Callin, I have not yet decided.' Callin nodded with a big smile and held up his mug to Tyr.

'Whatever it is my friend, I wish you well of it,' he said, ' and in truth I wish us all well of it and I hope that in some far distant season yet to come, we can all sit here once again and talk of what we did thereafter.' He paused and then added, 'Good luck on the path.' The three of them lifted their pots and brought them together, then they repeated the toast.

Chapter 13 – Choices

One of Lord Cullcoil's guards strode into the ale hut and up to Bethran.

'Lord Cullcoil will see you now,' he said, and he escorted them to the long-hut of the elder-man. Tyr and Callin stopped at the entrance, but were allowed to accompany Bethran to see the lord. Inside, Bethran was surprised to see Lord Cullcoil alone, seated at the table with many trinkets and decorative items strewn across it, and the floor. Cullcoil had his arms crossed and was wearing a thick frown as he stared at the items.

'Ah, Bethran,' he said looking up, 'a pretty haul would you say?' Bethran looked about him. There were all manner of items but he didn't see the iron chest.

'I was correct then my lord, he was living a life of great luxury it seems.'

'And he did not send anything north,' replied the lord, still frowning. 'He could have still lived a good life here, he could have sent some tribute and kept a great deal of this, but no, greed corrupts men's hearts.'

'What of the iron chest?' asked Bethran. Cullcoil looked up to Bethran and seemed to be thinking about something.

'Sit, sit, all of you,' he motioned. He then looked back to Bethran.

'You were correct, well, in a way you were correct, but I will tell you of that later,' he said, then continued with, 'you now know the full story of what happened here?'

'I think so my lord,' nodded Bethran, 'at least I am as sure as I can be.'

'Then let me hear it,' said the man with a glimmer of a smile.

'Most of the story revolves around the boat that a fisherman called Laman owned. The fishing in the settlement was quite a cutthroat business due to the fact that Laman was an accomplished sailor and fisherman. Several other fishermen were put out of business in various ways. This boat of Laman's was, and remains, unique, and is a special vessel. A man called Perst saw this new boat and wanted one like it for himself, but he had not the means to have such a craft built. So he asked Laman if his own boat could be altered and Laman suggested it could be improved in speed and seaworthiness, but it would remain of a narrow beam. Laman and his wife's brother altered the boat for a reasonable sum, but Perst was still unhappy and made it clear that the boat was no better, and in some way much worse. That probably was not the case, but the feud came to a head when Laman offered to race Perst in his boat and to make the race fair, they should swap boats.' Bethran stopped for a breath and to explain. 'I will not go into the complexities of sailing such craft but just add that Laman was an expert sailor. Either way, he won the bet, and thereafter, Perst no longer had his own boat and had to give a part of every catch he made to try to pay his debt.'

'And so he should,' nodded the lord.

'But one evening after fishing, the boats were returning and in the gloom they all saw a large blow fish on the beach to the north. They landed their catch, but it was too dark by then to examine the stranded fish. Laman sent Unust straight to bed as he knew he was employed at the quarry the next morning. When the other fishermen had left, Perst killed Laman by a blow to the head, probably in his own boat. They then launched the boat and took his body to the north beach and placed it to look as if the blow fish had attacked him.'

'But it would have done him no good unless Laman had no offspring,' offered the lord, 'as the debt would pass to the next owner of Laman's boat.'

'There was no offspring surviving, the boat would go to the widow, but Perst knew something about the elder-man that would secure him a way out of this fix,' continued Bethran. 'His brother, who was probably a half-brother, was also in the employ of the elder-man, and knew about a haul of treasure that had come to the man. He probably helped the elder to find it.'

'I do not understand,' said Tyr, but then he realised he shouldn't have spoken with the lord there, but Bethran explained anyway.

'You mean about the treasure?' Tyr nodded, but Cullcoil was the one to explain.

'We have found hidden treasure before, some

small collections and some large. We assume they were left by the Romans, but we do not know why.'

'Further south,' explained Bethran, 'it is thought that when the Romans left, some of their troops wished to stay, it is not unreasonable. This had become their home, some had families here, so over months, they gathered what they could, buried it and once they had deserted and the Roman ships had left, they would come out of hiding and recover it.'

'It seems a good explanation,' nodded Cullcoil, 'some would be caught, some would die, those unfortunates would not recover their treasure and it would remain where they had left it.'

'I wish I could find such a treasure,' interrupted Callin.

'So do I,' smiled Cullcoil, 'for a good portion of it would come to my coffers.' He looked at Tyr closely, as if he recognised the lad. 'Continue,' he said to Bethran.

'From that point, the elder-man and Perst began a feud too. Perst knew the elder-man had found some treasure and had not declared it, and the elder knew Perst had killed Laman. I think that the elder then offered Perst's brother Laman's boat, and though he probably told Perst his debt was no longer valid, Perst was angered that his brother was to get the boat. The elder-man was also bribing the merchants so they would not stand against him, I think the first one was the smith. He had a new smithy built to keep him quiet, and I also think that the elder-man used the old one for himself. The hut was never used for anything else, so he must have wanted it as a quiet place where he could melt down the silver as he required it.' This surprised Tyr, and he looked directly at the seer. Bethran raised his brows and then continued. 'Then, Unust, the lad who fished with Laman, began to make waves over the incident. He had somehow found that all the catches from the night Laman was killed, had gone to be weighed as Perst's. This was what sealed his fate. He began to tell people that he knew Perst had killed Laman. One night, Perst went to Unust's hut and slayed him in his sleep. He then forced his brother to help him move the body. This did not sit well with the brother, and they began to argue. It is likely that Perst considered that his brother was plotting against him with the help of the elder. In Perst's foolish mind, it was a good enough reason to kill his younger brother. It was then easy to take the younger brother out fishing, kill him in the boat and tie his body to the anchor. He then returned and made up a story about yet another blow fish tangling their nets.'

'So the elder-man had nothing to do with the deaths?' asked Tyr.

'I do not think he did, there is more evidence to suggest that he was angered by Perst's actions, I think he was already plotting to be rid of Perst in some way.'

'You have done well, all of you,' nodded Cullcoil, 'I would not have thought such a thing possible. You must, at some stage, tell me exactly how you unravelled this mystery.'

'We did not think such a thing was possible either,' nodded Bethran, 'there were times we were about to give up.'

'I am happy you did not, and now,' paused the lord, 'we have decisions to make. The boat of Laman will now go to his widow, and the boat of Perst will also be hers. The property of the elder will be divided between myself, and whoever are to be the new elders of Tall Bridges, for the other two will be driven out. I will also allocate some of it to put right a few wrongs.' He looked at Callin and Bethran, 'Is elder-man something the two of you may consider?'

'Not I,' said Callin immediately, 'I thank you lord, but I am no elder-man. I would become bored too quickly.' Cullcoil nodded and looked to Bethran.

'I think you know my answer, but I could suggest at least two for the post.'

'Go on,' nodded Cullcoil.

'The brother of Laman's widow is single-minded, but he would not falter from the injustice of the death of Laman, even though he had no like of the man. There is also a merchant, Bolder, the pot seller, who seems to have resisted the urge to take bribes, I think the two of them would take the position seriously.'

'Very well,' nodded Cullcoil, 'I will speak with them.'

'What about the elder-man, what is to be his punishment?' asked Callin.

'I have not decided what will become of him yet,' frowned the lord, 'but he will be detained at Camma to begin with. I may make an example of him.' Cullcoil then looked at Callin. 'So what are you to do if not an elder of Tall Bridges?'

'Oh, I will return to my hut and see this season

out, but then, I do not know,' he replied.

'Well,' offered the lord, 'I am obviously in need of a set of eyes here in the south of the kingdom, I should not be expecting a travelling seer to do the job for me. What about Warden of the South?'

'Me, a... a warden?' spluttered Callin.

'Why not? You have the training, you have the experience?'

'But I have no weapons, no armour and no horse. How could-?' but Cullcoil interrupted.

'If you wish to take the position, they will be provided.'

'I am honoured, my lord,' bowed Callin.

'Then that is the way it shall be. Return north when you are finished for the season,' smiled Cullcoil and then he looked at Tyr. 'I cannot help thinking that I have seen you somewhere before,' he said.

'I, I think,' stuttered Tyr, 'that I have that kind of face, my lord. I do not have enough importance for you to have ever come across me before,' and he ended with a slight bow of the head.

'Looks like you have taught this one well Bethran, he is as illusive as you with his tongue,' and then he stood. 'Now I need a moment alone with Bethran.' The two men understood and left the hut. When they had gone, Cullcoil paced the area behind the table and then slowly turned to the seer.

'As I have said my friend, you have done well here.'

'My duty, that is all,' replied the seer.

'Is there anything you need, anything you want?'

'I cannot think of anything, maybe a few supplies, that is all,' shrugged the seer.

'We are standing in a room packed with treasure. Choose what you wish, you are free to take what you require,' offered Cullcoil.

'For a man on the path, these things are of no use,' and he saw something on the table, 'though these two items I would like as a gift to someone I know.'

'Of course, take them,' insisted the lord, 'though when all this is offered, you choose the least of value.'

'Value is not always measured by the shine an object makes,' he smiled as he put the items into his pack.

'I suppose you wish to know about the iron chest?' frowned the lord, sitting once more.

'It is of interest, but I will not ask if you do not wish me to know.'

'It was full of silver as you expected,' nodded Cullcoil, 'and some gold. Most of the silver had been melted down into blocks. The golden trinkets had not. This treasure must have corrupted him so completely, that he thought that he could keep it without word getting out.' He shook his head curiously. 'What men do for riches.' He seemed to be thinking something, and then he said, 'So, what of you? What will you do from here?'

'Oh, I will go back south, overwinter at Seal Bay, and try to keep out of trouble,' he said, ending with a smile.

'And we will see you next season, I suppose?' asked Cullcoil.

'I do not think so,' frowned Bethran. 'I suspect, this will be the last time I make my journey to Camma. I grow tired and somehow, the road lengthens.'

'What of the summer rite, the people expect you?' insisted the lord.

'I think next year, Tyr will come in my stead, he is bright and I think he will equal my talents by then.'

'I would hope this is not to be our last meeting.'

'I am sure it will not, I feel we will meet many times before the Great Goddess calls me,' smiled Bethran. He stood and looked at Cullcoil. 'I should take my leave. We need supplies for the journey south.' The lord also stood and reached out his arm to the seer. They grasped arms and embraced, then Cullcoil lifted a purse from the table.

'This is yours,' he smiled. Bethran thanked him. It was the purse of silver the seer had sent north. Bethran left, and as he walked outside, he knew that the Kingdom of Cat was lucky. It had a good ruler in the shape of Lord Cullcoil.

The three men walked to the shore, the tide was almost in and just at the head of the surf sat the boats. One was on the hard ground, now covered with nets and lobster baskets. The other, just being kissed by the first touches of the sea, and they both belonged to a woman who had never set foot in a boat in her life. That legacy would ensure she was well kept, however. The three of them leaned on Boaan and looked out to sea.

'Warden of the South, quite a mouthful,' grinned Bethran. Callin folded his arms. He looked over to the seer.

'Aye, and next year when you come north, you will have to watch your step. That new warden is a bit of a hard nose from what I hear.'

'I shall not be coming next year,' said Bethran calmly. The two men looked shocked, and for a moment no one spoke.

'Why not, has his lordship given you a post?' asked Callin.

'No, he has not, I do not want a post. I want very little.'

'So why would you not come north?' asked Tyr with a dumbfounded expression.

'I think that new blood is required,' and he looked at Tyr, 'my apprentice will be ready by then.' Tyr swallowed, he never imagined that was coming, and now he had another dilemma. He was having supper with Coblaith that night. His spine suddenly prickled. How could his fortunes change so quickly? 'Oh, and while I remember,' Bethran continued, removing his pack from his shoulder and reaching into the top. 'Lord Cullcoil made a gift to me, but I have no use for them, can you use them?' he asked, and he handed Tyr a fine comb case and a shaving knife. Tyr gazed at the fine items. The comb was made from bone, strengthened with finely worked silver, and the knife had a decorated handle and blade. Tyr looked up with a slack jaw. He didn't know what to say. He looked back to the items and then glanced up. Bethran then handed him a small purse. It contained some silver.

'Thank you,' he said. There was nothing more *to*

say.

Tyr turned up for supper with a newly shaved face, plus a couple of nicks in his skin for his trouble. He sat with Coblaith and her father and enjoyed a fabulous dish made from peas and beans with herbs and a few other things he could not identify. He made a joke about it being blow fish and then regretted it, as it had been the staple diet for most of the settlement for some days. Fortunately, they took it as it was meant, but he decided not to joke anymore. It wasn't something he was good at. There were oatcakes, and some sweetmeats made from honey and oats, which Tyr had never had before. When they had finished, they drank some locally made wine, probably made from elderflowers, and they sat and talked. They spoke briefly about Lord Cullcoil and what had happened, and Tyr also mentioned that Bethran had put Bolder forward as an elder. Coblaith seemed more thrilled about this than her father, but he said if he was asked, he would consider it. Later in the evening, Coblaith asked him why he had shaved off his beard. He stalled in the conversation a little, wondering if she didn't like him clean-shaven.

'It is fine on the road, but I try to remove it when we stop. Is it not to your taste as it is?' he asked.

'Oh, it is not important,' she smiled, 'it was just that I hardly recognised you when you arrived.' He said the hair would grow back quickly enough and left it at that.

As he sat with her in the glow of the small fire, he looked around her face. He looked for imperfections.

He looked for flaws, but he found none. She seemed perfect to him, and that hurt. Here he was, in a position he felt was a gift from the gods and he had to choose between *it*, and a life on the road. Bethran had done it again. He had given him the keys to a life that he knew he wanted, a life doing what Bethran had done for many years. He would become another Bethran, and that had seemed impossible just a week or so ago. And yet, another option seemed available. Stay here in Tall Bridges and marry the loveliest girl in the kingdom, probably in the world. The daughter of a merchant, and maybe in the future, the daughter of an elder-man? This was another impossible option that had presented itself. What a choice, what a decision to make. Then something struck him that would make his choice for him. He was banished from Camma, and what was the most important event on the seer's travels? The longest day, and the celebration at Camma. A place he could no longer visit. So that was it. He could not take Bethran's offer, and he would have to stay at Tall Bridges.

The morning after, the weather was as fine as it could be, and promised to be very warm. The sun was rising to the deep blue of the heavens and was unobscured by anything other than a passing bird. Tyr had looked for Bethran but could not find him. Callin had said he was meeting them at Rook Point, as he had no farewells to make. Tyr took that as meaning Tyr had. Callin had packed his small pack and was going to the ale hut first, and would meet them at Rook Point. Tyr put his comb and knife along with a few items from the market into a small bag that he tied at his waist. He had a new belt that made his clothing look a little less drab. He then set off up to Rook Point to see Bethran.

The old seer was laid within a bowl-shaped ledge on the top of the rocky shore, with his head on his pack and his eyes closed. He was wearing his new clothes for the first time, and it was plain to see why he had put so much import to them. Tyr walked up to him and sat on the rock edge and looked out to the sea. Gulls mewed and wheeled around in the perfect blue of the sky. The sea reflected was a darker blue in contrast, and the sound of the surf on the shore broke the stillness of the moment.

'You look like a king in those robes,' announced Tyr.

'That wasn't the effect I was planning, but yes, they are good,' agreed the seer. The undergarments were of exquisite linen and a large hooded cloak made from fine woven wool, covered all. Tyr knew that when Bethran entered a settlement dressed in that way. He would command their respect and make them believe a powerful sage was in their company. Tyr looked back out to sea and gave a shallow sigh, unheard by Bethran who had not moved and still had his eyes closed.

'Can all men have luck in their lives?' Tyr asked after a moment of taking in the scene.

'Not all, no,' replied Bethran.

'Why not?' asked the young man.

'Because,' sighed Bethran, 'some men choose not to take the luck when it falls in their lap.'

'You do not believe in fate, or luck for that

275

matter.'

'Then let us call it, "fortunate opportunity" then,' replied the seer, keeping his eyes tight shut.

'In the past, I could not see myself ever doing this, sitting here with options in my life. I do not know how to deal with such a thing,' added Tyr. Bethran drew a long, deep breath.

'Do you smell that?' he asked.

'What?'

'Whatever it is you smell?' said Bethran.

'I smell the sea, the beach, the grass,' he paused, 'and maybe a slight amount of Seal Bay mixed with new cloth.'

'Being my apprentice does not mean I cannot punish you,' insisted Bethran, still warming in the sun. Tyr laughed.

'Well, yes, I suppose you could, but that is what I smell.'

'That is the thing,' said Bethran with another deep breath, 'what you smell is life, as long as you can smell it, you can live it. There are no set paths, most men do not have the chance to choose, so make sure the one you choose is what you want.'

'But that is it,' insisted Tyr, 'my life has always been steered by someone else, I do not know how to choose.' Bethran slowly sat up and looked out towards the ocean. He looked around in the poor grass that grew there and found two similar stones.

'Which stone would you choose?' he asked, holding them both out. Tyr looked at them for a moment.

'It depends why I was choosing them,' replied

Tyr. 'This blue one would skim across the water better than the brown one, but the brown one would be better for sharpening my blade.' Bethran threw the two stones away and returned to his reclined position.

'What was that about?' asked Tyr after a few moments of silence.

'I was just showing that you were wrong, you do know how to choose. Choosing comes easier than you think.'

'That was just two unimportant stones. This is my future, my life,' insisted Tyr. Bethran sat up again, this time seeming a little more irritated than previously.

'What do you want?' he asked.

'What do I want? With what?' asked Tyr.

'With life? What do you want with your life?'

I'm not sure I understand the question,' admitted Tyr.

'Well, for instance, Callin wants a life away from a small settlement. The elder-man wanted loads of treasure, whereas Lord Cullcoil wants to build fortresses. What do you want?' Tyr was stuck for words. He decided to use a tactic of Bethran's.

'You mentioned others, but what do you want, Bethran?' The old seer calmed his features and looked back out to sea.

'Lord Cullcoil asked me that, I told him I wanted nothing. That isn't true though,' and he paused, covering his eyes from the sun with his hand. He then turned around to Tyr. 'We people, we that are ruled by the Great King Bridei, are a singular race. We are good farmers, we are excellent sailors and brave warriors. We live in a land that gives nothing to us freely. Yet we fight it and we win, we survive. In all our kingdoms, we remain similar, and we survive. We have tamed the land and yet, we are essentially a people of the eastern coasts. That ocean is always close. Her salt almost runs through our bodies. The Romans came and did not subjugate us. Then, Northanhymbre tried to take us, and we took them instead. The Irish want our lands, but we drive them back. Now,' he softened his voice, 'Christians come, and they will change all of that.' He gave a little sigh, then stood. 'You ask what I want and I say, *nothing*. In some ways that is true.' He turned from the sea and looked directly at Tyr. 'What I truly want is for this land to remain as it is. I fear for the people, and I fear for our way of life. Other than that, I want nothing.' He paused, then added, 'as long as there is a mug of ale along the way.' He raised his hand as he saw Callin approaching from the settlement. He turned back to Tyr and slung his pack onto his back and smiled at the young man. Tyr didn't think the seer had ever smiled at him before, certainly not in that way. 'When I think of it, there are things I want, but not things that mortals can provide me with. We are surrounded by natural wonders, things that none of us understand, and I would like to understand them at some stage, but...' he paused again, this time to look back out to the sea and then up to the sky. 'So few of us get the chance to choose, that makes you unique.' He looked back to Tyr for a moment. 'I must take my leave. Calm seas and following winds to you Tyr,' and he climbed down the rock to Callin who was waiting. Callin looked up, and then he nodded, and the two of them set off south.

In the afternoon, they had reached Callin's hut and after a little food and a rest, Callin showed Bethran the problems he faced as a farmer in a small settlement. Bethran agreed that as a warden of Lord Cullcoil, Callin would have a better life.

'I thought Tyr would have gone with you,' said Callin as they sat on a bench by the little hut.

'He had talked of nothing else since I met him,' smiled Bethran, 'but the lad has a want of women like most men crave silver.'

'She is a fine-looking girl though, and if he has a chance of making a life with her…' but Callin broke off, he too thought that Tyr didn't quite have the means for such a match.

'He will find his way, he is bright, and he is young,' nodded Bethran, watching a buzzard, circling in the sky above them. 'A life on the road is hard enough, and I doubt he would want to return to Camma for the celebrations next year.'

'Of course,' nodded Callin, 'that would have been a problem for him.' The stocky man looked to Bethran and asked, 'I wonder if he had considered that, I mean, I wonder if that is why he stayed there?' Bethran nodded a little and shrugged. 'Well, my friend, I must continue. I would wish to be this side of the ferry before dark.' The two of them stood and said their goodbyes, then, the seer pulled his pack onto his shoulder and turned to the south.

Bethran began his journey towards Northferry and ultimately Flowfoot. He was planning to stay there for a few days or maybe a moon at the longest. He had silver, most of what Lord Cullcoil had given him. He had left some with Tyr, at least enough for the lad to get on his feet. Bethran had suspected that Tyr would stay at Tall Bridges. Maybe it was for the best. An apprentice in the seeing trade was going to be out of work soon enough, and he may find that settling down was what he needed. Bethran could not see anything in it, but he was... Hmm, what was he exactly? He would have to think on that one as he walked.

He glanced over to his left and the constant companion of the eastern sea. The sun was tinting the wispy clouds orange and reflecting a glow in the water. That view never failed to inspire him. He couldn't have walked this road for so many years if the sea had not been there for him. He stopped and pulled a lump of flavoured bread from his pack, then slung the full pack once more and continued, munching on the bread as he talked to himself. He hadn't noticed that before. He didn't recall ever talking to himself. Neither had he noticed the tiny bit of bread he dropped.

On the deserted track that wound its way along the coast, a man wondered off into the south, occasionally speaking to himself but getting no answer. A large crow circling above him, saw something fall at the man's side and he waited until the track had returned to its former silent condition. He then landed to see what the item was. The crow looked at it from a few paces away and saw that it was edible. He hopped twice, took

280

the bread in his mouth, then, flew off over the rocks without even a 'thank you' to the one who had dropped it.

The End

Glossary

1. Vitrification is a name given to the method of heating stone until it begins to melt and bond to other rocks.
2. If we use the Gaelic naming of places and in some cases the Viking system, we find that a name of a settlement was descriptive. For instance, Inverness translates from Gaelic to – mouth of the River Now.

Achtland – A Celtic goddess (Irish) that it was said could not find satisfaction from a man.

Arianrhod – Celtic goddess, moon and sky goddess, keeper of the silver wheel. (the wheel of life)

Athall – (fictional) A local name for north western Scotland.

Birchbay – (fictional) Close to the modern village of Dunbeath in Caithness, which translates to the Fort in the Birches. At this time it is unlikely there was a fort at the site.

Blodeuedd – A spiritual Princess conjured for the son of Arianrhod who was cursed never to have a human wife.

Boar, Kingdom of – The old kingdom of Orkney as it was known by the Irish.

Bog myrtle - An aromatic herb used as insect repellent and in brewing.

Broadbay – (fictional) A settlement where Wick now stands in Caithness.

Camma – (fictional) Larger settlement in the Clyth area of Caithness. Home to the local Lord Cullcoil.

Cat, kingdom of – Cat or Cait (sometimes Caith) is an early kingdom of northern Scotland, now called Caithness. Originally, the area was much larger than present day Caithness and may have reached as far as the River Fleet.

Ceromancy – Divination or reading the future of a person by studying melted wax. The particular method that Bethran employed was to get the subject to hold a lighted tallow candle and splash the tallow on a surface. Bethran would then interpret the shapes of the tallow for the subject.

Crummock – In England, skirret, is a perennial plant sometimes grown as a root vegetable. The English name is derived from middle English – 'skirwort' meaning white root. In Scotland where it grows well, it is known as Crummock.

Dalmar – (fictional) The King of the Kingdom of the Boar. (Orkney)

Derile of Limm - (fictional) A female seer on Orkney.

Dunat – Dunadd (Gaelic: Fort on the River Add) A hillfort in Argyll and Bute and believed to be the capital of Dal Riata

Dunwhin – (fictional) A small settlement below the Garrywhin fort near Ulbster, in Caithness.

Dragon Boat – Viking longship.

Fidach – Pict kingdom or shire, may have been ruled from where modern Inverness stands.

Flowfoot – (fictional) A large village on the site of modern day Tain in Sutherland.

Forced Fire – in folklaw, rubbing two sticks to create fire as a sickness remedy or to ward off plague.

Fortriu – Pict kingdom centred around Moray.

Gododdin – A large Pictish kingdom around Lothian and the Borders. By Bethran's time, some of the land was probably ruled by Northumbria, and it is likely the border was in constant change.

Gyre Carlin – Scottish, old goddess, sometimes a maiden, sometimes an old hag. She was thought to have formed the mountains and rivers. Mother goddess.

Hawthorne Moon Festival – Many festivals have come and gone but minor festivals named after trees remain popular to this day.

Keln – (fictional) Moiri of Keln a seamstress living by the Fleet River. See Moiri of Keln.

Lliefoot – (fictional) A settlement on the River Llihd which is now called Helmsdale River or River Ullie. The settlement is placed on the southern side of the river.

Lord Cullcoil – (fictional) A leader or minor king of Cat. (modern day Caithness and northern Sutherland)

Lyr – a pagan god of the seas.

Moiri of Keln – (fictitious) Women would be very able with needle and thread but it is likely that certain of these women would become well known for their skills. I have placed Keln around the Rogart area of Sutherland close to the River Fleet.

Nechtan – God of water – daughter - Boann water goddess

Needed Fire – see Forced Fire.

Northanhymbra – The Angle kingdom south of Scotland. This is now included in the county of Northumbria.

Oblate – Initiate to a religious order.

Oenology – The study and art of winemaking. It is doubtful that the word or anything like it existed at this time, but the church may have used something similar.

Pebbles – (fictional) A village close to present day Dornock. Dornock indeed, translates to 'Place of Pebbles'.

Pellar – old name for a healer.

Red Isthmus – (fictional) A name one of the characters uses for the Tarbat Peninsula in Easter Ross.

Rysgle – (fictional) A settlement in the deep bay at Lybster in Caithness.

Seal Bay – (fictional) The bay on the Moray Firth where Inverness now stands.

Please note: The fictional place names were not just plucked out of the air. They are based on research and formed by features of the area, lost names, or direct translations. Character names are either Pictish/Celtic or based on other names of the period.

Also by the Author.

FROM THE AVALON SERIES

The Drums of Drumnadrochit
Auld Clootie
The Brollachan
The Black Clan
Caledonian Flame
Plague Witch

OTHER TITLES

A Certain Summer
Sam's Kingdom
With Feeling

For more information, please visit:

www.petergrayauthor.co.uk
www.avalon-series.co.uk

Published by Trick Imp Publishers.